PRAISE FOR ROBERT BRYNDZA

SHADOW SANDS

"With its delightful detective duo, Bryndza's refreshing, twisty thriller stays upbeat even in dark moments."

—*Kirkus Reviews*

"Sharply written and wonderfully wrought, this crime thriller sings with every twist and builds to a more-than-satisfying bang."

—*Publishers Weekly*

NINE ELMS

"A heart-pounding series launch."

—*Publishers Weekly*

"*Nine Elms* is a taut thriller that sweeps up the reader into the world of Kate Marshall. Kate is a thoroughly realized character with troubles and virtues who will have you rooting for her through to the nail-biting end."

—Authorlink

"A taut thriller that will keep readers guessing, this is a powerful start to a new series."

—*Parkersburg News and Sentinel*

"While there are shades of *The Silence of the Lambs* in *Nine Elms*, due to a connection between an imprisoned monster and an investigator, Robert Bryndza has created wholly original characters and a story that is the very definition of a 'page-turner' and 'unputdownable'!"

—The Nerd Daily

"With *Nine Elms*, Bryndza proves that he's got another blockbuster saga on his hands. Kate Marshall is a bona fide superstar—an appealing mix of strength and vulnerability who shows that the damage of our past doesn't need to define us or defeat us but that it can spark our determination to be smarter, stronger, and singularly successful. That's a hero, and a notion, worth rooting for."

—Criminal Element

"Robert Bryndza's characters are so vividly drawn—even the slightest character—and fully human and uniquely imperfect. His plots are clever and original and cool, and his sense of timing is excruciatingly flawless. *Nine Elms* is Robert Bryndza spreading his already formidable wings to thrilling effect."

—Augusten Burroughs, *New York Times* bestselling author of *Running with Scissors*

"So chilling, with truly terrifying characters and a hard-hitting story line that is gripping from start to finish. I will wait with bated breath for the next Kate Marshall thriller."

—Rachel Abbott, Amazon Charts bestselling author

"Bryndza is my type of author, and *Nine Elms* is my type of book. Twisty, dark, and layered with a protagonist you root for from page one, this is a superb start to what promises to be another standout series."

—M. W. Craven, author of *The Puppet Show*

DARKNESS
FALLS

OTHER TITLES BY ROBERT BRYNDZA

Kate Marshall Series

Nine Elms

Shadow Sands

Erika Foster Series

The Girl in the Ice

The Night Stalker

Dark Water

Last Breath

Cold Blood

Deadly Secrets

Coco Pinchard Series

The Not So Secret Emails of Coco Pinchard

Coco Pinchard's Big Fat Tipsy Wedding

Coco Pinchard, the Consequences of Love and Sex

A Very Coco Christmas

Coco Pinchard's Must-Have Toy Story

Stand-Alone Work

Miss Wrong and Mr Right

DARKNESS
FALLS

A
KATE MARSHALL
THRILLER

ROBERT
BRYNDZA

THOMAS & MERCER

Text copyright © 2021 by Raven Street Ltd.
All rights reserved.

Published by Thomas & Mercer, Seattle

www.apub.com

Amazon, the Amazon logo, and Thomas & Mercer are trademarks of Amazon.com, Inc., or its affiliates.

ISBN-13: 9781542029629 (hardcover)
ISBN-10: 1542029627 (hardcover)
ISBN-13: 9781542005739 (paperback)
ISBN-10: 1542005736 (paperback)

Cover design by Caroline Teagle Johnson

Printed in the United States of America

First edition

For Nanna May

PROLOGUE

Saturday, September 7, 2002

Joanna Duncan stepped out of the office building and crossed the road with her head down against the rain. The rain was good, thought the man watching her from inside the car. People saw less with their heads down and umbrellas up.

Joanna was moving fast, marching up toward the old Deansgate multistory car park. She was petite with wavy shoulder-length blonde hair and strong, almost gnomic features, but Joanna was far from ugly. She had an earthy warrior-goddess beauty and wore a long black coat and brown leather cowboy boots. He waited for a bus to pass and pulled out of his parking spot. The bus left a spray of dirty water in its wake, and for a moment he lost sight of Joanna. He put on the windscreen wipers. She was close to the bus stop, where a line of people waited.

At five forty p.m., things were winding down, shops were getting ready to close, and people were clearing out and going home. The bus reached the stop and pulled over. Just as Joanna crossed behind it, he accelerated past, using the bus to shield him.

The gray cinder-block car park would be demolished in a few months, and Joanna was one of the last people who parked her car there. It was close to the office where she worked, and she was stubborn. This stubbornness helped realize his plan.

As he turned right into the car park entrance, he saw Joanna was just passing the bus. The car ramp twisted and turned, and he arrived, giddy from driving up in circles, on the third floor. Joanna's blue Ford Sierra was the only car on the level, parked in the middle of an empty row. The interior of the car park was dimly lit, and at intervals there were rough, wide windows open to the elements. In the fading light, a faint spray of rain was coming in and darkening the already-damp concrete.

He parked his car in the space to the left of the lift shaft and the stairwell. The lifts didn't work, so she would take the stairs. He switched off the engine and got out, hurrying over to one of the windows looking down on the high street. He saw the top of her head as she crossed the road to enter the car park. He hurried back to the car, leaned inside, and popped open the boot. He took out a small thick black plastic bag.

She was fast, because he'd barely prepared the bag when he heard the scuff of her shoes in the stairwell. This felt messy, and he was having to think on his feet. He positioned himself by the entrance to the stairwell. As soon as Joanna reached the top and stepped out, he slipped the bag over her head, yanked her backward, and used the handles to pull the plastic tight around her neck.

Joanna cried out and staggered on her feet, dropping the large handbag she carried. He pulled the bag tighter. The plastic sat flush over her skull and bulged at the mouth and nose as she fought to breathe.

Gripping her hair and the plastic bag together, he pulled tighter, and she gave a strangulated moan.

A cold breeze came through the windows, and he felt a spray of rain on his eyes. Joanna flailed and gagged, trying to scrabble at the thick plastic. He was much taller, but it took all his effort to keep hold and not overbalance.

It always amazed him how long it took for a person to suffocate. The will to live was too time consuming for TV dramas. After the first minute of fruitless clawing at the slick plastic covering her head, Joanna got clever, and she started to attack, landing two good punches to his ribs and aiming a kick toward the groin, which he managed to dodge.

He was sweating with exertion as he took one hand off the plastic, reached round, and grabbed her throat, lifting her clean off the concrete so the bag became a noose, quickening her death.

Joanna kicked in the air, then gave a terrible rattling moan, as if she were winding down. With a final shudder, she was still. She dangled in his grip for a moment, and then he let go. Her body hit the concrete floor with a nasty hollow thud. He was soaked in sweat, and he struggled to catch his breath. He coughed, and the sound echoed around the vast empty space. The multistory car park stank of urine and damp. He felt the cold air on his skin, and he looked around. He knelt, tied a knot in the plastic bag at the nape of her neck, and dragged her body over to his car. He laid her on the ground in the gap beside his car and the outer wall of the lift shaft. He opened the boot and picked up her limp body, putting one of his arms under her legs and the other under her shoulders, much like a groom carries his new bride across the threshold. He placed her in the back of the car, covered her with a blanket, and closed the boot. With a flash of panic, he saw that her handbag was still on the floor beside the stairs. He grabbed it and returned to the car. Her laptop and notebook were inside the bag with her mobile phone. He checked the call log and the text messages, and then he switched it off and wiped it down thoroughly with a cloth. He hurried over to Joanna's car and dropped her phone underneath.

He spent another minute with a flashlight, checking carefully over the patch of ground where he'd grabbed Joanna to see if she'd dropped anything, but all was clear.

He got into his car and sat for a moment in the silence.

What now? She had to disappear. Her body. Her computer. All DNA evidence had to vanish.

An idea came to him. It was bold and risky, but if it worked . . . He started the engine, and he drove away.

3

1

THIRTEEN YEARS LATER

Tuesday, May 5, 2015

"How expensive will it be to fix?" asked Kate Marshall, watching Derek, the elderly handyman, as he slowly measured the broken window frame. They were standing beside a 1950 Airstream aluminum caravan, and the midmorning sun was glinting off the curved edge of its roof. Kate squinted and slid her sunglasses down.

"We're talking about *round* glass windows," said Derek in his broad Cornish accent. He tapped the edge of his tape measure on the frame. "Expensive to fix."

"How expensive?"

He paused, sucking air through his lips. Derek seemed incapable of answering a question without an infuriatingly long pause. He rolled his top denture round his mouth. "Five hundred."

"You charged Myra two hundred pounds to mend one of these round windows," said Kate.

"She was having a tough time, what with the cancer. And round glass is more work for a glazier. The handle's embedded in the glass."

Myra had been Kate's friend for nine years, and they'd grown close. Her death, eighteen months ago, had been sudden and a shock.

"I appreciate that you helped Myra, but five hundred pounds is way too much. I can find someone else."

Derek rolled his dentures around his mouth again, and the pink gummy edge of the prothesis appeared fleetingly through his lips. Kate took off her sunglasses and met his gaze, refusing to look away.

"It'll take a week, with the specialist glass cutting and what 'ave you, but let's call it two fifty."

"Thank you."

Derek picked up his tool bag, and they walked back down the sloping hill through the caravan site to the road. There were eight static caravans, neatly spaced apart, in a hotchpotch of styles from modern white UPVC to the oldest, a Romani caravan with faded red and green paint. The caravans were rented out to people who came for walking or surfing holidays. Each caravan had a couple of bedrooms and a small kitchen, and some of the newer ones had bathrooms. The caravan site was on the lower end of the hospitality scale, but it was particularly popular with surfers because it was an inexpensive place to stay and a short walk down to the beach, which had some of the best surf in Devon and Cornwall. The holiday season would be starting in one week, and it felt like spring had finally arrived. The surrounding trees were bursting into leaf, and the sky was a clear blue.

When they reached the short set of concrete steps down to the road, Kate offered Derek her arm for support, but he ignored her, wincing as they slowly descended to where his car was parked. He opened the boot and heaved in his tool bag. He looked up at her; his watery blue eyes were piercing.

"I bet it was a shock when Myra left you her house and her business in her will."

"Yes."

"An' she left nothing to her son . . ." Derek tutted and shook his head. "I know they weren't close, but as I always say, blood is thicker than water."

It had been a surprise to Kate that Myra had left everything to her. It had caused a lot of anger from Myra's son and his wife, and it had generated a lot of local gossip and snide remarks.

"You've got my number. Let me know when the glass is ready," said Kate, not wanting to continue the conversation.

Derek looked annoyed that Kate wasn't going to give him any more.

He nodded curtly, got into his car, and drove away, leaving her in a wake of black smoke.

She coughed and wiped her eyes and then heard the faint tone of her mobile phone ringing. She hurried across the road to a squat, square building. On the ground floor was the campsite shop, still boarded up from the winter. Kate climbed a set of steps on the side of the building to the second floor and let herself into the small flat where Myra had lived, which Kate now used as an office.

A row of windows ran the length of the back of the building with a view out over the beach. The tide was out, exposing the black sea-weed-covered rocks. To the right, a row of cliffs jutted out, forming the edge of the bay, and beyond was the university town of Ashdean, which she could see clearly on this bright, sunny day. Her phone stopped ringing when she reached her desk.

The missed call was from a landline number with an area code she didn't recognize. She was about to phone back when a voice mail message popped up. Kate listened; it was from an older woman with a Cornish accent who spoke in a halting, nervous staccato.

"Hello . . . I got yer number online . . . I've seen that you've just started your own private detective agency . . . My name's Bev Ellis, and I'm calling about my daughter, Joanna Duncan. She was a journalist, and she went missing, almost thirteen years ago . . . She just vanished. The police never found out what happened to her, but she *did* vanish. She didn't run away or nothing like that . . . She had everything going for her. I want to hire a private detective who can find out what happened to her. What happened to her body . . ." At this point her voice broke, and she took a deep breath and swallowed loudly. "Please, call me back."

Kate listened to the message again. From the sound of the woman's voice, it had obviously taken a lot of courage to make the call. Kate opened her laptop to google the case and hesitated. She should call this woman back right away. There were two other long-established detective agencies nearby in Exeter, with slick websites and offices, and she could be phoning them too.

Bev's voice was still shaky when she answered the phone. Kate apologized for missing her call and gave her condolences for the loss of her daughter.

"Thank you," said Bev.

"Do you live locally?" asked Kate as she googled "Joanna Duncan missing."

"We're in Salcombe. About an hour away."

"Salcombe's very nice," said Kate, scanning the search results that had appeared on her screen. Two articles from September 2002 in the *West Country News* said:

DEVASTATED MOTHER OF LOCAL JOURNALIST JOANNA DUNCAN APPEALS FOR WITNESSES TO HER DAUGHTER'S DISAPPEARANCE NEAR EXETER TOWN CENTRE.

WHERE DID JO GO?

PHONE FOUND ABANDONED WITH CAR

IN DEANSGATE CAR PARK

Another from the *Sun* newspaper said:

WEST COUNTRY LOCAL JOURNALIST VANISHES

"I live with my partner, Bill," said Bev. "We've been together for years, but I recently moved in with him. I used to live on the Moor Side council estate on the outskirts of Exeter . . . Quite different."

Another headline, dated December 1, 2002, which acknowledged that Joanna had been missing for almost three months, caught Kate's eye.

Nearly all the articles used the same photo of Joanna Duncan, on a beach against blue sky and perfect white sand. She had bright-blue eyes, high cheekbones, a strong nose, and slightly bucked front teeth. She was smiling in the photo. There was a large red carnation tucked behind her left ear, and she held a halved coconut containing a cocktail umbrella.

"You said that Joanna was a journalist?" asked Kate.

"Yes. For the *West Country News*. She was going places. She wanted to move to London and work on one of the tabloids. She loved her job. She'd just got married. Jo and her husband, Fred, wanted kids . . . She went missing on Saturday, the seventh of September. She'd been at work in Exeter and then left around five thirty. One of her colleagues saw her go. It was less than a quarter of a mile walk from the newspaper offices to the multistory car park, but somewhere along the way, something happened. She just vanished into thin air . . . We found her car in the multistory; her phone was underneath. The police had nothing. They had no suspects. They spent nearly thirteen years doing God knows what, and then I got a phone call from them last week, telling me that after twelve years, the case is now inactive. They've given up on finding Jo. I have to find out what happened to her. I know she's probably dead; I want to find her and put her properly to rest. I saw an article about you in the *National Geographic*, how you found the body of that young woman who'd been missing for twenty years . . . Then I googled you and saw you've just started your own detective agency. Is that right?"

"Yes," said Kate.

"I like that you're a woman. I've spent so many years dealing with policemen who've patronized me," said Bev, her voice rising in defiance. "Could we meet? I can come over to your offices."

Kate glanced up at what was passing for their "offices." The space they were using had been Myra's living room. It still had the old 1970s patterned carpet, and their desk was an opened-out leafed dining table. Along one wall were bottles of urinal disinfectant and packs of paper towels for the caravan site. A large corkboard on the wall had a note that said ACTIVE CASES pinned at the top, but it was empty. Since the conclusion of their most recent job, a background check on a young man for his prospective employer, the agency had had no work. When Myra left her estate to Kate, it was on the condition that she quit her job and pursue her ambition to start a detective agency. They'd been up and running for nine months, but building the agency into something that could make a profit was proving to be tough.

"Why don't I come and meet you with my colleague, Tristan?" said Kate.

Tristan Harper was Kate's partner in the agency, and he was out at his other job today. Three days a week he worked at Ashdean University as a research assistant.

"Yes. I remember Tristan from the *National Geographic* article . . . Listen, I'm free tomorrow? But you're probably all booked up."

"Let me talk to Tristan, check our diary, and I'll call you right back," said Kate.

When she put the phone down at the end of the call, her heart was thumping with excitement.

2

At the same time Kate was finishing her call, Tristan Harper was sitting in his sister's small glass-walled office in the Barclays Bank on Ashdean High Street.

"Okay. Let's get this over with," he said, sliding the plastic folder containing his mortgage application across the desk. He had a sinking feeling in his stomach.

"What do you mean?"

"Your interrogation into my finances."

"Would you wear that if I was a stranger interviewing you for a new mortgage application?" said Sarah, opening the folder and peering at him across her desk.

"This is what I wear for work," said Tristan, looking down at his smart white V-neck T-shirt, jeans, and trainers.

"A bit informal for a bank interview, though," she said, adjusting her gray jacket and blue blouse. Sarah was twenty-eight, three years older than Tristan, but sometimes she seemed twenty years older.

"When I arrived, I didn't see many people lining up to cash their giros wearing three-piece suits. And these trainers are limited-edition Adidas."

"And how much did they cost?"

"Enough. They're an investment. Aren't they gorgeous?" he said, grinning.

Sarah rolled her eyes and nodded. "They're very cool."

Tristan was tall with a lean, muscular frame. His forearms were covered in tattoos, and the head of the eagle tattoo across his chest poked up from the V-neck of his T-shirt. They looked alike, brother and sister, with the same soft brown eyes. Tristan's chestnut-brown curly hair was now shoulder length and tousled. Whereas Sarah's hair was tied back and neatly tamed with straighteners.

There was a knock on the glass door, and a short balding man wearing a suit and tie came into the office.

"Has she started the interrogation yet?" he said. "She wanted to bring in a lamp to put on the desk so she could shine it in your face!"

This was Gary, Sarah's husband and the manager of the bank branch. Tristan got up and gave his brother-in-law a hug.

"Gary! Don't be so silly," said Sarah, now smiling with them. "I'm asking the same questions I would of any other mortgage applicant."

"Look how long your bloody hair is. Wish mine still grew like that!" said Gary, patting his expanding bald spot.

"I much prefer him with short hair," said Sarah.

"Do you want a coffee, Tris?"

"Please."

"A black coffee would be lovely, thank you, Gary," said Sarah. He left the office, and she took out the mortgage application form, scanned it, turned over the paper, and sighed.

"What?" said Tristan.

"I'm just seeing the pitiful amount you're now earning part time working at the university," said Sarah, shaking her head.

"I've got my contract for the agency, and my new tenant's agreement," said Tristan. Sarah looked in the plastic file and pulled out the two documents, flicking through them with a frown on her face.

"How much work has *Kate* got for you?"

Tristan noted how Sarah said Kate's name with an inflection, as she always did when referring to women she disapproved of.

"I've invested in the agency as a partner," said Tristan, bristling. "The agency pays us both a retainer, regardless of work. It's all there in the contract."

"And has the agency got any work right now?" she asked, looking up at him.

Tristan hesitated. "No."

Sarah raised her eyebrows and turned back to reading the paperwork. Tristan wanted to defend himself, but he didn't want to have another argument. In the nine months since he and Kate had started the detective agency, they'd had four cases. Two women had asked them to gather evidence of their husbands' infidelity. The owner of an office supplier in Exeter had asked them to find out if one of his employees was stealing stock and selling it, which she was, and they'd also done a detailed background check for a local businesswoman on a young man she wanted to hire.

Gary appeared at the door with a little tray filled with plastic coffee cups and leaned on the handle with his elbow. Tristan got up and opened the door.

"The agency income is irregular, and you haven't filed any tax returns yet," said Sarah, holding the Kate Marshall Detective Agency contract between thumb and index finger as if it were a pair of dirty underpants. Gary placed cups of steaming coffee on the desk.

"The agency also gets income from the caravan site," said Tristan.

"So, when detective work is low, Kate's got you changing beds and emptying chemical toilets?"

"We've started a business together, Sarah. It takes time to build it up. Kate's son, Jake, is coming back from university in a couple of weeks. And he'll be working for us helping to run the caravan site over the summer."

Sarah shook her head. She'd always been hostile toward Kate, but since he'd gone part time at the university to work at the fledgling detective agency, Sarah's dislike had gone up another notch. In her mind,

Kate was taking Tristan away from a secure job with good benefits. He wished Sarah would accept Kate as his friend and business partner. Kate was smart and never said anything derogatory about Sarah, but Sarah was happy to let rip and rant about Kate and her many faults. Tristan understood why his sister was protective. Their father had left when they were tiny, and their mother had died when Sarah was eighteen and Tristan fifteen. At a very young age, Sarah had had to become the breadwinner and parent.

"He's got a tenant now, haven't you, Tris?" said Gary, trying to lighten the mood. "That's a nice bit of extra income."

"Yeah. The tenancy agreement is there," said Tristan.

"How is it going with the yeti?" asked Gary. Tristan smiled. His new tenant, Glenn, had dark hair covering every visible piece of skin, as well as a thick, bushy beard.

"He's a good bloke. Very tidy. Stays in his room most of the time. Doesn't really talk," said Tristan.

"Not your type, then?"

"No, I like a guy with two eyebrows."

Gary laughed. Sarah looked up from the paperwork.

"Gary. Now he's left his full-time job at the university, it's going to be difficult to approve a remortgage on his flat with what he's earning . . ."

Gary went round the desk and touched her lightly on the shoulders.

"Let's have a look. Everything is workable, with a bit of Gary magic," he said. She got up and let him sit in the chair, and he pulled up the mortgage application on his screen.

"You're lucky that your brother-in-law is a bank manager," said Sarah. Tristan's phone rang in his pocket, and he took it out. Kate's name flashed up on the screen. "Who's that? This is important."

"It's Kate. I'll be quick," said Tristan, getting up and leaving the small office.

As he walked down the corridor, he heard Sarah's voice saying, "Kate's all right. She hasn't got a mortgage on *her* house . . ."

"Hello," said Tristan, answering the call. "Hang on. I'm at the bank." He moved past the line of people waiting for the cash desks, through the foyer, and outside onto the pavement.

"Did it all go through okay?" asked Kate.

"Sarah and Gary are just dealing with it."

"Do you want me to call back?"

"No. I'm good."

Kate sounded excited when she told him about her phone call with Bev Ellis.

"This could be a high-profile cold case?" said Tristan.

"Yes. But it looks complicated. Joanna Duncan's disappearance was featured on *Crimewatch*, and after twelve years, the police still had very little to go on."

"Do you think this woman can afford a long investigation?"

"I don't know. I've been googling. The press made a big thing about Bev being a single mother on a low income."

"Right."

"But that's the press, and you know how they like to distort things. She's recently moved to Salcombe and lives with her long-term boyfriend. Their address is on the millionaires' row. I'd like to go and meet them, tomorrow, if you're up for it?"

"Of course."

When Tristan came off the phone, he felt a little burst of excitement. He turned to see Sarah emerging from the front entrance of the bank.

"You owe Gary a pint," she said, crossing her arms over her blue blouse against the breeze. "He got your remortgage approved *and* on a much better fixed rate for five years. You'll save eighty quid a month."

"That's great," he said, giving her a hug, feeling relieved. "Thanks, sis."

"What did *Kate* want?"

"We could have a new case, missing person. We're going to meet the client tomorrow."

Sarah nodded and smiled. "That's good. You know, Tris, I don't like being hard on you. I just want you to be okay. I always promised Mum that I would take care of you. And when I bought that flat, it was the first time anyone in our family had owned property. You need to make sure you can keep paying the mortgage."

"I know, and I will," he said.

"One day, when you've paid it off, you'll own it properly and you'll be looked after."

"*Or* I might meet some gorgeous millionaire and he'll sweep me off my feet," said Tristan.

Sarah peered up and down the high street at the smattering of miserable-looking locals. "Do you see any millionaires in Ashdean?"

"Exeter is close by . . ."

Sarah rolled her eyes and laughed. "Where are you meeting this new client?"

"Salcombe. She lives in a big house overlooking the bay."

"Well. Make sure you don't solve the case too quickly if she's paying you by the hour."

3

Kate didn't sleep well that night. The meeting loomed large in her mind. Had Bev Ellis contacted other private detectives? Exactly how much information had she discovered about Kate online? It was all in the public domain. One click of a mouse, and the Google search results spoke for themselves.

She tossed and turned in bed, running through her past failures. Kate had been a young Met Police officer in London when she discovered that her colleague Peter Conway, a senior police officer, was responsible for the rape and murder of four young women in Greater London. To add to the mess, she'd been romantically involved with Peter and was pregnant with his child when she cracked the case. The tabloid stories had been lurid and intrusive, and the scandal put an end to her career in the force. She subsequently struggled with alcohol addiction, which resulted in her mother and father being granted custody of Kate and Peter's son, Jake, when he was six years old.

She'd moved to the south coast to rebuild her life, and for the past eleven years, she'd worked as a lecturer in criminology at Ashdean University.

During this time, Myra had been her rock. A good friend and her sponsor in Alcoholics Anonymous, and Kate felt a responsibility to herself, and to Myra, to make her detective agency a success.

At five a.m., Kate got up and went for her regular early-morning swim in the sea. It calmed her to swim out through the still water, with just the sound of a far-off group of seagulls cawing, and as the dawn broke, the sky blazed with blue, pink, and gold.

Kate was waiting outside the house when Tristan pulled up in his blue MINI Cooper.

"Morning. I got you a coffee," he said, holding up a Starbucks cup when she opened the passenger door and got in.

"Lovely. Double shot?" she asked, feeling the warmth emanating from the cup on her cold hands.

"Triple. I didn't sleep too well."

He was wearing a dark-blue suit with a white shirt open at the neck, and Kate thought how handsome he looked. She had taken care with what she wore, choosing dark jeans with a white blouse and a smart royal-blue jacket in light wool. Kate took a sip of the coffee, enjoying the hit of caffeine.

"That's good; I didn't sleep that well either."

"I'm nervous about this one," said Tristan as they drove past the caravan site. "I still feel like a rookie."

"Don't be nervous. Bev Ellis is desperate to find out what happened to her daughter, and we're the people who can find her. Yes?"

Tristan nodded. "Yes."

"Think about it like that and you won't be nervous," said Kate. She'd been telling herself this as she'd swum and got ready for the meeting and was close to believing it.

"Did you look Joanna Duncan up online?" asked Tristan. "No one has any clue what happened to her. She disappeared from that multistory car park on Exeter High Street on a busy Saturday evening. There's something creepy about it. That she vanished into thin air."

"Once I got past all the stories about her disappearance, there was some interesting stuff about her career as an investigative journalist," said Kate. "She published an exposé on the local member of Parliament at the time, Noah Huntley. He was taking cash bribes to award council contracts. The national tabloids picked up the story, and it triggered a by-election, and he ended up losing his seat."

"When was this?" asked Tristan.

"Six months before she went missing, March 2002. It will be interesting to find out from Bev what other stories she was working on back then."

———

The day quickly warmed up, and for the first time that year, they didn't need the car heater. They drove along the coast for a few miles, and the Jurassic coastline was breathtakingly beautiful. Kate never took it for granted. It was almost Californian compared to the rest of the UK. They left the coast road to join the motorway for the next forty minutes and then rejoined the coastline when they turned off toward Salcombe. The road wound its way down toward the bay, and the houses became grander. Fishing boats and yachts sat on the calm sea, which reflected the sun and the blue sky, like plate glass.

Tristan's GPS indicated they should take a right turn, which led onto a narrow private road. The trees thinned out, and they reached a high white wall and a gate. Tristan opened his window and pressed a button on a console.

"What did she say Bill did for a living?" asked Tristan.

"I don't know. Something lucrative, I presume," said Kate.

"He likes his privacy. Look at those huge trees," he said, indicating a line of giant fir trees behind the wall. The console crackled.

"Hello. I can see you. I'll just buzz you in," said Bev's voice through the intercom. The gate opened, sliding soundlessly to the right. Kate looked up and saw a security camera mounted in a glass dome on one of the gate pillars. They followed a winding paved driveway, which sloped up through a landscaped garden with palms, fig trees, and an assortment of evergreens. The path was lined with beds of evenly spaced tulips in red, white, yellow, and purple, all of which were about to open. The driveway passed along the side of the house and then turned sharply to the left and opened out to a paved parking area. Up close the back of the house was a huge, minimalistic white box. There were no windows at the back, just a small oak door.

They got out of the car, and the door opened. Bev Ellis appeared with a very tall man. Kate noted he was almost half a head taller than Tristan, who was just over six foot. Bev barely came up to his shoulder. There was a strong resemblance with Bev and her daughter. Like Joanna, she was rail thin, with the same strong nose, full-lipped mouth, prominent cheekbones, and blue eyes, but Bev's skin was pale and crepey, and she had huge bags under her eyes. Her hair was cut in a short pixie crop, which accentuated her prominent ears, and it was dyed a little too dark. She wore a pair of pink Crocs, jeans, and a grubby green fleece. She looked completely out of place, like a lottery winner or a poor out-of-town relative. Kate banished the unkind thought.

Bill looked younger than Bev, thin and muscular with thick gray hair clipped short in a buzz cut. He wore a faded Rolling Stones T-shirt with a gold necklace lying over the top, stonewashed jeans with ripped knees, and bare feet. He had a kind, ruddy face, emphasized by beautiful green eyes.

"Hello," said Bev. She offered a trembling hand to Kate. "This is Bill. I want to call him my boyfriend, but we're a bit past it for all that, ha ha. We've been together forever."

"Nice to meet you, Kate, and you too, Tristan," said Bill, shaking their hands. He was calm in comparison to Bev. Any nerves Kate had about being judged evaporated.

"I hope you found the 'ouse okay?" Kate went to answer, but Bev carried on, "Of course you did. You're here! Come in."

The front door led right into a huge open-plan living area. Floor-to-ceiling glass lined the front of the house, looking out over a terrace and the bay. The floors were white marble with delicate threads of gold and black in the pattern, and there was very little furniture in the vast space. To the left was a living area with a large concrete fireplace. A long white leather sofa sat on top of a white carpet, facing a flat-screen television above the fire.

To the right was a spacious, minimalist kitchen, which was completely white and devoid of anything on the surfaces. Kate wondered how long Bev had been living here. She was a chatty, nervous person. From Kate's experience, chatty, nervous people liked their space filled with furniture and knickknacks, mirroring their need to fill empty silences.

"Bloody hell, look at this view!" said Tristan as they moved closer to the windows. The sweeping panoramic vista looked out over the bay and the sea, uninterrupted by any other houses. The far-off undulating rocks of the Jurassic coastline stretched away into a haze of blue. "Sorry. Excuse my language."

"It's okay, love. I think my first words were *fucking hell* when I first saw it!" said Bev. There was an awkward silence, and Bev blushed. "Sit down; I'll make some tea and coffee," she added, indicating the sofa.

Kate and Tristan sat down and watched as Bill and Bev got things ready. Bev had trouble opening the white cupboard doors, which sat flush, with no handles, and twice she got the wrong door for the fridge.

"How long has she lived here?" murmured Tristan. Kate shook her head and busied herself with getting out her notebook and pen.

A few minutes later, Bill and Bev brought over a large french press of coffee and a three-tiered cake stand filled with cupcakes and biscuits. Bill sat on the floor, with his back against the stone fireplace. Bev perched on the edge of an armchair next to him.

"Do you mind if we take notes?" asked Kate, indicating her notebook. "Just so we don't miss anything."

"Yeah, go ahead," said Bill. Bev pushed the plunger down on the french press and poured the coffee. The room was suddenly thick with silence. Bev's hands were shaking so badly that Bill had to take over, passing Kate and Tristan their cups.

"It's all right," said Bill, leaning forward to rub her leg. Bev grabbed his hand. Hers was tiny and birdlike in comparison.

"Sorry. I've been dreading having to talk about this," she said, pulling her hand away and wiping it on her trousers. "I don't know where to start."

"Why don't you tell us about Joanna?" said Kate. "What was she like?"

"I always called her Jo," said Bev, sounding surprised at being asked such a simple question. "She was a wonderful baby. I had an easy pregnancy. A quick birth, and she was so good and quiet. Her dad was an older guy I dated for a bit. He was twenty-six to my seventeen. He died when Jo was two. Heart attack, unusual for such a young bloke. He had a heart defect he never knew about. We never married, and he was never really in the picture, so I brought Jo up on my own. We were very close. More friends, really, especially when she was older."

"What job did you do?" asked Kate.

"I was a cleaner for Reed, the company who rent out offices. They had two big spaces in Exeter and Exmouth . . . I had a council flat for years, on the Moor Side Estate. Then I rented a flat a bit closer to town. I only moved in here two months ago. My landlord gave me notice he was selling up. This is all Bill's."

Bill looked up and smiled at her. "This is your home now, girl, as much as mine."

Bev nodded and pulled a ratty piece of tissue from her sleeve and wiped her eyes.

"How long have you two been together?" asked Tristan.

"Gawd. On and off for, what? Thirty years? We never married. We liked having our own space," said Bev. Bill nodded. She blushed again, and Kate thought how hollow it sounded. Like a practiced line.

"Did Jo always want to be a journalist?" asked Kate.

"Yes. When Joanna was eleven years old, there was this kiddies' typewriter. The Petite 990. It worked like a proper typewriter. Do you remember the advert? There was this young girl dressed up like Dolly Parton typing away, and the song '9 to 5' played."

"I remember," said Kate. "When was that?"

"1985."

Kate did a quick calculation. If Joanna was eleven in 1985, she'd been born in 1974. That meant she had been twenty-eight when she went missing in 2002.

"In 1985, I was still four years off being born," said Tristan, putting up his hand. They all laughed, and the tension in the room eased a little.

"As soon as Jo saw that advert, she wanted that typewriter for Christmas, but back then, it cost an arm and a leg—thirty quid! I said to 'er, 'What are you going to use a typewriter for? It'll just end up in the cupboard on Boxing Day, collecting dust.' And Jo said, 'I can be a news reporter.' I scraped together the thirty quid, begged and borrowed, mainly from Bill . . ."

Bill chuckled at the memory, nodding.

"And I got Jo the typewriter for Christmas. And she kept her word. Every week, she'd type out a newsletter, silly stuff about what had happened to us, or at school. She never stopped writing and asking questions . . . She was clever. Passed the eleven-plus and got into the grammar school. Jo went on to study journalism at Exeter University and worked as a reporter at the *West Country News*. Back then, it sold half a million copies a day . . . She'd been applying for jobs up in London at one of the national newspapers, and she even got an interview . . ." Bev's voice trailed off. "And then, she went missing."

"In the months or weeks leading up to Joanna going missing, did her behavior change? Was she depressed or worried about anything?"

"No. She was happier than I'd ever seen her."

"And you saw her a lot?"

"A few times a week. We'd talk on the phone most days, more than once. She'd just bought a house in Upton Pyne, a small village on the outskirts of Exeter, with her husband, Fred."

"What did you think of Fred?"

"Fred was—*is*—a lovely guy. He didn't do it," said Bev instantly. "He was home all day. And there were so many witnesses. He was painting their house, and up a ladder . . . Lots of people saw him in the village and gave him an alibi."

"Did anything unusual happen in the run-up to her going missing?" asked Kate.

"No."

"What was she working on? I read that she was an investigative journalist."

"She was working on lots of stories," said Bev, looking at Bill.

"But nothing that would have got her killed or abducted," he said.

"She went to work on Saturday, September seventh, and then left at five thirty. It was only a short walk to her car, but somewhere along the way, she vanished. Me and Bill had been out that day at Killerton House, about an hour's drive. We came back in the afternoon. Bill stopped in at the office block his company was remodeling in Exeter; I went home. Then, around seven, I got a call from Fred that Jo hadn't come home. We called round; no one knew where she was. In the end, Fred drove over and picked me up, and we started looking for her. The police wouldn't treat her as a missing person for the first twenty-four hours, so we drove round the local hospitals, and we checked the car park near her office, and her car was still there. We found her mobile phone underneath the car, switched off. There was no fingerprints on it. Not even hers, which made the police think that whoever took her switched it off and wiped their prints off it."

"It was the Deansgate car park, and it was demolished a few months later, in 2003?" asked Tristan.

"Yes. There's flats there now," said Bev.

"Joanna, Jo, was an investigative journalist involved in exposing a local MP, Noah Huntley, of fraud. This was back in March 2002, six months before she went missing?" said Kate.

"Yes, Jo's story was picked up by the national newspapers, it triggered a by-election, and Noah Huntley lost his seat, but that was in May, four months before Joanna went missing."

"And after he lost his seat, he landed a load of private-sector work, which paid him much more than he ever got as an MP," said Bill, shaking his head in disgust.

"Was Joanna working on any other story which might have put her in danger?" asked Kate.

"No, we don't think so," said Bev, looking to Bill. He shook his head. Bev went on. "Jo didn't talk much about stories she was working on, but there was nothing that her boss, her editor, was concerned about . . . The police talked to that Noah Huntley; I think they were getting desperate because they had no other suspects, but there was no motive for him to do anything to Jo after the article was published, and he had an alibi."

"Were there many witnesses who saw Jo before she went missing?" asked Kate.

"A couple of people came forward to say they'd seen her come out of the newspaper office. Another old lady remembers her passing the bus stop up to Deansgate. The police got hold of a CCTV image from a camera on the high street, which she passed around twenty to six that evening, but it was facing the other direction from the car park. No one knows what happened after that. It's like she vanished."

There was a long silence, and Kate noticed for the first time a clock ticking in the background. Bill put his cup down on the table.

"Listen. Bev means everything to me," he said. "I've watched her suffer for too long. I can't do anything to replace Jo, but if Jo was murdered, I want to help find her so Bev can put her to rest . . ." Bev looked down at the tissue she was twisting in her lap, tears running down her crumpled cheeks. "If I hire you, I know your investigation isn't going to take just a few hours. I'm prepared to pay for your time, but I won't just sign off on a blank check. Is that understood?"

"Of course," said Kate. "We never make false promises, but every case we've taken, we've solved."

Bill nodded for a moment and then got up. "If you come with me, there's something I want to show you."

4

Past the stark-white kitchen was a wide corridor with five doors leading off it. The doors were all closed, and the hallway was dimly lit.

Six or seven black-and-white framed prints of naked women lined the walls. Tristan was no prude, but he found them quite shocking as they walked down the corridor. Bill led the way, followed by Bev, and then Tristan and Kate. The models were artfully lit, but the photos were explicit. One print was a close-up of a woman's vagina and next to it was a man's hand, holding an unpeeled banana.

Tristan glanced back at Kate to see what she thought, and she raised an eyebrow. When he turned back, he saw Bev had noticed their exchange, and she laughed nervously.

"Bill's an art collector," she said. "They're all limited-edition prints. Worth a lot of money. The artist is very high profile. What's his name again?"

Bev seemed keen for them to think that the pictures on the wall were art and not porn. Tristan wondered if Bev had objected to them being on the wall when she'd moved in.

"Arata Hayashi. He's a very inventive Japanese visual artist. I was invited to his exhibition when I was there on business last year," said Bill.

"What kind of business are you in?" asked Tristan.

"Construction. I started out with office buildings, and more recently we've moved into roads. I own a company that supplies all the building materials for large motorway construction projects."

"Bill's company just resurfaced the M4 motorway," said Bev, proudly.

Tristan thought how long the M4 motorway stretched—two hundred miles, from London into South Wales. That was a lot of cement and tarmac.

Bill opened the door at the end of the corridor that led to his office. It was dark in comparison to the rest of the house, with lots of heavy wood furniture, and bookshelves, and a gun cabinet on the wall where a row of shotguns sat behind the polished glass.

Mounted on the wall above the desk was a large stag's head. Tristan felt a pang of sadness at seeing its open mouth and mournful eyes. He was about to ask Bill if he hunted, when he noticed a pile of cardboard police evidence boxes stacked up beside a black marble fireplace. Each was labeled JOANNA DUNCAN CASE FILE and had a number.

"Are these official police case files?" Kate asked, moving over to the pile of boxes.

"Yes," said Bill.

Tristan saw Kate was frowning.

"Bill got them for me," said Bev, as if they were something he'd ordered for her online.

"In the past I've known the police to allow a family member to view parts of a case file, under supervision in the station . . . I've never known of case files out on, what? On loan?" asked Kate, raising an eyebrow at Bill.

"Yes. I have them for three months," said Bill.

"Officially?"

Bill went over to his desk and picked up a piece of paper and handed it to Kate. Tristan joined her and saw that it was an official letter from Superintendent Allen Cowen of the Devon and Cornwall police. The letter thanked Bill for writing and expressed gratitude for his donations to the Golden Lantern, a police benevolent fund, and said that considering the support he'd given for the families of fallen police officers, they would grant access to the Joanna Duncan cold-case files to pursue civil investigations.

"The case is now inactive, a cold case. That letter confirms we have police consent to access the case files," said Bill.

Tristan went over to the boxes. He counted twenty.

"Have you had a look through the files?" he asked.

"Yes," said Bill.

"Did the police take Jo's laptop and her files from work?" asked Kate.

"No. We think Jo had her laptop and her notebooks with her when she went missing," said Bev. "They've never been found."

"The police took away some other work files and paperwork that was on Jo's desk. They're in the case files, but they're vague notes about other stories she was working on," said Bill.

There was another long silence. The office was warm and stuffy, and there was a gamy whiff coming from the stag's head, which made Tristan feel queasy.

"I tried to look through all this. I thought it would help me and give me some answers, but there's so much there," said Bev. "All questions, too many questions and no answers . . . It shows me that the police really didn't have a fucking clue. I need a drink . . . sorry," she added, moving to a globe bar to the right of the desk and opening it to reveal a selection of bottles inside. She poured a large measure of whiskey into a cut-glass tumbler, took a sip, and wiped her mouth with shaking hands.

"Can I get either of you a drink?" asked Bill, joining Bev and pouring himself a whiskey to try and defuse the situation. There was a pause, and Tristan quickly said no. The cut-glass crystal tumbler was so large that Bev had to cradle it in both hands.

"Look. I'm no good at negotiating and playing games," she said. "I need to know if you'll take on this case and help me find out what happened to Jo. There's so much in those case files—witness statements, a timeline the police put together in the hours before she vanished."

Bev pulled out the chair behind the desk and slumped down into it. She looked exhausted. Tristan looked at Kate. As far as he was concerned, he'd wanted to take on the case the moment Kate had called him at the bank. She nodded.

"Okay. We're on board," said Kate. "I have contacts in the police and in forensics. And having the case files here gives us a huge advantage."

"Oh, I'm so happy," said Bev. "Thank you." Tristan could see how raw the emotions were about the loss of her daughter.

"Let's start with six months," said Bill. "Then we'll review where you are." He held out his hand first to Kate and then Tristan, and they shook on it. Bev got up and came over to them and gave them both a hug. Tristan could smell stale booze on her breath.

"Thank you, thank you so much," said Bev.

"We'll do everything we can to find Jo," said Kate.

Bev nodded and burst into tears, moving to Bill, who put his arm around her protectively.

"Can we take the case files with us?" asked Tristan.

"I'll give you a hand to take them down to your car," said Bill.

"I can't bear having all this in the house. It gives me the creeps," said Bev. "Please. Take it all away."

5

The next morning, Kate and Tristan started to go through the Joanna Duncan case files. They were also planning to scan all the documents. It would be time consuming, but it would also help if they both had electronic access to the files, and Kate figured it would be worth having a backup. They had permission to use the files, but police bureaucracy could be fickle. The police had granted access but could withdraw it at any time.

When they started on the first box, Tristan found a cassette tape tucked inside the file containing the official statement from Joanna's husband, Fred Duncan.

"It's dated September twelfth, 2002," he said, reading the handwritten label on the side of the plastic box. "That's five days after Joanna went missing."

"Have any of the other statements from early in the investigation got cassettes in them?" asked Kate. Tristan flicked through the other files from the first box.

"These look like written statements from Joanna's family, friends, and work colleagues, but no cassettes," said Tristan.

"So, at the beginning of the investigation, they only brought in Joanna's husband for official questioning. Next of kin are usually the first suspects."

"How long is an audio cassette? I've never really come across them," said Tristan, turning the plastic box over in his hands.

"Bloody hell. You make me feel old," said Kate with a grin. She took the cassette box and checked it over. "This one is thirty minutes on each side, and it says it's one of one, so it wasn't a long interview."

Kate got up and went to the filing cabinet where they kept an old radio cassette machine inherited from Myra. She took the cassette from its box and put it in the machine. She started the audio recorder on her phone, switched on the cassette player, and put the phone next to it.

There were two voices on the tape. A DCI Featherstone—an older, gruff-voiced male—and Fred Duncan, who had a pronounced Cornish accent.

"You said you were painting the house all day on the seventh of September, at the home you shared with Joanna in the village of Upton Pyne. Your neighbor Arthur Malone told us that a young woman arrived just after two p.m. and went inside your house, but he didn't see her leave," said DCI Featherstone on the tape. "Who was she?"

"A neighbor. Famke," said Fred.

"*Famke*—sounds foreign? What's her second name?"

"Van Noort . . ." There was a bit of back-and-forth as Fred spelled it out for DCI Featherstone. "The name is Dutch. She's an au pair working for a family a few doors down."

"Do people in your area have au pairs?" asked Featherstone, a mocking tone in his voice.

"Yeah. It's a doctor and his wife. Paulson is their name. Dr. Trevor Paulson. I don't know his wife's name. They own the big manor house at the end of the village. Famke looks after their kids," said Fred.

"And can you spell their names?"

"The names of their kids?"

"No. The doctor's name," said Featherstone, sounding annoyed. There was more back-and-forth about this.

"Why did this au pair visit you?" asked Featherstone. There was a long pause.

"Why do you think?" said Fred.

"I need you to state it, for the benefit of the tape."

Fred let out a long sigh.

"For sex," he said. "She came round for sex. She stayed for a couple of hours or so, then left out through the back garden."

"There's a footpath running along the bottom of your garden?"

"Yes. That's the way she left."

"And Famke will confirm this?"

"Yes. Please, don't be hard on her. She's only young . . . Well, she's not that young," he added.

"How did you meet her?" asked Featherstone.

"One day at the corner shop . . . She was giving me the eye," said Fred. "I've been unemployed since we moved to the village. Feeling pretty shit about myself."

"Why do you feel that way about yourself?"

"Me and Jo just got a mortgage, and I can't contribute."

"Joanna earns a good wage, then, up at the *West Country News* in Exeter?"

"Yes."

"That must have caused tension," said Featherstone. There was a goading tone in his voice.

"What do you think?" Fred shot back.

"That gives you a motive. Your wife dies. You get her life insurance, pay off the mortgage."

"Do you know she's dead? Have you found her body?" asked Fred, his voice cracking.

There was a silence that lasted almost half a minute. Kate checked the cassette player to see if the tape had stopped.

"How many times have you met for sex with this Famke?" asked Featherstone.

"Three or four times over the past couple of months. It's not a crime to have an affair."

"Of course not, Mr. Duncan. Does Joanna know you've been entertaining the local au pair in her bed when she's out, hard at work, paying the mortgage?"

There was another long pause.

"No," said Fred in a small voice. "But that's all stupid. I've been so stupid. I just want her home safe, and I'll tell her everything, if she just comes home."

"Can you think of anyone who would want to hurt her?" asked Featherstone.

"No."

"Could she be having an affair of her own? You've strayed."

"What? No. No. She's obsessed with her job. She spends all her time with me, or her mum, or she's at work. She's spoken before about a woman at work who had an affair with a colleague and how everyone talked about her in derogatory terms."

"Who's that?"

"Rita Hocking; she's another journalist at the *West Country News*."

"Your wife might have run away."

"How am I supposed to answer that? That's not a question. You're the bloody police. You should be doing better than that . . . She wouldn't just leave. She would never leave her mum. They're close. Too close sometimes."

There was another long silence, and then DCI Featherstone started to go through Fred's official statement. Kate stopped the tape and the voice recorder on her phone.

"Why didn't Bev tell us about Fred's affair?"

"Maybe she has this idea of them being happy together," said Tristan. "She didn't mention that Fred was questioned. The police thought he had motive."

"The neighbor and Famke gave him an alibi. Is it there?"

Tristan flicked through the files and found a piece of paper. "Yes . . . She gave the police a written statement . . . She arrived at Fred's house just after two p.m. and stayed for two hours, until just after four p.m.," he said, scanning the signed statement. "Then she left via the back door, along the footpath running behind the row of houses, and went back home."

"How far is Upton Pyne from Exeter?" asked Kate.

"Not far, about four miles," said Tristan, flicking through the other files in the box.

"Fred had an alibi until four p.m. the day Joanna went missing, but Bev told us Joanna didn't leave work that day until five thirty p.m. . . ."

"Fred's neighbor Arthur Malone gave the police a statement to say he saw Fred on and off all day on Saturday, September seventh, and Fred's car didn't move from outside the house until later that evening, around seven thirty . . ."

"Which is when Fred got concerned why Joanna hadn't come home from work, and he drove into Exeter to go to Bev's flat," said Kate.

Tristan was looking through another file and whistled. He held up a contact photo sheet with four images taken from a CCTV camera.

"What's that?" asked Kate.

"The police took a statement from Noah Huntley, the MP Joanna did the exposé on," he said. "These are photos of them meeting at a petrol station."

Kate took the contact sheet from Tristan. "Look at the time stamp; the CCTV is dated August twenty-third, 2002 . . . ," she said.

"Two weeks before Joanna went missing."

"And the CCTV images were taken from the Upton Pyne Texaco petrol station. Why would Joanna be meeting Noah Huntley two weeks before she went missing, and so close to home?"

"Noah Huntley says in his statement that Joanna asked to meet him because she had applied for a job at the *Daily Mail* newspaper and he was on the board of the company, and she wanted to make sure that there wasn't any bad blood between them," said Tristan. "He also had an alibi for when Joanna went missing. He was away at his house in France."

He handed Noah Huntley's statement to Kate.

"We need to talk to Fred and get his side of things. Bev mentioned none of this. It makes me wonder what else she hasn't told us."

6

Fred Duncan agreed to talk to Kate and Tristan on the following Monday afternoon. He still lived in the same house he'd shared with Joanna, in Upton Pyne, a village twenty minutes from Ashdean, on the outskirts of Exeter.

The house was on a narrow lane of cottages and houses set back from the road and bordered with high redbrick walls and hedges that were bursting into leaf. Fred's house looked very different from the run-down, grimy little place they'd seen in the case file pictures. The thatched roof and windows looked new, and the brickwork had been sandblasted, cleaning away the staining from years of smog to reveal the original deep-red color of the bricks. There was a large front garden surrounded by a high redbrick wall with a curved top. A giant tree dominated the front lawn, its enormous bare branches reaching out over the garden to create a canopy. The spring sun was warm, but in the shade cast by the branches, the air felt chilly.

Kate pressed the doorbell, and a distant clanging bell rang inside. Moments later, Fred opened the door. In the case file photos, he'd been a thin, wiry man who wore baseball caps and casual clothes and had a permanent dark stubble. The man in front of them looked filled out and healthy with a light tan. He was barefoot and clean shaven, and his thinning hair was cropped close to his head. To Kate, he looked like a new-age guru. He wore loose white linen trousers and a baggy linen shirt open at the neck, showing a hairy chest with a chain of rosary beads and a small silver cross around his neck.

"Hello, welcome," he said, smiling broadly. "Please take off your shoes. Do you want slippers?" he added, indicating a rustic wooden box by the door filled with identical sheepskin slippers. Kate and Tristan both removed their shoes but declined the slippers.

"I've got the underfloor heating cranked up, so you should be fine in your socks," he said. "My wife, Tameka, didn't want to be here." He led them through to the kitchen. "She's taken our little girl, Anika, into the city."

On the wall above the kitchen table was a collage of wedding photos. At the top was a large group photo of Fred's wedding. It had been a traditional Indian affair, and the guests looked to number a hundred or more. Fred and his pasty-white elderly parents stuck out among Tameka's Indian family and friends. There were two photos of Fred and Tameka in brightly colored traditional Indian dress. She was taller than Fred and strikingly beautiful.

"When did you get married?" asked Kate.

"We just had our third anniversary," said Fred, following Kate and Tristan's gaze over to the photos. "Tameka has a big family, lots of relations came over from Mumbai. Would you like coffee? I've only got soy milk," he added. "We're vegans."

"I'll take it black," said Tristan.

"Me too," said Kate.

"Have a seat," he said, indicating a long wooden kitchen table with a bench on each side next to a patio window.

Kate and Tristan perched on the bench facing the window. The back garden was large and dotted with silver birch trees, which were still small. A soft, undulating path of white gravel led to a huge wood-framed structure with glass walls at the bottom of the garden. It was empty inside, and the floor was covered in dark-green mats.

"That's Tameka's yoga studio," said Fred. Kate noticed the gate in the wall at the bottom of the garden. Tristan noticed it, too, and glanced sideways and raised his eyebrow. It was the gate Famke had used for their affair.

Fred came over to the table with three steaming espresso cups on a little tray. "Tameka is an Ashtanga yoga teacher, and she does lessons from home."

"Do you work now?" asked Kate, taking two of the cups off the tray and handing one to Tristan. "The case files say you were unemployed when Joanna went missing."

"Yes, I work now," he said with an edge of sarcasm in his voice. "I'm a website designer. We both get to work from home and share the responsibility for Anika." He pulled a packet of biscuits from the pocket of his baggy trousers and opened it with his teeth, spreading out the plastic packet on the tabletop. The biscuits spilled out. "Damn, I didn't think that through, did I?" he said. He went back to the kitchen and started searching through the cupboards to find a plate. Kate sensed that he was a stranger to food preparation and the kitchen in general. He returned with a plate and tipped the biscuits onto it. He then fussed around some more, clearing up the crumbs and then checking to see if any mess remained. Kate presumed that Tameka ran a tight ship.

"Right," he said, sitting down opposite them. "Joanna . . ."

"Yes. Bev said she contacted you," said Kate.

"Yeah. She sent me a text," said Fred. "Do you think you'll find her?"

"I hope so," said Kate. "Do you support Bev's decision to hire a private detective?"

Fred rubbed his eyes. "I'm not against it. I've mourned for Joanna. And I think I'm lucky that I've been able to move on. I had to, for my sanity. I think Bev's still trapped in the same place she was the night Joanna vanished. Just talking about it again is giving me the shivers.

Look at my hands—I'm shaking . . ." He held them out. He had long, thin fingers, but his fingertips were slightly bulbous.

"Is it difficult to still live here, in the same house where you lived with Joanna?" asked Tristan.

"I've only been back for three years. A year after Joanna went missing, I rented the place out and got a flat in Exeter."

"Why did you rent it out?" asked Kate.

"I couldn't afford the mortgage on my own. I had to rent it out. When people go missing, there's no law in place to say what happens to their assets. We had a joint mortgage, but I couldn't change it without Joanna's signature. It wasn't until eight years later, that we, well, *I* went to court so Joanna could be ruled as death in absentia. Presumed dead."

His face looked pained at the memory.

"You said *we* and then corrected it to *I*?" asked Kate.

"Bev was against it. She accused me of giving up on Joanna, but in the end, she came around to it. We were able to get a death certificate, have a funeral. My marriage to her was annulled. I bought out what Joanna put into this house. I gave the money to Bev."

"What did Bill think?"

"Bill tends to think whatever Bev thinks. He's devoted to her . . . They look after each other. Bev had a bad time when she was with Joanna's father. He was violent and controlling. Bill is the opposite of that—calm, dependable. But after Joanna's dad, Bev vowed that she'd never get married or give up her independence to a man. I thought they might be married by now, after all these years. I suppose moving in together is a step in the right direction . . . Bill's a good guy. He helped me out with money after Joanna went missing. And when they finally ruled Joanna as dead, he bought the plot of land in the cemetery next to Bev's mum's grave and paid for a beautiful headstone . . ." His voice trailed off. "We had a lock of Joanna's hair interred."

Kate thought back to when they'd met Bev and Bill, how Bev had spoken of Joanna like she still might be alive. She hadn't mentioned any of this. Fred took a sip of his coffee and went on.

"I met Tameka six months after Joanna was ruled dead in absentia. I proposed six months later, and she fell pregnant. We wanted to live somewhere nice, and this is now a good area with a good school. We had this house completely gutted. New floors, roof. We added this kitchen on and two more rooms upstairs with an en suite bathroom. The garden was landscaped . . . It's unrecognizable from before. Weirdly, it helped with the neighbors too," he said.

"How did it help?" asked Kate.

Fred raised an eyebrow.

"As you probably know, the police questioned me, but that's as far as it went. My alibi came from Famke, a neighbor who I was having an affair with, so a lot of the neighbors still think I bumped Joanna off. When we remodeled, the whole house was ripped apart. Floors pulled up, walls stripped back to the brick. We dug up the garden for a new ground-source heat pump, and the village is now on the main sewage system, so we took out the old septic tank . . . Someone in the village called the police when they saw the tank being craned out of the garden. I don't know who. The police showed up and asked to look inside before it was taken away. They'd checked it already, three times over the years. It was good to get rid of it and make a new start. I think the rumors that I killed Joanna and stashed her under the floorboards or buried her in the garden have hopefully been put to rest."

"Are you still in contact with Famke?" asked Tristan.

Fred frowned. "Of course not. No."

"Do you know where she is?"

"The last I heard, years ago, is that she went back to the Netherlands," said Fred.

"What did Bev say about your affair?"

"What do you bloody think she said? She was angry at me for a long time, but we found peace . . ." There was a long pause. "We send each other Christmas cards."

"My bank sends me a Christmas card every year," said Kate.

"Okay. Yes. We're no longer close," said Fred. "But you would expect that. Joanna was the glue that held us together."

He took a sip of his coffee.

"On the day Joanna went missing, you were here all day. Your neighbor saw you gardening, and in between that you were . . ." Kate hesitated. "Here in the house, with Famke?"

"Yes."

"You didn't leave the house until just before eight?"

"Yes. When Joanna didn't come home from work, I tried her mobile, but it was switched off. I phoned Bev around seven, but she didn't know where Joanna was. Bev phoned Joanna's friend Marnie; she didn't know either. Joanna didn't have a lot of friends, and she didn't socialize with people from work. She'd been planning to come straight home, so we were concerned . . . Our first thought was that she'd had a car accident. Bev rang the police, but they weren't much help and told her to ring back after twenty-four hours. Bev asked if I could pick her up, so I drove over to her flat. She wanted to check the two local hospitals, but we went to the Deansgate multistory car park first."

"Why?" asked Kate.

"That's where Joanna parked. It was due to be demolished, and not many people were parking there because it attracted a lot of dodgy types, drug addicts. We'd told her to park up by the Corn Exchange, which was more expensive and further away from her office, but she stubbornly refused and carried on parking at Deansgate. When we arrived at the car park, I drove up the levels to check, and that's when we found Joanna's car. Her mobile phone was underneath it and switched off, and that's when things turned very dark, and the police opened a missing persons case."

"Did Joanna have any enemies?" asked Kate.

"No. She didn't have a lot of friends, and kept herself to herself, but no one who she hated, or hated her in return," said Fred.

"Six months before she went missing, Joanna had written an exposé about a local MP, Noah Huntley. Her investigative article triggered a by-election, and he lost his seat," said Kate.

Fred smiled. "That made me proud. It's always nice to see a Tory get a good kicking any day of the week, but to know Joanna caught that bastard and held him accountable . . . That was the point where she should have made the leap and gone to work at one of the national tabloids . . ."

"Why didn't she?" asked Tristan.

Fred paused and rubbed at his face. He slumped back and sat up again.

"This is all a bit much, raking over it again. It was because of me," he said. He looked down and bit his lip. Kate glanced over at Tristan, and for a moment she thought Fred was going to cry. He let out a deep breath. "I wasn't in a good place. I was unemployed and feeling disorientated. Joanna wanted to make the move to London, rent out this house, and try applying for one of the tabloids. She'd had interest from one of the national papers. I refused and said I didn't want to go, which is something I regret, deeply. If we'd gone, she'd probably still be alive."

Kate took a folder from her bag.

"We asked you about Joanna having enemies. Could Noah Huntley have been classed as an enemy? Joanna's article ended his career in politics," she said.

"That happened months before she went missing," said Fred.

"We've been given access to the original police case files. Did you know that Noah Huntley attended a voluntary police interview when Joanna went missing?" asked Kate.

"No. I didn't know that. When did they arrest him?" asked Fred. His surprise at this information seemed genuine.

"They didn't arrest him. He wasn't a suspect. And they spoke to him nine months after Joanna went missing: June fourteenth, 2003," said Kate. "The police requested to speak to him after some CCTV images surfaced of Joanna and him meeting two weeks before she vanished."

Fred sat back, surprised. "She'd talked about writing a follow-up story about Noah Huntley, but she never mentioned that she met him."

"What kind of follow-up story?" asked Kate.

"When she was doing the investigation into the council contracts, she'd also heard some rumors that he liked to meet men, after dark, pick them up in his car."

"Why didn't she write about this in her original article?"

"She didn't have enough evidence. Her editor didn't want it to distract from the fraud story."

"Did she discuss her work with you?" asked Tristan.

"She would talk about stuff after the event, but if it was a story she was working on and involved sensitive stuff, she wouldn't talk about it . . . Hang on, what kind of CCTV video surfaced of them meeting?"

"You've got a Texaco petrol station close by, on the main road into Exeter," said Kate. "It was held up by a gunman with a sawn-off shotgun nine months after Joanna went missing. The police asked for their CCTV tapes, and for some reason, a tape with footage from an evening nine months previously was amongst the footage. The police officer who was logging it recognized Joanna's number plate. He'd been working on the case, and it had stuck in his mind. Then he saw that the time stamp of the video was just after eight p.m. on the twenty-third of August, 2002."

"That doesn't make sense," said Fred. "Joanna used to joke she was probably the last person Noah Huntley would want to spit at, let alone speak to, after the story broke."

"We've looked on the map, and this petrol station is on the main road, the A377 to Exeter. Was that the route Joanna took from Upton Pyne to work?"

"Yeah."

Kate opened the folder and took out four still photos from the CCTV tape and laid them out on the table. In the first photo, Joanna's car, a blue Ford Sierra, was parked in one of the spots reserved for drivers at the side of the petrol station. It was parked facing the camera, and Joanna could be clearly seen through the front windscreen alone. The second photo showed Noah Huntley, who was tall with dark hair and a pronounced widow's peak, getting in the passenger side. The third photo showed a freeze-frame of them deep in conversation. The fourth showed Noah Huntley getting out of Joanna's car. The whole exchange lasted fifteen minutes. Fred stared at the photos, still lost for words.

"What did Noah Huntley say to the police about their meeting?" he asked.

"He told them that he was on the board of the *Daily Mail*, and he was also an occasional columnist. Joanna was being courted by the *Mail* to join their team, and she wanted to meet with him and get his assurance that he wouldn't block her hiring," said Kate.

Fred shook his head.

"That's bollocks. She would never go crawling to someone like him."

"We've looked through all of the case files, and the police confirmed that this was true—Joanna had applied for a post at the *Daily Mail*. There was confusion as to why the petrol station kept the CCTV tape. Usually, they recorded a month's worth of CCTV, then wiped and reused the tapes," said Kate. "They say it was a mistake—the tapes were badly organized. Once Noah's story checked out, the police didn't pursue it."

"Can you think of any other reason why Joanna could have met him?" she asked.

"I don't know," said Fred. "I thought I knew Joanna, but as more time passes, I don't think I knew her at all."

7

"That's the petrol station," said Tristan, pointing up ahead at a Texaco sign. After they left their meeting with Fred, Kate wanted to drive the route that Joanna took to get to work in Exeter. It was less than a mile from Upton Pyne to the bypass, and the petrol station was another half mile along the road. Kate slowed the car as they passed. It was in a lonely spot, surrounded by trees and open fields. A woman was filling up her car under the giant flying canopy.

"I don't buy it that the reason Joanna met with Noah Huntley at the petrol station was to talk about a potential job conflict of interest," said Kate. "She had a mobile phone, and presumably so did Noah Huntley. Why meet in person, after office hours, for something like that?"

The petrol station was now shrinking in her rearview mirror, and the road wound its way through remote and hilly countryside.

"And presumably, he came out of his way to meet her," said Tristan. "Noah Huntley moved back to London when he lost his seat in Parliament."

They drove in silence. Kate was mulling things over in her mind, imagining Joanna driving to work on the morning of September seventh. Was it just an ordinary day?

Five minutes later they left the motorway and drove into Exeter town center. As they turned onto the narrow high street, Kate slowed down so that she could squeeze past a bus, where a line of miserable-looking pensioners waited to board.

A couple of courier bikes zipped between the traffic. Kate stopped at another set of red lights.

"Okay. That was the offices for the *West Country News*," said Tristan, indicating a five-story building on the left that was now a John Lewis department store.

"When Joanna left work around five thirty, this street was still quite busy. It was a Saturday evening. The shops would be closing, but the bars and pubs would be filling up," said Kate, peering up between the traffic at the rows of shops and the four pubs that stretched along the high street. The lights changed to green, and she pulled forward, having to weave between two buses. Kate glanced to the right and left. There were a few side streets leading off the main road. They were quiet in comparison, and some had loading bays for the shops.

"Yeah. There must have been lots of people around, but no one saw what happened to her," said Tristan, following her gaze.

They sped on and came to a set of traffic lights. To the right of them was a big block of flats with *Anchor House Apartments* written in curling font on the front.

"And that's where the old Deansgate multistory car park stood," said Kate, their view blocked as a blur of people crossed in front. "Jesus, that's hardly any distance at all from the newspaper offices."

Tristan took the folder that was poking out of Kate's bag and found one of the photos from the case file. It was taken from a CCTV camera a little way down from the crossing where they waited. It was the last known photo taken of Joanna. She wore a long black coat and a pair of brown leather cowboy boots. Her shoulder-length blonde hair was wavy and parted in the middle. The pavement was empty, and a couple were a little way behind her on the street, with their backs to the camera, huddled down, sharing an umbrella.

"She looked stressed out," said Tristan, holding up the photo. Joanna's brow was furrowed, and both hands were clutching the handle of her bag hooked over her shoulder. It looked like she was deep in concentration.

"She would have crossed right here," said Kate, keeping one eye on the road as the last couple of pedestrians hurried across. "What was the multistory car park like? Was there an entrance on foot, here on the road?"

"Yeah, there was a car entrance in the middle, just further up," said Tristan, indicating what was now the center of the apartment block. "And to the right of that was a poky little door for pedestrians."

The lights turned green, and Kate drove past the Anchor apartment block. Tristan went on, "The car park was nasty, concrete, constantly damp. I used to get very scared the few times my mum parked there. Druggies hung around in the stairwell, and it was creepy if you had to go back to your car after dark. There were no windows, just holes in the concrete sides at intervals. It was six stories high, and over the years quite a few people jumped off and committed suicide on the road here. By the time they demolished it, most people were using the NCP multistory car park on the other side of the one-way system—we'll go past it in a sec. Or they used the Guildhall Shopping Centre down the other end of the high street."

"If Joanna got as far as crossing the road back there in that photo, then logically, she could have been grabbed or attacked by someone using the cover of the multistory car park. The traffic is so loud on the high street, it could have drowned out any sounds of screaming when she was inside," said Kate, glancing back down at the CCTV photo in Tristan's lap. It made her shiver to think that Joanna could have been moments away from her fate in this picture.

They reached the top of the high street, where there was a small park. The cathedral appeared to rise out of the ground as the one-way system curved around to the right onto Market Street, past the NCP car park and the Corn Exchange theatre.

"It just seems like such a risky place to make her vanish," said Kate. "Joanna lived in Upton Pyne, which is so tiny and out in the sticks. She had to drive across all that countryside to get to work. If I was going to make someone vanish, I wouldn't do it in the middle of Exeter with its busy one-way system and part-pedestrianized high street. I'd grab her in the countryside. Force her car off the road. We hardly saw any other cars when we drove into Exeter from Upton Pyne, and that road was probably even quieter back in 2002."

"There were no CCTV cameras facing the exit or entrance ramp of the multistory car park, were there?" asked Tristan.

"No. Just the camera that caught this last picture of Joanna. The next CCTV camera is up by the Corn Exchange around the corner."

"There are plenty of other side roads you could turn off before you get to the Corn Exchange."

They were now leaving the town center and heading back toward Ashdean. There was so much paperwork in the case file, and Kate wanted to have another look at it all. It was taking time to absorb all the details.

"I want to track down her colleagues at the *West Country News*," said Kate. "And her editor. I don't think DCI Featherstone pushed him enough to talk about what Joanna was investigating when she went missing. As far as I can see from the case file interviews, they never talked to him again . . . What was his name?"

"Ashley Harris," said Tristan.

"Yes, and we need to talk to Jo's friend Marnie. And Famke. She could give us more insight into the state of Fred and Joanna's marriage, and Fred's alibi is a bit of a patchwork."

Tristan looked at Kate. "You really think Fred could have done it?"

"At this stage I want to keep an open mind." Kate indicated the photo, still in Tristan's lap. "The case files say that Joanna logged out of her work computer at five thirty p.m. The time stamp on that photo is five forty-one. What if Fred came to pick her up in his car? She got in willingly . . . He managed to drop her phone without her noticing . . . Okay, that part's still unclear. But if she got into a car willingly with him, there's six miles of lonely countryside where he could have dumped her body, come back home. It's not a long journey from Upton Pyne to Exeter."

"The neighbor said Fred's car didn't move until seven thirty that night, when he left and went searching for Joanna," said Tristan.

"Shit. Yes. That's right. Let's get something to eat and go back to the case files again."

8

Tristan arrived home at seven that evening. He'd worked through the afternoon with Kate, putting together a timeline of Joanna's last day. They couldn't find contact details for Famke, but they'd managed to track down the doctor who Famke had worked for as an au pair. He now had a surgery in Surrey, and they'd emailed him.

Tristan's flat was on the ground floor of the esplanade on Ashdean seafront. He loved the location and being able to cross the road and walk on the beach, but he was still trying to adjust to having a roommate.

Glenn was already in the kitchen stirring a steaming stir-fry in a wok on the stove. Glenn was a tall, beefy bloke with a Desperate Dan face; thick, bushy eyebrows; and a permanent five-o'clock shadow. In repose, his face was menacing, but he broke into a grin when he saw Tristan and suddenly looked like a big cuddly teddy bear.

"Yerite, mate? I'm almost done here," he said.

"What are you having?" asked Tristan. The smell of spices and meat made his mouth water.

"It's Delia Smith."

"You've managed to chop her up very small."

"No, it's her hung shao pork with stir-fry greens," said Glenn, not getting the joke. "I think I could make it stretch to two."

"No. Thank you. I'm heading back out and meeting a friend for a drink."

Glenn had moved in a month ago but worked shifts as a prison warden, and with Tristan juggling his two jobs with the agency and the university, he hadn't had time to get to know him.

Tristan went for a shower, and when he came back downstairs ten minutes later, the kitchen was empty, the dishwasher running, and the counters were wiped down. Glenn was the fastest eater Tristan had ever seen. He almost swallowed his food whole.

Checking he had his phone and wallet, Tristan called out, "Bye," up the stairs as he left but didn't hear a response.

Ashdean was a student town, and even though it was the students' end-of-year exams, the seafront was busy with people. It wouldn't get dark for a couple of hours, but there was already a group of students building a fire on the beach from driftwood.

There were bars and pubs along the seafront nestled among the terraced flats and houses, and occasional hotels that still had the aura of a 1950s boardinghouse. Tristan lived at the top end of the seafront, close to the university building, where the esplanade curved sharply away from the beach and then doubled back on itself and became the high street.

He walked in the opposite direction, down toward the end of the esplanade, past a couple of pubs where groups of people sat outside on the pavement eating dinner.

The Boar's Head was at the very end, and it backed onto the steep hill that led up onto the cliffs.

It was a small pub with a raised stage next to a DJ booth, where Pete the DJ was playing Atomic Kitten's Spanish cover of "The Tide Is High." It was still early when Tristan entered, and there was a mix of guys and girls, old and young, standing by the bar.

He noticed his friend Ade playing on an ancient *Who Wants to Be a Millionaire?* slot machine. He was a large man in his early fifties, wearing baggy jeans, a white T-shirt, and an orange down vest. His black hair was long and lustrously styled, flowing down over his shoulders, and a thick, dark beard.

"Well hello, Miss Marple," said Ade, looking up from the machine. He leaned over and gave Tristan a hug. *Miss Marple* was the nickname Ade had coined when he heard Tristan worked as a private detective. "Haven't seen you for a few days. Has it been busy in Saint Mary Mead?"

"We've just started working on a new missing persons case. Very complex. What are you drinking?" asked Tristan.

"Alcohol, Miss Marple!" said Ade, holding up his empty pint glass. "Get me a lager top."

Tristan ordered a pint of Guinness and another lager for Ade, and they went to sit in one of the booths to the side of the bar.

Their friendship was easy. Ade went drinking most evenings at the Boar's Head, and they never arranged to meet, but it had become a regular thing for them to meet for drinks a couple of times a week.

Ade had been a police officer for twenty-five years, but then an attack when he was on duty left him with PTSD. At fifty, Ade had taken early retirement, and he was trying to write a science fiction novel. He'd taken Tristan under his wing after Tristan had come out as gay almost three years earlier.

"Did you ever work on the Joanna Duncan missing persons case?" asked Tristan.

Ade took a long pull on his lager. "No. Who was she?"

Tristan had known it was a long shot that Ade might have worked on the case.

"She was a journalist at the *West Country News*. She went missing in September 2002."

"Oh yes, I remember. I was working with the Devon and Cornwall vice squad at the time. Which I know probably sounds like a contradiction in terms, but I'm telling you, it's a hotbed of sex and scandal just like the rest of the country."

"I wanted to know if you ever heard any gossip about a guy called Noah Huntley? He was the local MP round here. He won his seat in the '92 election and then lost it in a bribery scandal . . ."

Ade raised an eyebrow and took another sip of his lager. "I know that he's been 'happily married' for twenty years but prefers to spend his nights with handsome young men. Why? Has he given you his number, Miss Marple?"

"No, nothing like that."

Tristan went on to explain that Joanna Duncan had also been investigating Noah Huntley's use of rent boys, but that part of the story hadn't been published.

"I caught him cruising once, years back," said Ade. "It was August, a few weeks before Princess Diana died, 1997. It was a hot night, and we were doing a big round of two housing estates and some nicer residential areas, and we'd go past a gay pub on the outskirts of Exeter called Peppermintz. It was a bit rough and ready. It was actually my local, and an ex-boyfriend of mine used to do some gigs there. He was a Lorna Luft impersonator . . ."

"Who's Lorna Luft?" asked Tristan, regretting it the moment he asked.

"Oh my Lord—call yourself gay? Or do you say *queer*?"

"No. I don't say *queer*."

"Good. Why are the young using *queer*? *Queer* is the slur that was hurled at me for most of my younger years. *Queer* is what the bullies and the homophobes called me when they beat the crap out of me."

"But some people use that word to describe themselves."

"And that's fine, all power to them; just don't call *me* queer. I want to be called gay, and I have the right to ask that."

Tristan could see Ade was getting worked up.

"Okay, so you were saying about Noah Huntley."

"No, I was telling you that Lorna Luft is Judy Garland's daughter. *Please* tell me you know who Judy Garland is."

"Yes, of course."

"I don't know *why* he chose to impersonate Lorna Luft. I said to him, 'Have some ambition. Be Liza.' I got into a similar row with a queen last Halloween who came dressed up as Tamar Braxton."

"Anyway," said Tristan impatiently. "You saw Noah Huntley at this gay club, Peppermintz, in August 1997?" he asked, guiding Ade back to the subject.

"No, he wasn't in the club. I was a beat officer, and our beat took us past the club, on to an old bit of scrubland by the motorway underpass. On this night, there was a smart-looking car parked up by the curb in this completely desolate area, with overgrown bits in the road and just a few blinking streetlights. We'd been briefed that evening that one of the other teams would be doing surveillance on a local drug gang. I thought at first the car might be one of theirs. It was a BMW. So we held back, and the officer I was on shift with, I forget her name, called in the number plate to Control, and it came back that the car was registered to Noah Huntley. We then went to take a closer look and found our local Conservative MP was on the back seat with George, one of the lads who worked at Peppermintz."

"Having sex?"

Ade rolled his eyes. "Yes, Tristan. *Having sex.* Either that or it was a particularly enthusiastic naked Heimlich maneuver."

Tristan laughed. "What did you do?"

"I knocked on the window, and then we stood back and gave them enough time to make themselves presentable. After a few minutes, Noah opened the door. It didn't help that the barman, George, said, 'Hiya, Ade,' whilst he was still doing up his belt buckle. I told them to move on and be careful and reminded them that what they were doing was a public-order offense."

"Why didn't you arrest them?"

"Labour had just won the election, and the whole issue of how the police dealt with gay rights had changed radically. They were in a deserted, lonely spot at night. Noah also looked shaken up and was very apologetic. If he'd been an arsehole about it or tried to use his clout as an MP, we'd have booked him and taken him down to the station."

"Are you still in contact with this barman, George?" asked Tristan.

"I was never *in* contact with him—I used to see him around, but he went missing a few years later," said Ade.

"What do you mean, *missing*?" asked Tristan.

"Vanished without a trace."

"Were the police involved?"

"Oh, it was nothing like that. Some people thought he'd met a bloke with a bit of money and done a midnight flit. George was behind on his rent. Another rumor was that George turned a few tricks on the side—you know, the job called blow—but he hadn't taken any money from Noah Huntley, or so he said."

"Can you remember George's second name?"

Ade took a sip of his drink and thought for a moment.

"No, he was George. He was Spanish, and he'd been living here for a few years, but I can't remember his surname. I think I might have a photo of him somewhere at a fancy-dress party. It was before social media, and I'm not sure he even had a mobile phone. He was employed cash in hand at the bar, and I'd known quite a few young guys like him who'd done a midnight flit to avoid the rent."

"Can you remember when he went missing?"

"Bloody hell. I know it was a while later, after the millennium, cos he was at all the parties . . . erm, maybe a year or two later, summer 2002."

"Do you know if Noah Huntley was ever arrested or had a police record?" asked Tristan. Ade swilled the last dregs of his pint in the glass and downed it.

"Not when we caught him in 1997. I checked just after to see if he'd been caught cruising before. Do you think he had something to do with Joanna Dobson—"

"Joanna Duncan," corrected Tristan.

"You think he had something to do with her going missing?"

"I don't know. If she knew about him being in the closet. And knew he was using rent boys?" asked Tristan.

Ade shook his head.

"By the time Joanna Duncan went missing, being gay in government was no longer a sackable offense, and Noah Huntley had left politics. He was probably earning three times as much money as a well-paid consultant traveling around, able to have his pick of Spanish barmen. He didn't have to worry about being exposed and then trotting out the wife, two kids, and the Labrador on his front lawn for a happy family photo shoot."

"Yeah, that's true," said Tristan. "It would have been more believable if he'd made her vanish to bury the story."

"What if that's *not* the real story?" asked Ade.

9

After Tristan left, Kate was locking up the office when she remembered that a delivery of clean bedding was coming the next morning, and the case files were all over the office.

"Bloody hell," said Kate. She'd been looking forward to sitting down with a cup of tea and egg on toast. She took the key from her pocket and unlocked the door.

It didn't take long to move the boxes to one side. There was three months' worth of bedding for the eight caravans coming, so she shifted the boxes against the right-hand wall, having to pile them three high. She was excited to see Jake when he finished university in two weeks. He'd be home for the whole summer and was coming back to help with running the caravan site, and he'd be able to deal with things like bed linen.

The last box that Kate moved was a blue one that had belonged to Joanna, and it held her paperwork and diaries from work. The box was from a stationery shop and made from a shiny blue cardboard. There were small steel brackets on each corner to help keep it from tearing. When Kate picked up the lid to put it back on, the bright fluorescent strip light from above bounced off the shiny surface of the cardboard inside the lid, and she noticed there was an impression of handwriting.

Kate studied it more closely, tilting it under the light, and saw there were three lines of writing. The box lid had been used as a writing surface, to hold a sheet of paper against. Kate turned the lid over and saw that the top of the box was a little battered and scuffed, but there was no writing. On the front of the box there was a small label in a metal frame that said *Notes 6/2001–6/2002* in faded blue handwriting.

Kate carried the box lid over to the filing cabinets, where there was a bright lamp next to the long window. She switched it on, and as she tilted the box lid from side to side under the dazzling light, she could make out a few letters but nothing she could decipher. She'd recently bought an iPhone, and Jake had shown her how good its camera was at enhancing the light in photos. She put the box down on the desk and took some photos of the writing inside the lid.

When she enhanced the picture on her iPhone, it didn't make a lot of difference. She opened her MacBook and transferred the photo over from her phone, then opened the iPhoto app and started to play with all the detailed picture settings, sharpening the contrast, increasing the definition, reducing the noise. She wasn't sure what the latter two settings meant, but as she moved the slider back and forth, the shading and shadows in the picture altered, and the indented writing on the back of the box started to become clear.

"Bloody hell," she said, feeling a tingle of excitement.

Pick up at 10am or later? Check

David Lamb

Gabe Kemp

Meet at the catering truck 07980746029

She saved the image, printed it off, and googled both of the names. There were scores of results for both on social media and LinkedIn.

It was just after seven thirty p.m., and Kate tried the phone number, which was a British mobile number, but it was out of service.

Kate hesitated and then phoned Bev. When she answered, her voice sounded thick with alcohol. Kate knew then that she was being impatient and should have waited until the next morning to ring.

"Oh, hello, Kate. Is everything all right?" asked Bev. She sounded like she was in a small, echoing room.

"Sorry to bother you at home," said Kate. "I just wanted to ask you about a couple of names that have come up—David Lamb and Gabe Kemp. Do they ring a bell?"

There was a pause, and she heard water running. She wondered if she'd caught Bev when she was in the toilet. From the noise, she imagined some poky downstairs loo, but their house in Salcombe was palatial, all that marble and high ceilings.

"No, love, I'm sorry. I can't remember Jo having any friends or colleagues with those names . . ."

"No. They're written on the inside of the blue box that you gave us with the evidence. It was the box of Joanna's paperwork. It looks like the same writing on the label on the front of the box."

"Right," said Bev, still sounding a bit confused.

"I'm thinking that Jo could have used the box to write on as a rest for a piece of paper. Although . . . the box has probably been with the police for years. If I text you a photo of it that I just took, can you just confirm it's Joanna's writing?"

"Yeah, okay."

Kate took the phone away from her ear to send the photo. Moments later she heard a ting on the end of the phone. "Hang on, love . . ." There was a rustling and then a clatter where Bev dropped the phone. Then a moment later she came back on the line. "Yes, that's Jo's writing . . . ," she said, her voice quavering. "Is this a clue?"

"It could be."

"Oh. You think those blokes could have had something to do with her going missing?"

"I don't know. I've just found it . . ." Kate's voice trailed off, trying to find something she could say to comfort Bev. "This will all take time, but I promise you we're working hard every day on this."

Yuck. That sounded so corporate, thought Kate.

Bev sighed.

"I just had a row with Bill. He stormed out. Took off in his car. I wanted to follow 'im, but I've had the best part of a bottle of Jacob's Creek . . ."

"Oh, I'm sorry," said Kate.

"Yeah, well. We have these ups and downs. It's the stress. We've never lived together before, after all these years . . . You will tell me the moment that you find something out, won't you, about those names?"

"Yes," said Kate.

"Okay. I sent you over the first payment. I did it online."

"Thank you."

"I'm staying in tonight . . ." She gave a bitter laugh. "Listen to me—I stay in every night. I'm going to open another bottle, bugger it, and watch telly. There's no bloody curtains here. I know I shouldn't moan, but I miss my curtains. I've got all these huge windows looking out to sea. I know we're high up, but I can't shake the idea that someone's peering in."

"Do you think someone's outside?"

"Course not. No. All the other houses are far away, and if some fisherman wants to peer at me through a telescope, he won't see much, just me getting plastered in front of *Coronation Street* . . . It's just my thing. I like closing curtains. I like having a cozy room . . . Bill'll come back when he's calmed down. What did you have for your tea?"

"Nothing, yet. I'll probably have egg on toast."

"Nice, with a bit of brown sauce. Okay. I won't keep you. You can phone me, whenever. Night, love."

"Good night."

When Kate came off the phone, she thought how lonely Bev had sounded, and she kept hearing her words echoing in her head.

Bottle of wine, bottle of wine, another bottle of wine, and the sound of a cork popping from a good bottle of wine. Red wine, rich and full bodied, that delicious sound when the first drops pour out of the bottle.

Myra had been Kate's AA sponsor, and after she died, Kate hadn't tried to find another, but she did keep going to meetings.

Kate pushed the image of a large glass of red wine from her thoughts, sat back down at her computer, and started to search through the Google results for David Lamb and Gabe Kemp.

10

The Brewer's Arms was a small gay bar situated on a stretch of the canal in Torquay, twenty miles down the coast from Ashdean. In its past life, it had been a brewery, and the entrance was nestled under a long line of brick arches. On this quiet Monday evening, the sun was starting to set on the canal bank, reflecting orange on the still water.

Hayden Oakley approached the front entrance and smiled at the bouncer at the door. The bouncer, a thick-set man with a boxer's nose, returned the smile and stood to one side to let him in.

In the dimly lit interior, Hayden felt the warmth and the pounding music on his skin and smelled the scent of a thousand aftershaves clashing in the air with a sweet chemical tang. It was a real meat market. Propping up the bar was a group of older guys, sitting with ice buckets of champagne. They were watching with studied intensity, like fishermen waiting for a bite on the end of a hook, as a group of attractive young guys danced on a small dance floor bathed in the scattered shards of light from a glitter ball.

All heads turned to look at Hayden. He was tall and lean with an athlete's build and a smooth, fresh face. He guessed that most of the older guys at the bar didn't have more than a few pounds between them, but the prospect of a night with a twenty-year-old with a slim waist was worth putting on your good jeans and T-shirt and forking out for a few drinks.

There was one guy that Hayden was hoping to see at the bar, and he smiled when he saw him, sitting on the end. His name was Tom. He wore jeans and a tight T-shirt, and he had a baseball cap over his thick, dark hair, which hung down to his shoulders. He wasn't the best-looking guy, but he had a slightly battered straight-guy look about him, and more importantly, he had money. He was the only one who had a bottle of proper champagne in his ice bucket. They'd met here the previous week. Tom had bought a bottle of vintage champagne, and they'd chatted and flirted for a couple of hours, and Hayden had hinted at more. That was the key, thought Hayden—play a little bit hard to get. Tom worked in finance, business, or something. Whatever he did, it made him lots of money.

"Hi, sexy," said Tom as Hayden approached. Tom was shy and soft spoken. "You thirsty?" He held up a spare champagne glass.

"Always," said Hayden. He leaned over to kiss him, and Tom pulled him close, squeezing his waist. Hayden put his hand on Tom's waist, which felt thick and solid, and trailed it down to his firm backside. There was a thick square in the back pocket of his jeans. *Money.* Last time they met, Tom had pulled out a wad of fifty-pound notes to pay for their drinks, and it felt like he'd brought even more with him this time.

Hayden pulled away and smiled at Tom. The older man's brown eyes twinkled mischievously in the multicolored lights from the dance floor. A slow song started to play, and a few of the young guys who'd been dancing left the floor and started circling around the row of barstools. Three of them already had drinks on the go with the older guys, and they chatted and flirted and had their glasses topped up.

"You had a good week?" Tom asked.

"Yeah, I bought these jeans," said Hayden, pulling up his tight T-shirt to reveal his washboard stomach and the top of his new Levi's. Tom's eyes lit up.

"Nice," he said, tipping the flute of champagne back and downing the contents.

This is going to be so easy, thought Hayden.

A lad with a ratty face and hair dyed far too dark for his skin tone came dancing over to them. His name was Carl. His eyes lit up when he saw the bottle of Moët.

"You guys want a third?" he shouted, in the same throwaway manner as if asking for a portion of chips. His pupils were dilated like two large inkwells, and he had a cold sore on his bottom lip.

Hayden shook his head.

"Go on," said Carl, leaning close. "Champagne makes me really slutty."

Hayden turned so his back was to Tom, and he leaned over and said, "Get the fuck away from him, Carl. Or I'll tell the bouncer on the door that you're a rent boy hassling the punters."

"All right, I was only up for a laugh!" replied Carl, his eyes wide with alarm. He reached into his jeans to get out his phone, staggered on his feet, and moved away to one of the other older men. Hayden had heard that Carl had recently been chucked out of his bedsit and needed to find a bed for the night. Hayden turned back to Tom.

"What did you say to him?" asked Tom.

"I told him to take it easy. He's fallen off the wagon again. Do you want to go and sit down?" he said, indicating a long leather bench lining the sidewall.

"Sure," said Tom with a smile.

They sat chatting for the next half hour and drank another bottle. Hayden did all the talking, telling Tom about his crazy roommate, Amy, who had recently dyed her blonde hair red with henna from a new-age shop in Torquay and then gone swimming at the leisure center.

"It was like a scene from *Jaws*," finished Hayden. Tom laughed. He poured the last of the bottle into their glasses. "Would you excuse me a moment?" Hayden added, getting up and going to the toilet.

The gents' toilet in the Brewer's Arms was always a bit of a shock to the system. The bar was warm with dim-colored lighting. The toilets, in comparison, were starkly lit and freezing cold. Hayden blinked in the brightness as he went to the urinal and took a pee. The toilets were empty. When he finished, he washed his hands and studied his reflection in the mirror. Even in the bright fluorescent light, he looked good. He took a deep breath and dried his hands on a hand towel. He reached into his pocket and took out a small resealable plastic bag. It contained the finely crushed powder of four Rohypnol tablets.

The door crashed open, and Carl came stumbling in. Hayden quickly pocketed the bag. Carl had looked rough in the bar, but the light in the toilet made him look positively cadaverous. He went to the urinal and unzipped his trousers and started to pee, swaying on his feet. Hayden could see that his jeans and trainers were filthy.

"I know what you're up to," said Carl, shaking and zipping up.

"And what's that?" asked Hayden.

"You're going to put something in that guy's drink and then rob him," slurred Carl, adjusting his spiky hair in the mirror.

Hayden kept his face neutral. "You need to lay off the crystal meth, Carl," he said.

Carl raised his eyebrows. "*Do I?* I got chatting to a guy at the Feather's the other night, telling me about a tall blond from up north, with blue eyes and a metal bar through his bell end, who he took home . . . He woke up the next morning and all his cash and credit cards were gone. He thinks someone spiked his drink. I've peed next to you enough times to know that's you."

Hayden hesitated and then grabbed Carl by the throat and slammed him against the tiled wall.

"If I hear you talking about me, I'll kill you. I'm not joking," he said, pressing his thumb into Carl's Adam's apple. "I'll cut you up. Break your skull. Happens all the time to scally little rent boys like you."

Carl's dilated eyes were wide, and he was gagging. Hayden held on for a few more seconds, then abruptly let go. Carl coughed and spat and slid down the wall to land in the damp pools of water on the dirty tiles. Hayden stepped over him and left the toilets.

Tom looked up and smiled when he came back into the bar.

"Can I get us another bottle?" he said. Hayden noticed a thick gold ring on his finger.

"Why don't you take me back to your place?" said Hayden, sliding his hand up Tom's thigh. Tom's face broke into a sheepish grin.

"Okay. My car's parked by the canal."

It was dark outside when they left the bar. Hayden's eyes grew wide when he saw Tom's expensive Land Rover waiting in the shadows in the car park next to the water. The headlights flashed invitingly when Tom unlocked the car.

"This is gorgeous," said Hayden, stroking the tan leather seats as he climbed inside.

"Thanks. It's new."

"It smells new. I love the smell of leather. I love leather, full stop."

"Good. I've got more leather back at my place. Buckle up," said Tom, grinning as he started the engine. They pulled up the hill to the main road.

"And where is your place?"

"Quay Apartments, on the other side of town."

Hayden smiled. He'd hit the jackpot. You didn't get much change from a million quid at Quay Apartments.

"You want a drink?" asked Tom.

"At your place?"

"No. Now," he said, tilting his head toward a leather square between the front seats. "Open it."

Hayden opened the lid, and nestled inside was a small box fridge containing miniature bottles of Moët and Coca-Cola.

"You've got a bar in your car—that's a bit naughty," said Hayden.

"I don't like my friends to go thirsty."

For the first time, Hayden felt a pang of guilt. Tom seemed like a nice guy. He pushed the thought away. He picked up one of the small Moët bottles. The foil had been removed, and he untwisted the metal cage from the cork, teasing it out with a small pop.

"There's straws in the bottom of the fridge," added Tom. They reached a junction that sloped down to the empty motorway.

Hayden took out one of the paper straws, put it in the bottle. Tom leaned over with one eye on the road. "Give us a sip." Hayden held out the bottle and watched as Tom put his lips to the straw and swallowed. "Lovely."

Hayden took a sip from the straw. It was cold and deliciously tart. The pang of guilt came back to him again. What if this Tom could be someone good in his life? A boyfriend who'd love him and look after him? For the next five minutes, they chatted and laughed. The only other vehicle they passed was a small white van tootling along in the slow lane.

Hayden finished the bottle quickly, and as he put it in the cup holder, a wave of lethargy came over him, and he started to feel dizzy. The lights of the town on the horizon were starting to streak and flare when he moved his head. His tongue felt thick in his mouth.

"How are you enjoying that champagne? Want another?" asked Tom, looking over at him. An alarm was going off in the back of Hayden's mind, but everything felt far away. He shifted in his seat, but his legs were heavy.

"Was that champagne I drank?" he slurred. He looked down, and a ribbon of drool was hanging off his bottom lip.

"Champagne. With a little added extra," said Tom with a laugh. Hayden put his head back against the leather headrest, but it felt like his skull was melting into the soft leather. He pulled his head away. The lights outside were now trailing long lines in his vision. "Did you know, Hayden, that you can push a syringe through a champagne cork down into the bottle?" Tom looked different. In the bar he'd seemed like a big, bashful teddy bear, but now his brown eyes were hard, and he had a hungry stare. "The cork is fairly soft, but you really have to fight against the pressure of the carbon dioxide in the bottle when you get the needle in. You can feel it trying to force the plunger part of the syringe back out . . . The cork reseals itself; it really is a marvel." He laughed. It echoed and reverberated around the inside of the car. There were no streetlights, thought Hayden. Why were they on the motorway? They'd left town, but Tom had said he lived in town.

Hayden's head was now too heavy to hold up. It slid to one side, and he felt his cheek against the cold of the window, and he had that melting feeling again, like it was going through the glass. Tom reached over and gently ruffled Hayden's hair. Then he grabbed a handful and pulled him upright, pushing his head back against the headrest. "Sit up straight."

Tom checked the mirror, signaled, and took an exit off the motor-way. The sign was a blur of letters. Once they were off the brightly lit motorway, the dark country road seemed to swallow the car, and Hayden saw the edges of fields and trees lit up in the beam of the head-lights. He could hear a far-off voice in the back of his head, shouting at him, *Open the door; jump out of the car!* But he couldn't move.

Tom pulled off the country road and parked in a lay-by. He switched off the headlights, plunging the inside of the car into darkness. There was just the dim glow on the horizon from the motorway. He unclipped his seat belt and took a pair of latex gloves from his pocket and pulled them on. He leaned over Hayden, searching the pockets of his jeans, taking out his mobile phone. The screen saver activated, lighting up the inside of the car. Tom put the phone on the lid of the leather icebox. He found the small plastic wallet where Hayden kept his bank cash card and a ten-pound note, and then he found the little plastic bag of white powder.

Hayden opened his mouth to explain, but his tongue was too thick, and just a groan came out.

"You evil little bastard. The rumors I'd heard about you were true," said Tom, holding up the bag of powder. The phone screen saver went dark. Hayden heard a crackling sound, and his eyes adjusted to the dim glow coming off the motorway. Tom opened the seal on the bag, and pinching Hayden's cheeks to open his mouth, he tipped out the contents onto his tongue. Hayden tasted how bitter it was as Tom closed his mouth.

"Swallow," he said. "Swallow it!" Hayden felt Tom's hand on his throat, squeezing, and he swallowed involuntarily, wincing at the bitterness.

Tom leaned over the controls on the driver's side, and Hayden felt his chair start to recline and tip back. The view of the glowing horizon disappeared, and he was lying horizontally. There was another whir as Tom used the controls to recline the driver's seat. Tom slid back onto the back seat behind Hayden. He hooked his hands under Hayden's limp body and dragged him into the back of the car. The back seat seemed huge, and then Hayden worked out why. Tom had reclined the back seats so he could pull him into the boot of the car.

Tom rolled Hayden onto his left side, and he felt pressure on his wrists as they were fastened behind his back with tape. Tom did the same with his ankles, pulling up the bottom of his jeans. The tape felt cold on his skin.

Tom rolled Hayden onto his back, and he felt the pain of lying on his bound wrists. There was a rustling sound, and Tom appeared above him in the dim light, holding up something long and curved. Hayden thought with alarm that it was a sex toy, but then he saw it was a small plastic tube with a rounded ending. It was an oropharyngeal airway, used by paramedics to keep a patient's airway free.

"I don't want you choking to death on me," said Tom as he pushed the curved plastic tube between Hayden's lips. Hayden gagged as the long tube of the oropharyngeal airway pushed down on his tongue and came to rest at the back of his throat. It protruded from his mouth and over his lips like a pacifier. A square of gaffer tape was pressed over his mouth, and then he felt a violent burst of dizziness as Tom pulled him farther back into the car boot, and then everything went dark as he was covered with a blanket.

———

Tom ignored the muffled moans from Hayden as he crawled back into the driver's seat. He righted all the car seats. The back seat was now empty. He'd been able to move Hayden to the car boot without getting out of the car, and he'd done it in pitch darkness.

He worked quickly with Hayden's mobile phone, switching it off, removing the SIM card, and snapping it in half. He placed the phone, SIM, and wallet in a clear plastic bag and sealed it shut.

He peeled off the white T-shirt he was wearing and put on a dark-blue shirt, which he left open at the collar. He lifted off the backward baseball cap, pulled out six hairpins, and carefully lifted the dark wig they were holding in place. He reached into his mouth and unclipped the top set of dentures, which were larger and whiter than his own teeth, and put them in a bag. Finally, he took a small contact lens holder from the glove compartment and carefully peeled the brown contacts out of each eye and placed them in the solution. It took only a few subtle changes to completely alter his appearance. Tom wasn't his real name, and this was his favorite disguise, with the long hair and baseball cap. He was sad that he would now have to retire it. It gave him an all-American look, like a hunky lumberjack. He switched his headlights back on, then pulled out of the lay-by and started driving across country along the B roads, vanishing into the darkness.

11

Kate stared at the two photos on her computer screen. Gabe Kemp and David Lamb were both handsome young men—or they had been.

There had been a surprising number of men called Gabe Kemp online, scores of Facebook profiles, and there were even more David Lamb profiles. Kate had started to make a list when she thought her first search should be the UK Missing Persons Unit. When she'd been a police officer, the first place she always looked were criminal records, and then missing persons. She didn't have access to the former, but the UK Missing Persons Unit was a free public internet search site where you could find the details of any person who'd been reported missing in the UK. Kate had only their names and that they were male, but she instantly found one missing person profile for David Lamb and one for Gabe Kemp.

The photo used for David was from an instant passport photo booth. He had short, spiky brown hair, brown eyes, olive skin, and a confident, pouty stare. He wore a white V-neck T-shirt and a gold chain. David Lamb had been reported missing in June 1999 in Exeter, but the address listed was "No fixed abode." His birth date was June 14, 1980.

"Just nineteen," said Kate, staring at the photo. There were two photos on the profile, and she clicked forward to the second. It looked to be taken from the same photo booth at the same time. In the second,

David was grinning. He had beautiful teeth and dimples, and he was looking to one side. Kate stared at it and wondered if there had been a friend on the other side of the photo booth curtain, making him laugh.

Gabe Kemp had been reported missing in Plymouth, forty-three miles from Exeter, in April 2002. He was also listed as living at "No fixed abode." Like David, he was dark haired and over six feet tall. There was one photo of Gabe where he was sitting on a set of steps, smoking a cigarette. It looked like it had been cut out of a larger photo—one side of the picture was square, but the opposite side had a curved edge running past Gabe's head and shoulder. He had a harsh beauty. Chiseled features, and a shaved head. It said his eyes were brown, but the photo must have been taken at night, because the flash had given him red-eye.

Kate saved both images and then went back to Google, inputting the details of the two young men. There were no social media profiles for either of them, and there were no articles about them going missing.

Kate sat back and rubbed her eyes, feeling tired and hungry. Her urge to drink was itching at the back of her throat. It was like an old friend, the craving for alcohol. She looked up at the calendar and counted back. Her last meeting was eight days ago. Kate checked her watch. It was eight forty-five p.m.; if she left right away, she could just make the nine o'clock AA meeting in Ashdean.

Kate grabbed her bag and car keys, pulled on her thick fleece, and left the office.

———

It was just after ten p.m. when Tristan left the Boar's Head with Ade. They'd ordered food, and the conversation had moved on from Noah Huntley and George, but Tristan was turning it over in his head when they parted at the bottom of the seafront and he started back to his flat.

There was still the faint glow of dusk on the horizon, and the bars and clubs were now busy with students queuing up outside. He ran into Kate just before his flat.

"Hey," he said, surprised to see her.

"Evening," she replied with a smile. "The only parking spot I could find was outside your flat. I've just been to a meeting."

Tristan didn't feel the need to comment on it. Kate going to meetings was now par for the course.

"I was going to ring you; I've just had a very interesting conversation with my friend Ade about Noah Huntley," he said.

"Yeah? I have some news too," said Kate. She looked across the road. There was a burger van that set up on the esplanade to catch the students who got the munchies when the pubs closed. The smell made her stomach rumble. "I haven't had dinner; do you fancy a burger?"

Tristan had already eaten, but the smell of the grilling meat was making his mouth water. He smiled and nodded. They joined the short line at the burger van, ordered cheeseburgers, and then took the steps down onto the beach.

The air was still, and the tide was now far out. A group of students had lit a fire close to the water's edge, and a couple of dreadlocked young men were throwing logs onto the bright blaze. Sparks flew up into the air, and voices whooped and laughed. They found a quiet spot and sat down on the dry sand. Kate bit into the huge steaming burger.

"My God, this is good," she said, adding through a mouthful, "The sesame bun is the pièce de résistance." Tristan took a big bite and nodded. The juicy, tender beef and cheese melted in his mouth. He ate fast and finished when Kate was still halfway through her burger. He told her what he'd found out about Noah Huntley.

"And who is this friend, Ade?" she asked, finishing the last of her burger.

"He was a policeman, now retired. Early retirement. I think he's fifty."

"How long have you known him?" There was something in the way Kate asked—it was as if she were gently probing to see if he and Ade were an item.

"Oh. It's nothing like that," said Tristan. "I got to know him at the Boar's Head, during gay bingo."

Kate smiled. "That sounds much more fun than straight bingo, not that I play bingo."

"Ade's the bingo caller . . . He's one of those people who knows everybody. He told me that Noah Huntley was well known on the gay scene for sleeping with guys behind his wife's back, and that ties in with what Joanna found when she was researching her story about Noah. This whole George-the-barman thing could be something and nothing. He thinks it's more likely that George did a midnight flit to avoid paying his rent."

"Does Ade know George's second name?" asked Kate.

"No. He said he's going to ask around."

Kate told Tristan about finding the names David Lamb and Gabe Kemp on the inside of the box. She took her mobile out of her pocket and showed him the photos.

"And Bev is sure that the writing on the inside of the box belongs to Joanna?" asked Tristan.

"She sounded a bit drunk when I phoned her, but she also said the writing on the box label was Joanna's. They match . . ."

"Do you think that David Lamb and Gabe Kemp were talking to Joanna about Noah Huntley?"

"David Lamb was reported missing June 1999, Gabe Kemp in April 2002. Joanna didn't publish her exposé on Noah Huntley until March 2002, but she could have been working on it for a long time," said Kate.

Tristan's phone pinged in his pocket.

"It's from Ade," he said, looking at the message.

LOVELY TO SEE YOU,

AS ALWAYS, MISS MARPLE.

I HOPE YOU MADE IT SAFELY

BACK TO ST. MARY MEAD.

I JUST SPOKE TO MY FRIEND NEIL. HE HAS THIS PHOTO FROM HALLOWEEN '96

NEIL SAYS HE WAS GEORGE 'TOMASSINI,' HERE DRESSED AS FREDDIE MERCURY WITH NEIL, AS HIS ALTER EGO, MONSTERFAT COWBELLY ☺ x

Tristan showed Kate. Ade had taken a picture of the photo in the album. It was taken behind the bar of a pub. George was tall and slim, dressed in a blue tuxedo with black lapels and a black bow tie. A crude mustache was drawn on his face, and his long brown hair was swept back in a ponytail. Beside him was a large drag queen, dressed in a powder-blue caftan covered in glittering crystals, with her jet-black hair coiffured and swept back off her heavily made-up face.

Kate smiled. "Oh, Freddie Mercury and *Monsterfat Cowbelly* . . ."

"I don't get it," said Tristan.

"Freddie Mercury did the duet 'Barcelona' with the opera singer Montserrat Caballé. She didn't look dissimilar to this . . . Neil in drag . . . Hang on, let me check George's surname."

Kate handed back his phone and picked up hers. She typed "George Tomassini" into the UK missing persons database, but no results came up. Kate sighed. "That would have been too easy."

The glow had left the horizon, and the students were piling more logs onto the raging fire. There was a yell of excitement as a big wave broke and reached the fire, extinguishing the flames with a loud hiss.

"That stinks, boiling seawater," said Tristan. He checked the time on his phone. It was almost eleven p.m.

"Shall we reconvene tomorrow? I'm getting cold, and I could do with some sleep," said Kate. "Good work, Tris."

"Thanks, but I think you made the real find with those names on the box."

"Let's see," said Kate. She sounded like she was being cautious. They got up off the sand and started to walk back to the promenade. The road was now busy and noisy with students moving between bars.

"Saint Mary Mead?" she asked, when they reached her car.

"It's the village where Miss Marple lives," said Tristan, trying not to show his embarrassment.

"Ah, of course. You're working tomorrow?"

"Yeah, unfortunately," said Tristan, his heart sinking. "I could come over after work."

"Yes. Let's meet then," said Kate, getting into her car.

He looked back along the seafront to the university building, which sat at the opposite end, like a medieval castle. He wished he didn't have to go to work, taking him away from the detective agency, especially after such an exciting day of small but significant breakthroughs.

12

Kate was lost in thought about the missing young men as she drove home. The last few miles of the journey were in pitch darkness surrounded by empty fields. A bank of clouds had now come in from the sea, blocking out the light from the moon.

She thought back to her early days in the Met Police, when the head of a missing persons charity came to give a talk. The woman told them that in the UK, a missing person is reported every ninety seconds, which worked out as one hundred and eighty thousand people every year. Ninety-eight percent of them were found within a few days, but that still left thirty-six hundred people every year. That had been back in 1994, twenty-one years ago . . . Kate did the calculation in her tired brain: 75,600 people.

Joanna had been interested in David Lamb and Gabe Kemp, but why? Why had she written their names down? And why had she ended up joining them with the thousands of other people on the missing persons list?

When Kate turned onto her road, the other houses along the cliff top were dark. Three of the houses were holiday homes, and two of them were up for sale. Whatever time of the year, Myra's house had always had a welcoming light glowing behind the curtains, and Kate missed that. There were lights for the caravan site, but there was no one staying until next week, so she hadn't programmed them to come on.

Passing the dark windows of the office and shop, she pulled into the driveway behind her house. When she switched off the engine and headlights, she was plunged into darkness. It wasn't until she got out of her car and moved closer to the back door that the security light came on.

She was about to put her key in the lock when she heard a rustling sound coming from behind the house, on the cliff edge. The sound of footsteps on the small sand-covered terrace. She gripped the door key in her fingers and froze. She just wanted to go inside, into her warm house, switch on the lights, and lock the doors. The security lights went out, and noise came again, a thud of someone landing on the sand, and more footsteps, coming closer.

Kate had been attacked by intruders in her home twice before, once by Peter Conway and again fifteen years later by a stalker. She'd suffered from panic attacks and PTSD over the years, and Kate felt her heart thud in her chest at the sound of an intruder. She moved back to her car, her movements activating the security light again. She got inside and locked the doors.

A tall figure came loping through the gap and came up to her window.

"Mum! It's me. Mum!" said a voice, and it took her a moment to recognize the face looming close to the glass. It was Jake. Kate felt her body flood with relief and opened the car door.

"You scared the life out of me!" she said, feeling her heart still thumping in her chest. Jake was now nineteen, and he was over six feet tall. His hair was past his shoulders, and he had a beard. He was wearing jeans and a warm fleece jacket, and had on a huge hiking backpack. Kate and Jake shared the same genetic quirk, called sectoral heterochromia, that gave one of his blue eyes a burst of orange around the pupil.

"Just give me a minute." She took slow, deep breaths as Jake looked on, not knowing what to do. He crouched down beside her and took her hand.

"Sorry, Mum. I thought I'd surprise you."

"You did," she said with a smile, concentrating on her breathing to stave off the panic. He helped her out of the car, and they moved to the front door. Her breathing was easier. Jake used Kate's key to unlock the front door, then switched on the hall light.

"Do you want a cuppa?"

"That would be good," said Kate, relieved that she'd managed to get her shock under control and avoid a full-on panic attack. "You look so grown up since Easter! And the beard! It suits you."

He gave her a hug.

"I just FaceTimed Grandma. She says it makes me look like a hippie . . . I was asking her where you kept your spare key. She said to try under a flowerpot."

Kate went to the security alarm on the wall and typed in the code.

"What planet does your grandma live on if she thinks I keep a spare key under a flowerpot?"

Jake eyed the alarm and looked guilty.

"Sorry. I'll phone next time," he said. He shrugged off the huge backpack and propped it up by the radiator.

"It's so good to see you," said Kate, grabbing him for another hug. She pulled away. "I thought you were going to stay at uni for two more weeks?"

"Four of my mates got jobs as holiday reps, and the company asked if they could start tomorrow. And Marie and Verity both have been hired back in London at the Apple Store. They've got to go for training. I didn't fancy staying there on my own."

They slipped off their shoes and came through to the living room. The house had originally come with her job as a lecturer at Ashdean University, but with her savings and inheritance from Myra, Kate had been able to buy it from the university. The furniture in the living room was chintzy, left over from a previous tenant, and an old piano sat against one wall. Kate's favorite part was the living room and the row of windows that looked over the cliff top out to sea. The kitchen was slightly more modern than the rest of the house, with a large island, blond wooden countertops, and cupboards painted white.

Kate and Jake moved through to the kitchen, and she sat on one of the stools opposite the kitchen window as he filled the kettle.

"Are you still going to your AA meetings regularly?" asked Jake.

"Yes. I've just been to one."

"This late?"

"I met Tristan afterward . . . ," said Kate, and she briefly told him about the new case. Jake listened and made them tea and himself some toast.

"Have you found another sponsor?" he asked.

"I've just told you about my first proper case with the agency, and that's the first thing you ask!" said Kate.

"It's great about the agency; I just wanted to know if you've found another sponsor, after Myra?"

"No. Not everyone has a sponsor," she said, hearing the defensiveness in her voice. Jake didn't say anything and took a bite out of his toast. He chewed and swallowed.

"Only asking cos I love you," he said. He got up and put his plate and mug in the dishwasher. "I'm knackered. I'm going to bed. Love you."

He gave her a kiss on the top of the head and left the room.

Kate had been sober for thirteen years, but there had been many years before this when she'd lost people's trust. The guilt and the feeling of people doubting her were hard to shake off, especially coming from Jake. The way he'd kissed her on top of the head made it feel like the roles were reversed. He was the responsible adult, and she would always be trying to gain back his trust. It made her all the more determined to stay sober, and never drink again.

13

It was a long drive back to the house with Hayden in the back of his car. Tom took the B roads, avoiding the traffic cameras on the motorway. He'd needed to pee since they left the bar and was only halfway home when he could hold it in no longer. At the next lay-by, Tom pulled off the road to pee. The darkness was absolute as he stared into the trees. They creaked and swayed in the light breeze.

He felt sick with what he'd done. There was always a point where he could stop, and not go through with it, but he was past that now. Years ago, there had been times when he'd put the brakes on. Stopped and let them go, none the wiser. But Hayden wouldn't be released back into the wild. Tom would have to see it through to the end. The thought of this always held a tingle of excitement.

He zipped up and went to the boot. When he opened the door and pulled the blanket off Hayden, he lay very still, trussed up with his chest rising and falling. That was good. He was still alive. Tom put his finger to Hayden's throat and traced down until he felt the boy's pulse. He held his finger there, feeling the short, urgent twitch of his pulse point, like a tiny clock. It was ticking down the heartbeats until his death.

It was time to change the plates on the car. Tom rolled Hayden onto his side and opened the well where he kept the spare tire. He took out a set of different number plates and a screwdriver. He closed the boot, and he changed the plates, working fast in a practiced set of movements. When he opened the boot, he rolled Hayden onto his side again. Hayden's left trouser leg rode up a few inches, displaying the meaty muscle of his calf. The boy was athletic, and he was wearing white-and-green-striped football socks.

Tom reached out and stroked the fine hair on Hayden's calf muscle. Delicately, he took two or three hairs between his finger and thumb and pulled. Hayden moaned, muffled by the gaffer tape. Tom pulled again and saw Hayden's face muscles twitch.

The sound of an approaching car shook Tom out of his game, and he quickly covered Hayden in the blanket, closed the car boot, and walked round to the driver's door. He climbed inside just as a car appeared on the road behind and its headlights lit everything up.

It was late when Tom pulled into the garage at home. Hayden was still unconscious as Tom lifted him out of the car boot and carried him up the stairs to the bedroom and placed him gently on the bed. He cut the tape from his wrists and ankles and massaged them, helping the circulation to bring back feeling.

He arranged Hayden on the bed, laying him on his back with his arms by his side, and then he lit candles. The bedroom seemed to pulse and glow in the soft, forgiving light. Only then did he feel comfortable peeling off his own clothes until he was naked. Ready on the nightstand was a pair of round-ended scissors. The kind used for cutting the clothes off patients in the hospital accident and emergency department.

He worked carefully, untying Hayden's shoelaces and slipping off each of his trainers. He took the tip of each long sports sock and pulled so that the material stretched out like bubble gum before sliding off Hayden's leg and foot and pinging back. He dropped them on the floor at the end of the bed. He ran a fingernail across the clean, soft sole of each bare foot, and Hayden gave a little moan. Tom set to work, slowly cutting him out of his jeans and T-shirt. He took care with the scissors when he sliced off Hayden's white briefs on each side of the waistband. Then stood back and admired Hayden's naked form, rolling him over onto his front and then back again. He was so muscular and lean. His body in that firm yet juicy stage that lasts fleetingly in the early twenties.

Slowly, he clambered up and lay on top of Hayden, their naked bodies touching. His older soft, crepey flesh molding around Hayden's sculpted muscles. He lay there for a moment, slowing his breath until they were breathing in unison and he felt the hot thud of Hayden's heart against his chest.

"Are you awake?" Tom whispered, his mouth close to Hayden's right ear. Hayden moaned, and his eyelids fluttered. Tom sat up and peeled the gaffer tape off Hayden's mouth from each edge and then pulled the oropharyngeal airway out of his mouth. Hayden swallowed, wincing.

Tom slapped him hard across the face and sat back, enjoying the thrill of hurting this tall, strong athlete. He slapped him again, harder. Hayden opened his eyes.

"Where am I?" he croaked, struggling to focus.

"You're in heaven, or hell. It depends how willing you are to make me happy."

14

Kate got up early the next morning for a swim and then had breakfast with Jake. They didn't mention what had happened the night before, and he was enthusiastic to start work clearing out the shop and sorting everything for the dive and surf hire.

The delivery of bed linen arrived at ten, and after Jake had helped stack it in the office, he went downstairs to work in the shop, and Kate turned her attention back to Joanna Duncan.

The day before, she'd emailed Dr. Trevor Paulson about Famke van Noort, who had worked for him and his wife as an au pair. She found a reply in her in-box that was short and to the point. Dr. Paulson said he had lost contact with Famke after she went back to the Netherlands in 2004. He included Famke's last known address in Utrecht and said that he was now retired and he'd told the police everything he knew, which wasn't much, and to please not contact him again.

Kate googled "Famke van Noort, Utrecht." Results came up for a "Frank van Noort" and an "Annemieke van Noort" on LinkedIn. Annemieke also had a Facebook profile, but the privacy controls were locked. There was only one "Famke van Noort" on Facebook, but on closer inspection, she was listed as "Famke van Noort (van den Boogaard)," which meant that "van Noort" was her married name. And this Famke van Noort was twenty-two, which meant that she'd been only nine or ten years old when Joanna went missing.

Kate tried a search through Google Netherlands, and lots more Famkes came up on LinkedIn, but none with the same name and right age. Just as Kate started googling the address in Utrecht, Tristan rang.

"How's it going?" he asked.

Kate told him about the email from Dr. Paulson, and about her search. "I'm going a bit cross eyed from all the 'Van' surnames: 'Van Spaendonck,' 'Van Duinen,' 'Van den Berg.' There's even a 'Famke van Dam,' as in Jean-Claude."

"Ahh. Good old Jean-Claude Van Damme. I remember watching *Universal Soldier* when I was thirteen and realizing I might be gay. Did you know that *van* in Dutch means *from the*?"

"I didn't know that," said Kate, with one eye on the search results generated by the address in Utrecht.

"The actor James Van Der Beek's name translates as James 'from the creek,' which is a weird coincidence, as he was Dawson in the TV show *Dawson's Creek* . . ."

"I can't find anything about our Famke. All I have is an email for an accountancy firm in the building where she lived," said Kate, picking up her pen and noting it down.

"Listen. I'm ringing to say that I won't be able to make it after work," said Tristan. "Two of the caretakers are off sick and I have to help out moving chairs and desks for the exams tomorrow." Kate could hear the disappointment in his voice.

"That's a pain in the ass." She clicked on another link and started reading. "Did you know that the first Dutchman to circumnavigate the world was Olivier van Noort, and he was also from Utrecht?"

"What's that got to do with Famke?"

"*Van Noort* could be a name associated with Utrecht."

"And Utrecht might be teeming with Van Noorts," said Tristan.

"This is the problem with searching online. There's too much information, and most of it is bollocks. We really need to find her because she's Fred's alibi for the day Joanna went missing."

"If she lied back then, do you think she'll tell the truth to us?"

"I don't know. I just want to talk to her. Often, it's the small details, the little bits of information that people don't think is relevant or important, that lead to something bigger," said Kate.

"Okay, good luck. Sorry again I can't help," said Tristan.

"Good luck with exam prep. See you tomorrow."

When Kate came off the phone, she wrote a short email to the accountancy firm that had its offices in the same building as Famke's last known address. She knew it was a long shot, but she explained who she was and why she wanted to get in contact with Famke. Kate had been given the email address for Marnie, Joanna's old school friend, and she sent an email, asking if they could meet.

After lunch, Kate started looking into David Lamb and Gabe Kemp, and for a couple of hours, she felt like she was chasing the same rabbit down a hole. Then she came across something, buried deep in the twentieth page of Google search results for "David Lamb." It was a JustGiving fundraising page from 2006. A woman from Exeter had put up a crowdfunding page to raise money for a small community garden in town, which was to be called *Park Street Garden of Memories*. It was one of the donations that caught Kate's eye.

> Shelley Morden has donated £25
>
> in memory of her dear friend, David Lamb.
>
> Missing, but not forgotten.

The JustGiving page had been aiming to raise £2,750, but it had fallen short of its target by £900. Kate googled "Park Street" and saw that it was a road on the outskirts of Exeter. She then googled "Shelley Morden, Park Street."

"Okay, this is better," said Kate under her breath when the first search result came up from the electoral roll. Shelley Morden lived at 11 Park Street in Exeter with a Kevin James Morden, presumably her husband. Kate sat back, her eyes hurting from staring at the computer screen for so long. There was an old BT phone directory that had belonged to Myra on one of the shelves on the caravan park side of the office, and Kate picked it up and blew off the dust. "Let's try the old-school way . . ."

Kate hadn't used a phone book in years. She flicked through the pages to the *M* section, and there was a Kevin James Morden listed at the same address. Kate dialed the number.

After this breakthrough, she was disappointed to get a generic answerphone. Kate left a message explaining who she was and that she wanted to find out what had happened to David Lamb. She went to the little kitchen at the back of the office and made herself a cup of coffee and was about to go outside for some fresh air when her phone rang.

When Kate answered, she could hear children shouting in the background.

"Hello, it's Shelley Morden," said a harassed-sounding woman. "I'm sorry I missed your call."

"Thank you for calling back," said Kate.

"I knew David. I was the one who reported him going missing, but no one seemed that interested . . . I'm free tomorrow at two p.m. if you want to come over and talk," she said. "I can tell you all about him."

15

Hayden's hands were cuffed to the wooden headboard of the bed, each ankle tied with thin rope to the bedposts. His body was rigid and jerking from side to side, trying to fight.

Tom was kneeling above Hayden, and his hands were wrapped tightly around the young man's throat, gripping and squeezing.

"Yes, yes. Fight me," he whispered, leaning closer to Hayden's ear. "You can't, can you? Because I'm in charge. I'm the bully, and I'll win." He gripped harder, pressing his thumbs down onto the boy's Adam's apple. This was the magic spot to press if you wanted to keep the eyes open, thought Tom, and he needed Hayden's eyes to be open. It was coming. That powerful moment just before death, when darkness falls in their eyes.

Tom liked to throttle his victims whilst he raped them. The first few times it was play throttling, enough to instill fear and deprive the body of oxygen. But then he'd squeeze harder, bringing them to the edge of consciousness before reviving them.

The night had passed too quickly, and the sun had crept up on him. He'd only noticed when the light blazed through a chink in the curtain and a strip illuminated Hayden's face, swollen and bruised. The whites of his eyes were crisscrossed with burst blood vessels.

Tom was shaking from the exertion, the sweat dripping off his chin, slick down his back. Hayden's body was starting to shake and tremble in concert. Tom leaned forward, pushing down with all his weight.

The bed creaked, and he gripped and squeezed, feeling the pain of the exertion in his fingers and wrists.

The moment was close.

Hayden's eyes were wide and bulging, bloodshot. His pupils dilated. He gave a rattling moan, a passive sound at odds with his fear and the violence. Tom leaned close. Their faces were inches apart, and the tip of his nose touched Hayden's. The sunlight seemed to dance in his eyes, reflecting a final burst of defiance, of life force, and then came the realization that death was here. All the tautness and resistance in Hayden's body fell away. The light faded, and the darkness fell into his eyes, and the sunlight bounced off them, reflecting emptiness.

The house had been silent since he brought Hayden home. He hadn't switched on any music or the TV, but as he sat back on his haunches and looked at the dead body, the silence was thick, like it had suddenly descended on the room.

Tom flexed his fingers to work away the stiffness in his joints. He was out of breath, but the air was fetid with death, and as he gulped it into his lungs, he felt his stomach turn and had to run to the bathroom, where he threw up.

He was shaking uncontrollably as he knelt on the cold tiles in front of the toilet. He always went into shock afterward, after the darkness fell in their eyes. The fear and elation and the release of tension made him sick. He stayed crouched on the floor for a few minutes, retching and coughing, and when he felt his stomach was empty, he got up and splashed his face with water in the sink. Avoiding the mirror, Tom went back into the bedroom.

Hayden was still. The color had drained from his creamy, soft skin; his muscles looked deflated; and his skin had a yellow hue. Tom moved to the window and threw it open. He had to let Hayden's spirit free from the confines of the room.

Tom stood by the window for a few minutes, looking out into the bright sunshine, feeling the cool breeze on his naked body.

He went back to the bathroom, put the plug in the bath, and turned on the taps, adjusting the mix of water so that it was very hot. The steam rose, fogging up the air, and condensation began to form on the white tiles. A memory came back to him, still fresh and painful after so many years.

———

He's thirteen, at school, lining up naked by the communal showers with all the other boys after a football match. There's triumph and the camaraderie of sportsmen in the air, but he's been on the losing team. He kept to the edge of the football pitch during the game, dodging the ball, hoping that the team he was on would win. It was easier being on the winning team. He could be invisible on the winning team, but today he was on the losing side, and his teammates need someone to blame.

The cheers and shouts echo off the grimy tiled walls of the shower, and he can feel the anger rising in his teammates behind him. The losers need to blame the ultimate loser.

Tom stands shivering among the naked bodies. Among the smells of feet and sweat, flesh and mud. He wills Mr. Pike, the PE teacher, to hurry and switch the water on so he can run through the shower and then envelop himself in a towel. He tries to shield his own nakedness with his arms. His underdeveloped body feels vulnerable next to the athletic boys who are almost men . . .

Amid all this, he feels shameful lust at the sight of their toned bodies. He hates himself for desiring them as much as he fears them. He wants the cold tiled floor to open and swallow him.

Mr. Pike appears at the end of the long corridor through the showers, and he turns a huge metal dial on the wall. There's a hiss and a spatter, and a moment later, the water runs and the steam rises.

"Go on, wash! Get in there," Mr. Pike shouts. The steam cuts through the cold air. Tom is behind Edwin Johnson. Captain of the losing team. He has a broad, muscular back and firm buttocks. The jeers grow louder through the steam. Tom feels himself jostled from behind, hears a murmur, a loud

mocking laugh, and a cold hand plants itself in the center of his back, and he's shoved forward. His inadequate body makes contact with Edwin's firm, meaty rump. Skin to skin . . . and he leaps back. Edwin turns with his face flushed with anger.

"What the fuck are you doing?" he says.

Tom shivers and feels a cold trickling in his nerves and tendons, and he feels sick. It's fear.

"Sorry," he says, stepping back, but there's laughter again as another hand presses at his back and pushes harder. Tom trips and crashes into Edwin face-to-face. Naked.

"Get off me, fucking fairy!" cries Edwin. He's angry, but Tom can see the anger in his eyes is mixed with fear.

"He fancies you, Ed . . . ," says a voice.

"You shouldn't let him touch you like that," says another.

"Yeah, people will get ideas about you two!"

The steam is now curling up around them. Edwin's fist seems to come out of nowhere and hits Tom in the jaw. His head snaps back and smashes into the tiled wall. The pain is intense, and he slides down the wall and lands on the concrete floor, hitting his tailbone with a sickening thud. There's a thin line of blood where he hit the tiles.

Tom looks up. Edwin's face is a mix of hatred and terror. Tom tries to get up, but it hurts; he's numb.

"Get up, you fucking queer!" someone shouts. Getting up would be the thing to do. It would restore order. Getting up would be the mannish thing to do. Tom can see that lying on the ground makes them angrier.

Hormones raging. Looking for a fight. He hears his father's voice in that moment before the attack: "Whatever happens in a fight, you must stay on your feet, even if you get the shit kicked out of you. Never let them knock you to the ground or you'll be finished."

The full force of a punch slams his head against the concrete and shatters his front teeth. A foot kicks him in the guts. Edwin reaches down and grabs

91

at his ankles, and he's dragged naked along the concrete floor. Hot water, fists, and feet raining down on him.

He remembers Mr. Pike's part in all this. The glimpse of his red face at the end of the showers. The wild-eyed look of excitement at what's happening. He does nothing and watches as the steam and the rest of the boys swarm over Tom, kicking, punching, stomping.

———

Tom didn't know how long he had zoned out. When he looked down, he was in the shower cubicle next to the bath. He was washing and scrubbing at his skin. He ran his fingers over the left side of his rib cage, where there was a long, thick scar. The bruises and broken bones had all healed, but where Edwin had stomped on his rib cage, causing the bones to break and push through his skin, there would always be a scar.

Tom dried off and stepped out of the shower. From under the sink, he took out a set of white hazmat coveralls, long white socks, latex gloves, a bottle of antibacterial hand soap, and a scrubbing brush with a long wooden handle.

He placed them neatly in a pile on the chair by the bath and dressed in the socks and then in the hazmat suit, pulling the hood up over his head and adjusting the face mask so that only his eyes were showing through. Then he pulled on the latex gloves.

The large bath was now two-thirds full. Tom was glad for the fog on the mirror. He still couldn't look at himself. He came back to the bedroom and carefully untied Hayden's legs and unlocked the handcuffs on his wrists. He picked him up and carried him to the bathroom, where he gently placed him into the bathtub.

There was a fresh set of clothes waiting for Hayden after his bath. When the police found him—eventually found him, if at all—it would be impossible to gather DNA evidence.

Tom was planning to tuck him neatly away.

16

Kate and Tristan arrived at Shelley Morden's house at two p.m. the next day. Eleven Park Street was a pebble-dashed terrace house on a sloping hill looking out over Exeter. The street was quiet, and the path in front of the gate was covered with chalk drawings and hopscotch grids.

The door was opened by a small, plump lady who looked to be in her midthirties with shoulder-length blonde hair and oversize red-framed glasses. She had an open, smiley face and soft brown eyes, and when she welcomed them inside, there was a tinge of Birmingham in her accent. Music came floating out behind her from a kids' TV show, a song about counting to ten. Kate noticed she had a Chinese symbol tattoo on her wrist, and her fingers were adorned with silver rings, two of which were set with large amber stones. "I was about to put the kettle on, if you'd like a cup of tea?" she said.

"Thank you," said Kate.

"Lovely," said Tristan.

There was a large antique sideboard in the hallway with a spotted mirror. The shelves were filled with secondhand books, and a row of naked Barbie dolls were propped up against the books. They were all in stages of undress with hopelessly tangled hair, and one had a shaved head.

"This is Megan and Anwar," said Shelley as they reached the entrance to the living room, where the floor was strewn with toys. A boy and a girl, who must have been around seven or eight, were watching the CBeebies channel on TV. They looked up at Kate with cautious eyes.

"Hello," said Kate. She liked children but never knew how to speak to them. She always felt she was being formal and standoffish.

"Are your toys enjoying watching TV?" asked Tristan, indicating a LEGO fire station where a mixture of LEGO men, Barbie dolls, and cuddly toys were lined up on the roof, facing the TV. Anwar grinned sheepishly and nodded.

"After this program finishes, we're having a tea party," said Megan, picking up a teapot.

"With cake!" added Anwar, grinning. They turned to Shelley.

"Yes, I only just put the cake in. It'll be ready in a little bit," she said. "Will you two please watch telly quietly while we go in the kitchen?" she added. They nodded, and Shelley led Tristan and Kate down the hall toward the kitchen. "I'm a foster parent," she added. "When we spoke yesterday, I was in the middle of a chaotic playdate. Lots of fun but hard work."

The kitchen was just as messy and cozy, with a long wooden table and a bright-blue AGA, where the smell of a baking cake made Kate's mouth water. There were herbs in pots along the windowsill, which looked out over a large garden filled with a swing and climbing frame.

"Have a sit down, please." Kate and Tristan pulled out chairs at the end of the table. "I haven't heard anyone ask about David Lamb for a long time. Not that many people seemed bothered when he went missing," said Shelley, starting to make tea.

"How did you know him?" asked Kate.

"We grew up together in Wolverhampton. Lived next door to each other in the Kelsal Road. You know you live in a rough area when the locals put *the* on the front. It was one of the few terraces of two-up two-downs which weren't demolished during slum clearance in the sixties. In our terrace, you could climb up into the loft and get through to the house next door. Some of the neighbors put up partitions in their lofts. Between my house and David's, there wasn't one. I used to go up into the loft, and we'd meet up at night. No hanky-panky, of course—he was gay. He was a very good friend . . ."

"How did you end up in Exeter?" asked Tristan. Shelley hesitated. Kate could see this was hard for her to talk about.

"We ran away together. Neither of us came from loving families, to put it mildly . . . We pooled together what money we had. I had some from birthdays and my paper round. It was the best thing I ever did—probably saved my life—and I couldn't have done it without David."

"How old were you when you ran away?" asked Kate.

"We were both sixteen. We were going to go to London, and then we saw an advert for a commune in Exeter in the back of *Time Out* magazine."

"What year was this?"

"1996."

"What kind of advert did you see?" asked Tristan.

"The advert asked for young people of a liberal persuasion between eighteen and twenty-five to come and join a working commune." Shelley laughed. "It actually said that: *liberal persuasion*. We were very green and thought it was something to do with politics. The commune was on Walpole Street in the city. When we arrived and knocked on the door, we found it was mostly gay men. There were no women. I could make bread, which seemed to stand me in good stead, as the woman who cooked had just left to go traveling in India."

"Did anyone ask how old you were?" asked Kate.

"No. We lied and said we were eighteen, but no one seemed that bothered. I enjoyed it for a time, and we had very different experiences of it when we arrived. I was the lone girl, and David was fresh meat. He was very handsome . . . Nothing bad happened. The men weren't predatory, but David was quite the heartbreaker. I got a job almost as soon as we arrived, and I moved out after a year, when I met Kev, my husband . . ."

Shelley indicated a collage of photos on the wall beside the fridge that showed her over the years with a stocky ginger-haired man.

"He died, seven years ago. Cancer."

"Sorry to hear that," said Kate. There was a silence as Shelley went to the AGA and opened the door, checking the cake, which was turning golden on a shelf. She then poured them each a mug of tea and placed them on the long table.

"Who's hired you to look for David?" Shelley asked, sitting opposite them. This was the first time she'd looked less open and more cautious.

"His name has come up in conjunction with another person who's missing," said Kate. "A journalist called Joanna Duncan. She disappeared in September 2002."

Shelley sat back in her chair and frowned; they could see her thinking, like the name rang a bell.

"She was a journalist at the *West Country News*," she said.

"Yes. She vanished on Saturday, September seventh, 2002," said Kate.

"This is odd . . . Why was this journalist involved with David's disappearance?"

"She's not involved," said Kate. "We think Joanna was potentially looking into David's disappearance and the disappearance of another guy called Gabe Kemp. Does his name mean anything to you?"

"No, it doesn't," said Shelley. She frowned again, got up, and went to the window, looking out over the garden. It had started to rain, and in the quiet of her thinking, they could hear the droplets tapping against the glass. Tristan went to say something, but Kate shook her head. It was better to let her speak when she was ready. Shelley came back to the table and sat down.

"Okay, this is strange. Back in 2002, me and Kev went on holiday to the Seychelles. We always used to go later to avoid the school holidays. We came back in the second week of September, and there was a message on the answering machine from Joanna Duncan at the *West Country News*."

Kate and Tristan exchanged a look.

"I'm sorry to ask this, but are you sure it was Joanna Duncan?" asked Kate.

"Absolutely."

"Why did she leave a message?"

"It was a long time ago. She said that she was a journalist and wanted to talk to me informally. She said sorry she couldn't be more specific, but if I could call her back, she would explain. She left me her number," said Shelley.

"How do you remember this, after such a long time?" asked Tristan.

"The message on the answerphone was a week or so old when we got back from our holiday, and by then, it was all over the news that a journalist called Joanna Duncan had gone missing. I called back the number and left a message with someone at the newspaper, but they never got back to me."

"Do you remember who you spoke to?"

"No."

"Did you talk to the police?" asked Kate.

"No. I didn't know why she was calling me. I thought, at the time, it was to do with the Marco Polo House office block. Some local businessmen bought it and tried to cover up the fact that there was a ton of asbestos in the walls. They started to renovate it, and it's next to one of the biggest schools in the area. I'd been involved in a campaign to have it removed, and we'd got a lot of signatures. We'd written to lots of newspapers and the BBC *Watchdog* program. I assumed she was calling about that. Was she writing a story about David?"

"We're not sure," said Kate. "I found David's name written down by Joanna as part of the case files, and I only found you from the donation you made in David's name to the garden crowdfunder."

Shelley took another sip of her tea. "Have you got a photo of Gabe Kemp, in case I might recognize him?"

Tristan pulled out his phone and scrolled through to the photo he'd saved from the UK missing persons website. Shelley looked at it for a moment and then sighed and shook her head.

"No. Sorry. I never knew him."

"Could we show you another photo?" asked Tristan. He scrolled through and found a photo of George Tomassini. "He's in fancy dress there. The guy on the left, dressed as Freddie Mercury."

"I remember Monsterfat Cowbelly," she said with a smile.

"You do?"

"She used to do the rounds of the pubs in Exeter. I don't recognize the guy with her, though."

"Are you sure?" asked Kate, wishing they had a regular photo of George.

Shelley looked again and then shook her head.

"We think George Tomassini disappeared around the middle of 2002. We haven't got a concrete date, but he wasn't officially reported as a missing person like David and Gabe," said Kate. "What happened after you reported David missing in June 1999?"

"Nothing," said Shelley. "I don't think the police took it seriously. I chased it up a couple of times, but I never heard from them again."

"He's still listed on the UK missing persons database," said Kate.

"I know. I gave them a copy of passport photos I had of David, not that he ever got a passport . . . He'd been troubled for a while before he went missing . . . I presume you know that he was arrested for manslaughter?"

"No, we didn't," said Kate, exchanging a glance with Tristan.

"David was badly into drugs and putting himself in dangerous situations. It was all very intoxicating to him, to suddenly be adored by these older guys on the gay scene. Some of them would buy him gifts, and he'd jump into relationships, move in with them, only for it to go pear shaped, and he was knocking on my door, or back at the commune. There was this older man called Sidney Newett."

"How much older?" asked Kate.

"Must have been early fifties. David went back to his house one night, and they were partying. Sidney Newett's wife was away on holiday with the Women's Institute. David found Sidney dead in the back garden the next morning, panicked, and ran, but he left his wallet behind, and a neighbor saw him. The police eventually dropped the charges when they discovered Sidney died of a heart attack. It sent David off into a deeper depression. There were always parties at the commune, so it wasn't the best place for him to be."

"Are you in contact with anyone who lived at the commune?" asked Kate.

"Blimey, that's a good question. It was eighteen years ago. So many of the guys went by nicknames. Elsie and Vera and Liza . . ." Shelley chuckled. "They were a nice bunch, so different to the guys I'd known from my childhood. My father and my uncle were very *touchy-feely*, let me just say. It was nice to be in an environment where no one was interested in me that way. It was all run by an older guy, well, I say older—he was probably only thirty back when we were sixteen. Max Jesper. He'd been at the commune for the longest time, and he ran things. It was an old Georgian townhouse that had been empty for years. He became a squatter there in the early 1980s."

"Did you have to pay anything to stay there?" asked Tristan.

"There was a kitty, a big bowl which everyone had to contribute to. If you were working, you had to put in half of what you earned. If you didn't work, Max encouraged you to sign on at the Jobcentre, and you had to contribute half of what you got. No one ever had much money. And, of course, the guys would have to spend a night with Max to secure their room."

"Sounds sleazy," said Tristan.

"Oh, Max was. Luckily all I had to do was make him bread a couple of times a week, and I was earning and contributing the most. Max wasn't a bad-looking guy, but he'd often invite his mates over when a new lad wanted to move in . . ."

Shelley saw the look that passed between Kate and Tristan.

"I know, it sounds horrible, and it was, but so many young guys were coming from places far worse. And for me, it was such freedom."

"What happened to the commune?" asked Tristan.

"Max went to court to claim squatter's rights on the building, and he won. He became the legal owner of this huge old house. It was in the local paper."

"Can you remember when this was?" asked Kate.

"I don't know, four or five years ago. It's on the other side of Exeter, close to the new industrial estate they're building."

"When did you know that David had gone missing?" asked Tristan.

"Our birthday was on the same day, June fourteenth. I was living with Kev. We were having a party, and I'd invited David. He didn't show up. I wasn't too worried. As a rule, he was all over the place, but when I didn't hear from him for a week, that's when I got concerned. I went around to see the guy he'd been living with, Pierre, and Pierre said that he and David had split up ten days previously and David had moved out. I then asked around at the pubs in the area, and I went to the commune, but no one knew where he'd gone."

"How long had he been living with Pierre?"

"I can't remember, exactly. A few weeks, maybe."

"Do you have contact details for Pierre?"

"No. He died two years later of a drug overdose," said Shelley.

"Did David ever say that he'd been involved with anyone high profile, any politicians?"

Shelley considered the question.

"No. He was quite the blabbermouth. He would have been very proud of that."

"Could you give us the names of some of the gay pubs that David used to go to?"

"Yes, but I don't know how many of them are still open."

Shelley pulled out a piece of paper and had a think, then started to write. There was a long silence. Kate and Tristan looked to each other and didn't have any more questions.

"Okay. There's four that I can remember. I know for a fact I've got the first two right because we used to go there a lot; the other two, I'm not sure."

"Thank you so much," said Kate. "You've been really helpful."

Shelley took them back to the front door. They passed the kids, who looked up at them and smiled when they said goodbye.

"I had Joanna Duncan's message on my answering machine for quite a few weeks after she went missing," said Shelley when they were at the front door. "I had to delete it in the end. I didn't like hearing it and wondering what happened to her. It gives me the shivers that you've turned up on my doorstep all these years later mentioning Joanna Duncan and David in the same breath."

17

It had stopped raining when Kate and Tristan left Shelley's house, and the sun was now shining. They hurried to the car and got inside.

"The Spread-Eagle pub is closed," said Tristan, when they were inside the car. "I think The Brewer's too," he added, looking at the list Shelley had given them.

"I'm more interested to go and have a look at this commune on Walpole Street, in case this Max Jesper is still living there," she said.

It took them half an hour to cross the city. Walpole Street was by the river, and Kate remembered it for being part of a run-down area. She'd accompanied Myra there once when she put her clapped-out old car in for a service, and she remembered a row of boarded-up buildings next to an old car mechanic. The memory came back to her, bittersweet. Myra had had an aversion to discarding anything unless it was truly broken. She'd got rid of the old Morris Marina only when the engine had crumbled away. On the occasion Kate was thinking of, the car had lived to see another service.

Kate was surprised to see the car mechanic's was now a trendy barbershop with a tattoo parlor, and the rest of the area by the river had undergone a transformation. There was a row of small, independent shops, a beautiful public garden, a Starbucks, and an old art house cinema that she recalled being boarded up.

The row of shops curved sharply to the right and turned into Walpole Street, which was more residential and made up of terraced houses. At the end of the road was a large four-story house painted crisp white with a new roof of slate blue. The beautiful sash windows shone, and written on a sign above the door was a silver number **11** and **JESPER'S EST 2009**. There were five stars under the sign, indicating it was a hotel.

There was an elegant outdoor terrace on the pavement, and every table was occupied. Clear glass space heaters warmed the diners with the flicker of tall flames. Tristan found a parking space farther down the road and pulled over.

"How does a squatter end up having his name above a five-star hotel?" he said. Kate took her phone out of her pocket and googled "Jesper's hotel commune."

"Here we go, fifth result down: 'Exeter squatter wins right to prime property,'" said Kate, holding up the article on her phone. "'A local squatter has become the legal owner of an eighteenth-century townhouse on Walpole Street in Exeter, where he has lived for more than twelve years. Max Jesper, forty-five, was handed the title deeds to the townhouse, thought to be worth over one million pounds, after developers threatened to evict him. Mr. Jesper made a successful claim under squatter's rights, a Land Registry spokeswoman said. The property was previously owned and run as a boardinghouse. The owner died in 1974, and her descendant, who lived in Australia, inherited, and the property fell into disrepair. The property was sold to developers in 2009, and they sought to evict Mr. Jesper. He was able to prove he had been the sole occupier of the property for the past twelve years and made a successful claim under what is called squatter's rights.'"

Tristan moved closer as they peered at the photo. "He looks like a real hippie," he said.

The photo of Max Jesper had been taken on a gray, overcast day in front of the building. He had both thumbs up, and in one of his hands he held a lit cigarette. He was a wild-looking man with spiky black hair and ripped jeans. The building in the photo looked nothing like its current splendor. It was half-derelict with broken windows and big holes in the plaster, and there was a small tree growing out through a hole in the roof.

"Do you want to go inside and have a coffee?" asked Kate. "I'm intrigued to see what it looks like and if Max Jesper is there." Tristan nodded.

As they got out of the car, there was a rumble of thunder in the darkening sky, and it started to rain. The rain quickly turned into a downpour, and Kate and Tristan made a run for the hotel. Kate hooked the collar of her jacket over her head, but she was instantly soaked by the heavy rain.

The people who had been happily dining on the terrace were hurrying into the front entrance with bags and coats—some of them carried their plates of food and glasses, and a group of six handsome young waiters were helping to move people inside.

The main entrance opened out into a small reception area with a staircase. High above the desk was a stained-glass skylight that cast colored light across the pale-blue carpet. Tristan stood for a moment, dripping, in shock at the sudden downpour. He shook his head and wiped his face with his sleeve. Kate found a tissue in her bag and wiped her face. She watched as several heavily made-up women hurried through the reception area to the bathrooms to fix their hair and makeup and was glad for her low-maintenance look.

A door led into a large restaurant and bar. The crowd of people who'd come rushing inside barely filled a quarter of the tables. They passed a long glass bar backed by row after row of bottles all lit up in different colors. There looked to be every kind of alcohol under the sun, along with vintage champagnes and wines. Kate felt overwhelmed by it for a second and had to force herself to keep moving. She followed Tristan past the tables to a seated area next to a fireplace where a row of glass windows looked over a walled garden and, beyond, the river. They sat down in a couple of comfortable armchairs, close to where a large fire blazed in a stone fireplace.

A dark-haired waiter approached where they were sitting. He had a smoldering beauty and looked like he'd stepped out of a perfume advert.

"Blimey, it's chucking it down out there," he said in a sibilant cockney accent, his voice not quite matching the impression his looks gave. "What can I getcha, love?"

"Two cappuccinos, thank you," said Kate.

"Back in a jiffy." He smiled, pausing to look Tristan up and down, and went off back to the bar.

"This place is posh," said Tristan, looking around. "I've never been in a five-star hotel."

"Does Ashdean have a five-star hotel?" asked Kate, looking around at the opulent bar, trying to work it out.

"No. The only four-star hotel, Brannigan's, lost a star last year when they found rats in the rotisserie . . . How do squatter's rights work?"

"If a squatter is able to enter an empty or uninhabited building without breaking in and then lives in the building uninterrupted without legal challenge for twelve years, the squatter can apply for the right to own the property," said Kate.

"So when Max Jesper became the legal owner of this place, he would have been able to borrow money against it?"

"Yes, but to turn a derelict property into this would mean a huge investment," said Kate, looking up at the crown moldings on the ceiling. "And he did it so fast—in two years."

Tristan got up and went to look at a display of photos on the wall next to the bar. Kate followed him. The photos were of famous people who had visited the restaurant, ranging from the worlds of sports, acting, and reality television, and there were some politicians too.

"Who would know that so many famous people come to Exeter?" said Tristan. Max Jesper was in each photo. He was still recognizable but was now well groomed, with a full head of dyed brown hair, a tan, and a tailored suit. He looked to be in his fifties, and there was an old rock star vibe about him.

"Max Jesper has cleaned himself up," said Kate.

"New teeth too," said Tristan. "He didn't have those pearly whites in the other photo."

The waiter approached with their coffees on a silver tray. Kate and Tristan went back to where they were sitting.

"Is that the owner in the photos with all of the celebrities?" asked Kate, indicating the wall.

"Yes, that's Maximillian Jesper, the owner," he said reverently, taking two cappuccinos off the tray. The foam on each coffee sat four inches above the rim. "We had Joanne Collins in last week."

"Do you mean *Joan* Collins?" asked Kate.

"Yeah. She was nice. But all of those people are happy to have their photo taken if they come to stay or come for a function."

"What kind of functions do you do here?"

"All sorts: weddings, parties, conferences."

"Have you met many celebrities?"

"Loads. I've been here for three years while I study," he said, setting their cappuccinos down. The towering froth on their cappuccinos was now spilling over.

"Is the owner here? I'd like to talk to him," said Kate.

"Is there a problem? The steam arm is a bit unpredictable on the new coffee machine."

Kate smiled. "No. I'm trying to track down someone that he might know."

"I can ask. He's got a lot of meetings today, though," said the waiter. "What's the name of the person?"

"It would be great if we could talk to him," said Kate, not wanting to give Jesper the excuse to say he didn't know David Lamb before he saw them. The waiter looked nervous.

"Okay. I'll go and ask," he said and went off toward the back of the bar. Kate and Tristan got up and resumed looking at the wall of photos.

Tucked away in the corner, next to a light switch, were a couple of larger frames. One held a group photo of the staff in their uniforms with Max, standing in front of the bar. The second was taken at the front of the building. A crowd of people stood around Max, who was cutting a red ribbon across the main entrance. The obligatory mayor in his gold chain was standing next to Max, beaming. Kate peered closer, recognizing one of the faces in the crowd—a man, standing to the right and smiling broadly, his face a little red, presumably from drink.

"That's Noah Huntley," said Kate. She got out her mobile phone and took a photo of the picture and then another of the photo of Max with all the waiters.

"What's Noah Huntley doing in the photo? If the hotel opened in 2009, that was seven years after he got kicked out of Parliament," said Tristan.

They heard someone clearing their throat. They jumped and turned around. Max Jesper was standing behind them with the young waiter. He was taller than he looked in the photos. He wore tight black jeans, a white shirt open at the neck, and brightly colored trainers. A mobile phone and a pair of glasses hung around his neck on lanyards.

"Hello," he said in a fruity, refined voice with a rasping edge of cigarettes. "Bishop here said you were looking for someone?" He smiled, flashing a brilliant white set of veneers. He made no secret of looking them both up and down, almost as if he were scanning a bar code. "Who are you?"

"I'm Kate Marshall, and this is Tristan Harper. We're private detectives."

"Oh yes?" he said. His blue eyes had a hardness to them. He raised his eyebrows in anticipation.

"We're trying to find a young man called David Lamb. He lived here between 1996 and around June 1999, when this was a commune."

Tristan had his phone ready with the photo of David and held it out. Max slipped on his glasses, taking the phone from Tristan and peering at the screen.

"Blimey, that's a few years ago. Hmm, handsome lad, doesn't ring a bell."

"His friend Shelley Morden lived here with him between 1996 and 1997. They were from Wolverhampton," said Kate.

"Shelley said that she made bread," added Tristan.

"Now you're going even further back in the past. Lots of people made bread here, my dear. We were piss poor!" said Max. "And so many people drifted in and out of this place in those days. It looked very different, you can imagine, and I used to partake in the wacky baccy, so much of life back then is a blur," he said, handing the phone back to Tristan with a smile.

"Did the police ever come and talk to you about a missing person?"

"No," said Max. He was still smiling, but his voice was chilly. "In all my years, the police never felt the need to darken my door. We were all law abiding. We still are, aren't we, Bishop?"

"Yes," said Bishop, parroting his boss.

"Apart from the wacky baccy?" asked Kate.

Max dropped his smile. He rolled his tongue in his cheek. There was an awkward pause.

"What happened to this young lad, David Lamb?" he asked.

"He went missing in June 1999," said Kate.

"And you say he was living here?"

"No, he'd moved out a few weeks before," repeated Kate, frustrated that he wasn't paying attention.

"Ah, well there you go, then. If he'd been a resident, I'd have known about it. When people were under my roof, I was able to look out for them."

"Would you know anyone who can help us? Are you in contact with any other people who lived here around that time?"

Max took off his glasses.

"No, my de-ah. When I stepped over to the dark side and discovered the joys of capitalism, all my socialist, free-loving friends evaporated. I only claimed squatter's rights initially so I could insure the place and get things fixed."

"How did you find it?" asked Tristan.

"How did I find *what*? Be specific," said Max. The way he looked at Tristan, thought Kate, was a strange mixture of lust and loathing.

"How did you find the commune?"

"Back in the late seventies, I was homeless, and this place was derelict. You could just walk into the building through the courtyard out the back," he said, indicating with his glasses. "I joined a few others who dossed down inside to shelter. I was the only one smart enough to register myself as the bill payer. I also put in new doors and made it safer."

"And it had been a boardinghouse?" asked Kate.

"Yes, very dated. Some of the rooms still had chamber pots under the bed, gathering dust. I might have been a squatter, but I could never contemplate shitting in a pot."

Bishop laughed, a little too hard.

"It wasn't that funny," said Max. "Piss off and wipe some tables." Bishop blushed and went off to the bar. Max turned back to them. "I'm very sorry that lad, David, went missing, but back then was a different time. We had hundreds of young people come through the commune."

"Shelley said that it was mostly young men who lived at the commune," said Kate.

"Well, of course. You look old enough to remember the old days," he said pointedly. "It wasn't all fucking rainbow takeaway coffee cups back then. This was a safe house for many people, including young gay men who'd been thrown out by their parents . . . Anyway, I have work to do. Do you have a card, in case I remember something?"

Kate took out one of her business cards and handed it to him.

"The Kate Marshall Detective Agency," he said, peering at it. "Do you have a card?" he asked, looking up at Tristan.

"Yes," said Tristan, handing him one of his cards.

"I'll be sure to give you a ring, Tristan, if I remember anything. Now, if you'll excuse me."

He smiled and bowed his head and left before they could ask him anything else. He made Kate shudder a little, with his cold eyes and indifference.

18

It was still raining when they came out of Jesper's. They hurried back to the car and got inside. Tristan had paid for the coffee, and he got the receipt out and passed it to Kate. She noticed something written on the back.

"The waiter wrote his phone number, with a smiley face," she said, holding it up.

"Oh," he said. "I didn't ask for it."

"I doubt he wrote it for me," said Kate.

"He dots the *i* of *Bishop* with a circle," said Tristan, raising an eyebrow.

"I worked with a handwriting analyst once. It can mean someone has childish and playful qualities," said Kate.

"Not my type."

Kate fleetingly wondered what his type was, as she'd never heard him mention a boyfriend.

"It could be interesting, for the case, to meet him for coffee. He said he's been working at Jesper's for three years. Would you be comfortable doing that?" she asked.

"Okay. I would just be going for a cup of coffee."

Kate looked at the receipt again.

"Is that what a smiley face means? Do you want to go for coffee?"

"I presume so. What would you think if a waiter wrote that on your receipt?"

Kate laughed at Tristan's naivety.

"I'd think he's got my order mixed up. I'm past the age where a waiter's going to write his phone number on my receipt," she said. "If you're comfortable to contact him and go for coffee, then, it could give us more info."

Kate took over driving, started the engine, and pulled out of the parking spot. The smart shops and the cinema slid past, and they reached the end of the road and started toward the industrial estate. Tristan took out his mobile and typed a short message to Bishop and pressed "Send."

"What did you make of Max Jesper?" he asked, putting his phone back in his pocket.

"I thought he was cold and sleazy, and it wasn't even me he was interested in."

"I think he was lying. He knew David Lamb," said Tristan. "Shelley said very few women lived at the commune, so even if David, on his own, didn't stick out, the fact he arrived with Shelley and they were friends, that must have meant something. And Shelley said she went to the commune when David went missing. I don't buy the whole wacky baccy stuff. Max seems very sharp and on the ball. Like a sharp, inquisitive crow."

"It also troubles me how Max Jesper went from homeless dosser to the owner of a lucrative boutique hotel."

"What if it was luck?" asked Tristan. Kate smiled. He certainly saw the world more from a glass-half-full perspective.

"Luck is becoming the owner of a run-down squat by default. But there must have been serious investment involved in remodeling that building into a hotel. Look at all the people who he had at the opening. The mayor, all those Rotary Club types, and Noah Huntley. Of course, he could have just been attending as a local businessman."

"But it also brings us back to Joanna and her link to Noah," said Tristan. "I know neither of us have said this yet, but Joanna must have been investigating the disappearance of David and Gabe."

"Yes, but there's a chance that Joanna *did* phone Shelley to talk about that asbestos-removal story on her street. Which would mean she wasn't contacting her about David Lamb. It would have to be a big coincidence, though. Joanna happens to be looking for David Lamb, and she happens to contact his best friend, Shelley, on an unrelated story."

"What if the story isn't unrelated? We should look into that asbestos story," said Tristan.

Kate nodded in agreement, but her heart sank that they might be opening their investigation out even wider. This gave her an idea.

"Shelley said that David was questioned by the police about the death of that older man . . ."

"Sidney Newett."

"David was released without charge, but what if he has a criminal record? And what if Gabe Kemp and George Tomassini also have criminal records?"

"If they did, we might be able to find out more about them, their addresses, other stuff from their personal history," said Tristan.

"I'll give Alan Hexham a call and see if he can find anything for us," said Kate. Kate had first met Alan Hexham, the county pathologist, through Ashdean University. Alan had been a guest lecturer on her criminology course and had supplied cold cases for her students to work on. He'd known about her background in the police, and when they'd started up their detective agency, he had offered to assist her where he could.

"What about Noah Huntley? It would be worth doing a deep dive into his business links," said Tristan. "It could also be worth talking to him."

"Do you think he'd want to talk to us?" asked Kate.

"He might want to talk to me. I could be his type."

"I feel odd about pimping you out," said Kate. "I'd want to find a way to talk to him that included us both. We could let him think we're concentrating on Joanna and then surprise him with questions about David Lamb, George Tomassini, and the commune."

Tristan's phone pinged.

"Talking of whoring me out. It's Bishop," he said, checking the screen. "He wants to meet for coffee tomorrow afternoon at Starbucks in Exeter."

"I said *pimping*, not *whoring*."

"Is that better?"

"Why don't you suggest the Stage Door café behind the Corn Exchange?" said Kate. "Easier to have a quiet conversation."

Tristan nodded and started to text him back. They came to a set of traffic lights. Kate put on the hand brake and looked at her phone. She'd forgotten to take it off silent mode.

"Seems we're both popular," she said, reading a text message. "Joanna's old school friend Marnie has just got back to me. She wants to meet tomorrow afternoon," said Kate. The lights changed. She put her phone down in the console and followed the line of traffic onto the motorway.

"That's good," said Tristan. "We can do them separately and kill two birds with one stone. Where does she want to meet?"

"She's suggested her flat on the Moor Side Estate in Exeter. Her ex-husband has got the kids for their access day."

"Didn't Bev used to live on the Moor Side Estate?"

"Yeah. It's where she brought Joanna up. They were neighbors. It could be interesting to have a look at it."

"Be careful. The Moor Side Estate is pretty rough. Do you want me to come with you?"

"No. Go and meet Bishop. He could give us some more background about Jesper. I'll be going to visit Marnie after lunch. It'll be light."

"I'd still take your trusty can of pepper spray," said Tristan.

She sighed, a sudden gloom coming over her as it began to rain again and the motorway was reduced to a blur of gray. She remembered her days back in the Met Police, pounding the beat around the housing estates of South London, coming face-to-face with violence and despair.

It made her sad to think about Joanna Duncan. If she were alive now, she could be a high-powered newspaper executive living in London, happy and fulfilled. Joanna had almost escaped her upbringing.

Almost.

19

It was a long wait until nightfall. The sun didn't set until nine p.m. All the anger Tom felt toward Hayden had gone, because Hayden was no longer *anything*. He was just rotting meat to be disposed of.

Under the cover of darkness, Tom loaded Hayden's body into the car and drove toward Dartmoor. It had rained on and off all afternoon, but as he left the motorway, the rumbling sky erupted into a storm. Rain pelted the windscreen, lightning flashed, and he felt the Land Rover shift as it was pummeled by the wind.

It was now late, and the country roads were quiet. He'd passed a couple of small cottages, set back behind trees and hedges with light glowing in the windows, and then he went for a mile without seeing a house. The rain was now so heavy, the windscreen wipers couldn't keep up, and he almost missed the gate through the swamped windscreen.

He stopped the car, switched off the headlights, and immediately felt safer when he was swallowed by the darkness. The storm was right above him as he ran to open the gate, head down, glad of the thick waxed jacket and heavy boots he was wearing. The trees were creaking and keening in the wind, dark shadows high above his head. When he looked up, a flash of lightning lit up the skyline, and he saw that the row of large oak trees lining the road were bending far over in the wind.

He hurried to the car and drove through the gate, getting back out to close it.

The gate led to a piece of moorland popular with walkers. On a clear day, it stretched out for miles, dotted with trees whose branches towered and stretched out over the moor. An ancient Roman road ran straight through the middle. Its original stones had long ago been covered by moss and grass, but the road was built to last, and with the regular footfall from walkers, the grass, worn away in patches, revealed the shiny white granite flagstones.

Tom had explored this location before, and he'd planned to use the Roman road to drive deep into the moor without fear of the car getting stuck in the soft earth or sinking into the boggy marsh.

He put the car in a low gear and started across the grass toward the beginning of the road. Lightning forked across the black sky. Deep, rolling rumbles of thunder added to the symphony of the storm, and rain hammered relentlessly on the roof of the car with a low roar.

He usually felt safe on the moor, but as the storm raged around him, Tom felt scared for the first time.

As he passed under the canopy of a large tree, its branches bent and swayed, as if it were reaching out for him. The car stopped bouncing and lurching, and he felt the grass smooth out and firm up at the beginning of the Roman road.

There was a groaning, cracking sound up ahead, and the lightning lit up a huge hornbeam tree, which must have been several hundred years old. Its trunk was more than three meters wide, and its vast canopy of branches extended out over the road. It seemed to bend and rise up, and then the giant tree toppled toward the car. Tom hit the brakes, put the car in reverse, and had just pulled back when the tree fell across the road with a crash and a loud ripping sound, pulling up a wide circle of the earth with it.

Tom felt the impact of the tree falling, and the trunk blocked his view through the windscreen. He sat for a moment, shaking, and then opened the car door.

He could smell fresh soil mingling with the rain. The fallen trunk was like a tall wall, blocking his path. The tree must have stood at fifty meters tall. It lay across the road and seemed to stretch far out across the moorland into the shadows. The colossal ball of roots at its base seemed to reach up as high as a three-story house.

Tom found his mobile phone in one of the pockets of his jacket and, using the dim light from the screen saver, walked through the pelting rain to the huge muddy hole where the tree had been. It was deep, rapidly filling with rainwater, and the runoff from the edges was taking the loose earth with it.

Tom had planned to drive deep into the moor to dump Hayden's body, but with the Roman road now blocked with the tree, he didn't want to risk driving off into the soft moorland where the car could get stuck.

Tom looked up at the sky as the lightning flashed again. Steam was rising from the exposed roots, and the fallen tree creaked and groaned as if it were in the last throes of death, ripped from the soil and unable to breathe. He always believed that a higher power had brought him this far, had allowed him to do what he did. Had this higher power given him the perfect place to hide the body?

Tom looked down into the depths of the hole, where the soil and rainwater were pouring in. He went to the back of the car and lifted out Hayden's body. He cradled it in his arms and stood as close to the edge of the hole as felt safe, and then, like an offering to his helpful god, he tossed the body down into the depths. The noise of the storm was still loud, and he didn't hear Hayden's body hit, but a flash of lightning lit up the hole, and he saw the body was already half-submerged in the mud and filthy water.

Tom stepped back and looked up at the sky, enjoying the feeling of the cold rain on his face. Lightning flashed again, and he knew he wasn't looking up at God. He was God.

20

"Did you hear the storm last night?" asked Jake.

"No," said Kate. It was early the next morning, and she still felt bleary. They were walking down the cliff to the beach for a swim.

"It was like, *raging*. Thunder, lightning."

"I must have slept through for a change," she said. The sun was glinting golden off a bank of low clouds and scattering diamonds across the still water. Kate could see a tide line of rubbish on the beach thrown up by the storm. She was usually a light sleeper, so it was a refreshing change to feel rested.

Jake waded into the rolling surf and dove headfirst under a breaking wave. Kate waited for the next wave to break and dove in after him. The water enveloped her, and she kicked out lithely, moving through the growing swells, feeling her heart pumping and the zing on her skin from the salt water. The six-inch scar on her stomach tingled in the cold water, as it always did. It was an ever-present reminder of the night she'd learned that Peter Conway was the Nine Elms Cannibal and confronted him. She'd been unaware that she was pregnant with Jake at the time, and Peter's sharp blade had missed him by millimeters. But having Jake here with her, now a grown man, swimming out strongly beside her, made her feel that there was good in the world.

Kate stopped a hundred meters out and floated on her back. She looked over at Jake, his head bobbing in the water, smiling up at the sun, which had just broken over the horizon.

"You know, you're welcome to invite your friends to stay over," she said. Jake turned and swam back to join her.

"Sam might come for a weekend, if that's cool. He loves surfing," said Jake.

"Sam is one of your housemates?" said Kate, trying to remember. Jake had mentioned a lot of new friends in his English lit classes.

"Yeah. The others are off working in Spain . . ." Jake bit his lip, and Kate could see he wanted to tell her something. "I've made another interesting friend," he said.

Kate looked over at him and raised an eyebrow. "Oh yes?"

"Not like that. Her name's Anna. Anna Tomlinson. I met her on Facebook last year . . . We've been messaging back and forth."

"You kids are so lucky," said Kate, moving her arms lazily back and forward in the water. "I had to write letters to my friends during the holidays."

"Anna's the daughter of Dennis Tomlinson . . . I don't know if the name rings a bell?"

Kate sat up in the water. The name did ring a bell. Dennis Tomlinson had been one of the serial killers she'd lectured on in her Criminal Icons course at the university.

"Dennis Tomlinson who raped and killed eight women?" she said.

"Yeah."

"Dennis Tomlinson serving eight life sentences?" asked Kate. She didn't feel relaxed anymore.

"Yes. She contacted me, unexpectedly, asking if I wanted to talk to someone who knows what it's like to have a father like . . . *that*."

"Where does she live?"

"The north of Scotland. She lives on a farm in the middle of the mountains. She wrote a book fifteen years ago, and she used the money to buy the land."

Kate shivered. The water no longer felt zingy, and her fingers were numb.

"I hope you're not thinking of writing a book."

"No. Why would you think that? I'm happy working here. I love doing the diving lessons, taking the boat out, being here with you."

"Okay, I'm happy you're happy," said Kate.

"Did you think I wasn't happy?"

"I worry that I screwed you up."

"You didn't screw me up. You made me appreciate life," he said. Kate was surprised by this and didn't know what to say. "Anna wasn't lucky like me. She was all alone when her father was arrested. She was seventeen. Her mother died when she was sixteen . . . It's been good to meet someone who's had a similar experience . . ."

She looked at Jake treading water beside her. The sun glinting on his hair, shiny as a conker.

Why shouldn't he talk to someone who'd had the same experience? Peter Conway would always be his father; Jake would always be his son. Kate would always be the link between them, and it was her actions, her affair with Peter Conway, when he was her boss in the police, that had led to all this.

"Has anyone mentioned your . . . mentioned Peter at uni?"

"Not really. I've told my mates, and they've been okay. It's all right, Mum. I'm happy. Really happy. I just want to tell you everything. How are things with you? How's the case going?"

Kate told him that she had to go over and meet Joanna's childhood friend, Marnie, but she felt no closer to understanding the case.

"Just think. The longer it takes you to solve it, the longer they pay you!"

"That's what Tristan's sister said."

"She's not happy he's gone part time at the uni?"

"No. And she's having trouble with the whole caravan-site thing. She didn't love the fact that me and Tris repainted the toilet block ourselves a couple of weeks back."

"That reminds me. I've hired three local women to come and do the weekly changeovers, starting this weekend. If they're good, I'm hoping they'll do the season," said Jake.

"Well done," said Kate. She'd put the running of the caravan site to the back of her head now that Jake was home. The changeovers happened each week on Saturday between ten a.m. and two p.m., when one lot of guests left and the caravans were cleaned and the beds changed before the next group arrived. They'd taken a lot of bookings over the last week, which was good news, and the summer season would be starting the week after next.

"They're nice ladies. Local. A mother and daughter and their friend. They live in Ashdean and can all drive over together," said Jake. "It'll give me time to do more diving trips at the weekends."

It took a little of the pressure off Kate's shoulders, knowing that the site would be up and running and money would be coming in.

"Brrr. I'm starting to get cold. I'll race you back." Jake lurched forward and started swimming back to shore.

"Hey, you got a head start!" said Kate.

"You better start swimming, then!" he shouted back with a grin. "Last one home makes breakfast!"

Kate thought of all the years when Jake had lived with her parents and she couldn't make him breakfast. She hung back a little and then started swimming after him to shore.

21

Bella Jones was woken just after eight by her dog, Callie, licking her hand, and the thump of her tail on the bedclothes. Bella lived near the village of Buckfastleigh, in a tumbledown mauve-colored cottage.

They followed the same routine every morning. Bella rolled out of bed, dressed, and took Callie out before either of them had any breakfast. Bella's small cottage backed onto the eastern side of the Dartmoor National Park, and this was her route onto the moor each morning. As soon as the gate was open, Callie ran out, sniffing the air after the storm.

It had rained heavily, and the soggy moorland had almost made Bella turn back, but Callie had the new scents kicked up by the storm in her nose, and she ran off toward the colossal fallen tree on the Roman road.

Bella had lived in this part of Devon all her life, and the ancient hornbeam tree had remained a constant on the landscape for the past sixty years. Today, however, it looked like a giant who'd keeled over and died.

"Oh, bloody hell," said Bella, shocked and saddened to see the tree had fallen.

Callie ran ahead barking and stopped beside the wide hole left by the ripped-up roots. It was her angry, scared bark, which came out at a loud, yippy register.

22

The Moor Side housing estate was a grotty place with an air of menace. Kate parked her car on the edge of the estate and walked the last two streets to the high-rise tower block where Marnie lived. There were two burned-out cars in the car park and a group of young guys hanging around, sitting on a low wall, smoking. The lift was broken, but there was no one on the stairwell up to the second floor.

A tiny woman answered the door. She was barely five feet tall. She was painfully thin and leaning on a crutch. Her hair was bright red and styled poker straight in a bob with a blunt fringe. She wore a long multicolored tie-dyed skirt and a white long-sleeved T-shirt. She had pale hazel eyes, and her skin was bloodless, but her welcome and her smile were very warm.

"Really good to meet you," she said with enthusiasm. She led Kate through a narrow hallway filled with laundry drying on clothes racks, past a closed living room door, into the kitchen.

"I've got a couple of hours before I've got to pick the kids up from school," she said. Like Bev, Marnie had a strong West Country accent. "Tha's them both," she added, indicating a photo on the fridge of a boy and a girl sitting on the swings of a park with Marnie in between them. It was a bright, sunny day, and they were all wearing baseball caps.

"They're so cute at that age," said Kate.

It took a minute for Bella to reach Callie. The hole left by the tree roots was more than three meters across, very deep, and half-filled with rainwater. The root structure poked out from a muddy wall on the other side, stretching as many meters high and blocking out the light. Callie barked and shifted on her paws at the edge of the hole, causing large chunks of wet earth and grass to fall away and land with a splash in the muddy water.

"Heel; back!" said Bella, stepping away from the crumbling edge and seeing that Callie was dislodging the earth underneath her paws.

Bella managed to hook the end of her walking stick under Callie's collar, but Callie kept snarling and barking into the hole, and the hackles were up on the buttery-yellow fur on her back.

"It's just a tree," said Bella, understanding that seeing it from this bizarre new perspective might be a first for her beloved dog. The wall of wet earth and twisted roots looked alien to Bella too. There had been many times on their regular walks where Callie had seen something out of the ordinary and barked; most recently, a black bin liner caught on the edge of a barbed wire gate had floated, billowing full of air, in the breeze, like a mysterious hunched-over figure in a black cape.

Bella gripped the stick with both hands and dug in her heels to pull Callie back. She followed the dog's gaze downward, and that's when she saw the hand protruding from the dark, wet earth. Above it were an arm and the side of a face with its eyes closed. The rain had washed away some of the dirt, and the skin was pale and gray.

"Come on; back, Callie, back!" cried Bella, managing to pull Callie clear from the edge of the hole. The hair on the back of her neck stood up in the cold.

Bella didn't scare easily, but she had to take deep breaths and fight the urge to be sick as she found her mobile phone in the folds of her coat and called the police.

"I know. They think everything you do is wonderful . . . I'm waiting for that to wear off. How old is your son now?"

"How did you know I had a son?" she asked.

"I've read all about you," said Marnie.

"He's nineteen," said Kate, wondering what Marnie had read. "Just back from uni."

"What's he studying?"

"English."

"Do you have a photo?" she asked, a little too eagerly.

"I don't, I'm afraid," she said. Marnie looked disappointed as she put a cup of tea in front of Kate. She propped her crutch up against the radiator and sat down in the chair opposite. It was a warm, cozy little kitchen, with fogged-up windows from condensation.

"Thank you," said Kate, taking a sip of her tea.

"Is Bill paying for it, the investigation?" asked Marnie. She'd quickly assumed a familiarity, like they were close friends.

"I can't say. That's confidential."

Marnie nodded and tapped the side of her nose. "Course; mum's the word. He's been there for years, having Bev cry on his shoulder, paying the bills," said Marnie. "They never got married or even lived together. He was in and out at Bev's evenings and weekends, and she used to accompany him for work dinners."

"When you were growing up, Bev and Joanna lived here on the estate?"

"Yes. In Florence House, the tower opposite," said Marnie, tipping her head at the window. There was a pile of shoeboxes on the table. Marnie opened the top one and took out a couple of small photo albums. She picked up the first and opened it.

"Here. That's Jo and Fred's wedding," she said, flicking through photos of Joanna in a beautiful, simple silk bridal gown with Fred outside a church in a vintage Daimler. "That's Jo and Fred at the top table. Fred's parents to the left, and Bev with Bill on the right. This was 2000.

Bill was Bev's guest at the wedding, but he stumped up for most of the wedding too. It's one of the only photos I've got of him. *Hates* having his photo taken . . ."

She pulled out another photo album and opened it.

"Me and Jo were friends from when we were small. Our mums got to know each other cleaning the same office block. We were in the same class at primary school. My mum passed away eight years ago now . . . Here . . ." Marnie twisted the photo album around to face Kate and flicked through pages of photos of when Joanna and Marnie were small: trips out to the zoo, first days at school, fancy-dress parties, Christmases. She came to a photo that Kate had seen before, of Joanna, aged eleven, the Christmas that she'd got the mini typewriter, and then turned the page to another of her and Jo sitting on a brick wall in the car park of the tower block, wearing stonewashed blue jeans and white blouses.

"Bloody hell. Look, that's when we were Brosettes. Bev got those jeans for us from a bloke she knew on the market. Jeans were well expensive back then."

"Are you still on good terms with Bev?"

Marnie put the album down and took a gulp of tea.

"No. We've drifted apart. She was very good to me growing up, and when my mum died, we stayed in contact, but I don't know. It got difficult to be around her. We'd have the same *endless* conversations about Jo not being here, what happened to her. After eight years, I found it hard to be around."

"Did you get on with Bill?"

"Yeah. He was fine. Nice. A bit bland."

"Did Jo see Bill as a stepfather?" asked Kate.

"She did, but Jo had a *big* falling-out with him a few weeks before she went missing."

"What happened?"

"Jo was working on a story, investigating a development in Exeter. An office block had been bought by an investment firm, and it was being refurbished, but they found asbestos in the building."

"Marco Polo House?"

"Yeah. How did you know?"

"From someone else we talked to," said Kate, feeling her heart sink a little. It meant that Joanna could have been calling Shelley Morden about the asbestos and not about David Lamb.

"The investment firm Bill was involved with bought Marco Polo House to do it up and then flog it on to the council for a huge profit. When they found asbestos, they tried to cover it up, literally and figuratively, so they didn't lose money. Jo found out."

"How?"

"A whistleblower at the council. She started investigating it for the *West Country News*, and that's when she found out Bill was one of the three investors in the project. She went to him and told him that she was in this horrible position. Jo said if they didn't sort it out, she would write a story about it."

"Marco Polo House was next to a big primary school in the city?" said Kate.

"Yeah, and it was blue asbestos, the worst kind. It cost Bill and the other investors a lot of money to fix it safely. And then the sale to the council fell through. They ended up selling it privately at a loss."

"What did Bev have to say about it?" asked Kate.

"Oh, it caused tension, but Jo never published the story, which she could have. It would have been a much bigger scandal. She held back out of loyalty to Bill and her mum. Luckily, he did as she asked and got it fixed safely."

"Was Bill ever a suspect?"

"What? With Jo going missing? No . . . No . . ." It was as if the thought had never crossed Marnie's mind. She shook her head again. "No . . . And he'd been with Bev on the day that Jo went missing. They'd been out together, and then Bill went into work. People saw him. Two blokes he worked with confirmed he was there."

"What did Fred think of Bill?"

Marnie shrugged.

"They got on fine . . . It was all very weird because Bev and Bill were always so funny about their relationship. Fred would only really see him at Bev's place. I think Bill went to Jo and Fred's house only once when they moved in. It was like there was an unofficial rule that Bill only went to Bev's house. Bev wanted her boundaries. She'd lived with Jo's dad, and it hadn't been happy. She never wanted to sacrifice her independence."

"Where did Bill live?"

"He had a big flat over the other side of town. Bev didn't go there often. Nor did Jo."

"Why?"

"I don't have all the answers. Like I said: Bev liked her independence. So did Bill."

"Did you know they've moved in together?"

Marnie stared at Kate and sat back in her chair. "No way. Really? Where?"

"Salcombe. Bill has a very nice house there."

"Blimey. They took their time. I'm not surprised. He's done well for himself, Bill. He worked his way up from being a hod carrier. Started his own building firm and patented a new kind of tarmac that resists water. His company was bought out by a big European firm about six years ago."

There was a pause, and Marnie got up and filled their cups with fresh tea.

"What do you think happened to Joanna?" asked Kate. Marnie put the cups back on the table. "We've been over the evidence, and no one saw anything."

"Honestly? I think she was the victim of a multiple murderer," said Marnie. "And I think she was in the wrong place at the wrong time. I read a lot of true crime fiction, and statistics say that there are several active serial killers in the UK who haven't yet been caught. *You* caught a serial killer, though, didn't you?"

"Well, yes," said Kate, the comment taking her off guard.

"So many of them go on killing for *years* before they get caught. They think Harold Shipman killed two hundred and sixty people over three decades . . . Dennis Nilsen, Peter Sutcliffe, Fred and Rose West all killed people over several years and got away with it. In most cases, it was only a fluke or a stupid mistake that meant they got caught. Serial killers can manipulate people to see them as normal—nice, even. How long did Peter Conway get away with it until you worked out it was him?"

Kate was taken off guard again. "Officially, it was five years, but we think that there are other victims that have never been identified," she said.

"Exactly."

Kate suddenly felt chilly. The sky was growing darker outside the small kitchen window. She decided to change the subject.

"Did Joanna ever talk to you about her work? About stories she was working on?"

Marnie shook her head.

"No. We just used to talk about rubbish on TV, about the men in our lives. I got the impression that she liked to let off steam with me. I was easy to talk to."

"Did she ever talk in any detail about the Noah Huntley article she wrote?"

Marnie frowned.

"We did talk about that because it was such a big thing and the story got picked up by the national newspapers, and then he lost his seat."

"Did Joanna ever talk about meeting Noah Huntley again, or a job she was applying for in London?"

"No. Why would she have met Noah Huntley again? I should think she was the last person he'd want to talk to."

Kate hesitated and thought about her next question. She didn't want to lead Marnie.

"Did Joanna ever mention a story she was writing about missing people? Young men who'd gone missing?"

"She hardly ever talked about work. Like I said, she liked to have a laugh with me . . . Were these young men murdered?" she added, her interest piqued.

"I don't know. We're rather vague about the details."

Marnie rubbed at her face. "I remember Fred saying they took away all of Joanna's work stuff. They interviewed everyone she'd ever spoken to and combed through her whole life. And they came up with nothing. Like I said, I think Jo was abducted or killed by someone she didn't know. That's what happens with most of the victims of serial killers. Serial murderers are opportunists. Impulsive. Any number of creeps could have followed Jo and seen that she left her car in Deansgate. That was always empty and about to be demolished. It was the perfect place to grab her, stuff her in their car, and drive away. If you discount everything else, it's the only logical conclusion," said Marnie.

Kate was becoming irritated with Marnie, only because she could be right.

"Did you know about Fred having an affair with the neighbors' nanny, Famke?" asked Kate.

"Yeah, afterward I did."

"Were you surprised?"

"Not really. Jo was obsessed by work, and Fred was a bit lost. They'd just moved in together, and their lives were going in different directions."

"Do you think he did it?"

Marnie laughed.

"Fred? No. He couldn't organize a piss-up in a brewery, let alone, I dunno, killing Jo and stashing her body somewhere so good that no one has found her in almost thirteen years. Unless he hired a hit man, but he was skint."

"Did Joanna have any other friends from this estate, or enemies?"

Marnie shook her head.

"No, and Bev got on well with everyone. I know that this estate 'as got a bad name, but the people aren't all bad. There are good people. There was a real community spirit, and people rallied around. Bev's car got nicked the night Joanna went missing, right out on the road out front, and I had a crash the same day. And so many of the neighbors helped her out giving her lifts, and me too."

"Was the crash you had bad?" asked Kate, her eyes moving to the crutch propped up against the radiator.

"No. That's for early-onset arthritis," said Marnie. "The crash was my own fault. I backed into a posh BMW parked on the road below. My shit-heap MINI was okay, but I ended up having to pay a five hundred quid excess on the owner's insurance to have it fixed. I bet he could have paid for it easier than me, but that's life."

Marnie looked behind her, at the clock on the wall. "I'd better make a move in a bit. I need to pick up the kids from school. Can I show you something?"

"What's that?" asked Kate.

"It's in the lounge."

Marnie got up and picked up the crutch. Kate followed her slow walk down the hallway. Marnie opened the living room door. It was furnished with a dark leather sofa and a flat-screen TV. To the right of the TV was a giant bookcase filled with DVDs. To the left was a large wooden shelf unit with four tiers of shelves behind glass doors. On the shelves behind the glass were rows of foot-high collector's movie merchandise models: Freddy Krueger, Brandon Lee from *The Crow*,

Pennywise the clown, Ripley from *Aliens* holding a tiny Newt in one arm and a flame-throwing gun in the other. There were two versions of Chucky, one with and one without a knife, and three versions of Pinhead from *Hellraiser* and his Cenobites. There was also a group of figures that Kate didn't recognize.

"Wow," said Kate, trying to keep her voice light. It was all rather creepy.

"Yeah," said Marnie, misreading Kate's reaction as being impressed. "I've got a YouTube channel: Marnie'sMayhem07. I demonstrate film-merchandise toys," she said. "I'm waiting on a fifteen-inch talking Regan from *The Exorcist*, but she's stuck in the sorting office."

Kate smiled and nodded again. It was an oppressive room, and the smell of stale cigarettes was fighting with a cheap air freshener. Marnie had closed the thick curtains, and there was just a harsh overhead light, which bounced off the glossy cheap furniture. Marnie moved over to the DVD shelf, and at the bottom was a shelf of books, and as she picked up one particular book, Kate realized what was coming next. Marnie was holding a copy of *No Son of Mine*, the memoir written by Enid Conway, Peter Conway's mother. Kate could feel her chest tighten and her heart begin to thump as she saw there was a black felt-tip pen hooked over the book cover.

"Would you sign it?" She smiled, leaning her elbow on her crutch and opening the book to the title page. There were already two signatures. One in blue that read *Peter Conway*, and one in black that was illegible, but because Kate had been sent a signed copy of *No Son of Mine* when it was published, she knew it was Enid Conway's signature. Marnie held out the pen with an eager look in her eyes.

"But I didn't write it," said Kate.

"It would really help me out," said Marnie. "Do you know how much this book could be worth if a copy has all three signatures?"

"I've never signed a copy," said Kate.

"Exactly. I've helped you out, and if I remember anything else, I can help you out even more. Yeah?"

"Where did you get both of their signatures?" asked Kate.

"If you know the right person, you can get it."

This was abhorrent to Kate. The book, when it was published, had been a cheap ploy by Enid Conway to make money.

"There's a rare book dealer who's told me I can sell this for two thousand pounds or more if it has your signature. Do you know how much me and my kids could benefit from two grand? I've got black mold in this flat!" Her nostrils flared, and she looked angry. It suddenly made her look like one of her foot-high film-monster models.

Kate thought back to the conversation she'd had with Jake that morning, and it was oddly prescient. The reality of her life was not up for sale. It made sense now, why Marnie was so keen to talk to her.

"No. I'm sorry," said Kate. "I'm not signing that."

23

Tristan was the first to arrive at the café to meet Bishop and sat in a booth in the window. South Street in Exeter had one of the last independent coffee shops. Opposite were a home-ware shop, a betting shop, and a hairdresser with flats above them.

A few minutes later, Bishop the waiter—Tristan didn't know his last name—emerged from one of the doors opposite. He wore jeans and a tight white T-shirt.

"Hiya," said Bishop with a broad grin. He leaned over and pecked Tristan on the cheek. "Did you order?"

"Yeah. Americano," said Tristan, taken aback by the kiss on the cheek.

"You don't look like you need to watch your figure . . . although I could watch it all day," said Bishop. Tristan laughed awkwardly. Was Bishop naive enough to think this was a date? Kate and Tristan had already said they were private detectives and had asked to talk to his boss at Jesper's.

"I like your tattoos," Bishop added, indicating Tristan's forearms and the top of the eagle protruding from the neck of his T-shirt.

"Thanks."

"You want your usual?" said the owner, coming over to the table. She was an elderly lady with a stern face.

"Yes please, Esperanza. And a slice of that Snickers cheesecake . . . This is my local," he added when she'd gone. "You look even better than you did the other day."

"Thanks," said Tristan. "Listen. I've asked you here for a reason."

Bishop's eyes opened wider. "I thought I asked to meet *you*? My number on the receipt . . ."

"Yes, but to be clear, this isn't a date. Do you remember me and my colleague, Kate, saying to Max that we're private detectives and we're investigating the disappearance of several young men? One of them was living at Jesper's when it was a commune."

Bishop was quiet for a moment; he shifted the salt and pepper around on the table. He pushed his bottom lip out, which made him look a bit sulky. "Right. So this is . . . what?"

"This is me asking for your help to find someone from our community who we think might have been murdered," said Tristan. Bishop looked serious for the first time since he'd arrived.

"Yes. Okay. I thought Max told you that he didn't know anything?"

"David Lamb," said Tristan, placing his phone with David's photo between them on the table. "He went missing in June 1999. He'd been living at Jesper's when it was a commune, but he fell out with them and had moved in with a boyfriend. Did Max mention anything about David or the commune when we'd gone?"

Bishop studied the picture and shook his head. "No."

"Okay. Max Jesper. What can you tell me about him?" asked Tristan. "Do you mind if I take notes?"

"No, go ahead . . . Do you think Max is involved in this David going missing?"

"I'm interested to find out some background about him," said Tristan, taking a notepad and pen from his bag. "He doesn't have any social media accounts, and beyond the story of him opening Jesper's, there's not much else about him online."

"Max is a bit of an old queen, quite funny. He'll flirt outrageously, but he's not touchy-feely. He always pays on time, but he's not a warm person."

"Is he single?"

"No. He's got a long-term partner, Nick."

"Do you know his second name?"

"Erm, Lacey. I've only ever met him once or twice. He lives out at the house."

"What house?"

"Max and Nick own a house right on the beach in Burnham-on-Sea, on the Somerset coast."

"Max doesn't live at the hotel?"

"No. He commutes in most days. He'll sometimes stay the night at the weekend if things go on late."

"Is it a long drive?" asked Tristan.

"An hour or so each way, I think. He's always moaning about the M5, says he spends most of his time on it."

"What does Nick do for work?"

"He's a property developer. I've never, ever seen him at Jesper's. I only met him a couple of times at one of their parties. Max asked some of the waiters to travel up to the house to serve drinks at the party."

"What kind of party?"

"There were two, both costume parties." Esperanza appeared at the booth with their drinks. She put another espresso in front of Tristan and a huge milkshake in front of Bishop. It was garnished with pieces of fruit. "Thanks . . ." She smiled and left. "She's ever so good, makes up my protein powder for me," said Bishop. "You wanna try?"

Tristan shook his head. Whenever he worked out, he saw protein-powder drinks as something to endure, not have served with fruit in a sundae glass. He watched as Bishop eagerly started to suck it up through a straw.

"Do Max and Nick often have parties?"

"I don't know. I worked at their summer party last year," he said, wiping his mouth. "Three of us from Jesper's went to help out and serve food and drink."

"What kind of people were at the party?"

"Their friends. Rich ones. Local rich people."

Tristan scrolled through his phone and found the photo taken from the opening of Jesper's, of Max cutting the ribbon next to the town mayor and the group of local dignitaries.

"Were any of these people at the party?"

Bishop peered at the photo. "Where's this from? I kind of recognize it."

"It's on the wall in the bar at Jesper's."

"Oh yes. I've stopped noticing those photos, I spend so much time there . . . I remember him," said Bishop, pointing to Noah Huntley. Tristan didn't let his excitement show.

"Can you remember his name?"

Bishop rolled his eyes and smiled. "Yes. It was Noah. I'm not sure of his second name, but he got very drunk and asked me and Sam, one of the other waiters, if we'd like to go down onto the beach with him."

"And you're sure he's called Noah?"

Bishop nodded. "Yeah. He made some joke that he could make us come two by two, you know, like Noah did on the ark."

"What a smooth talker," said Tristan. "And did you?"

"No way! That's tacky, and I needed my job to pay me through uni. He offered us money, but that was a step too far."

"How much money?"

"A hundred quid each. He had the cash in his codpiece."

"Codpiece?"

"It was a Roman masked ball. He was dressed as Casanova, with white tights, a sort of bodice, and a Zorro-style mask, but then, so were most of the other men."

"Was Noah's wife there?"

"No. He didn't mention being married."

"Were women at the party?"

"Yeah, it was couples, all kinds of people."

"Did you talk to Noah much? Did he say how he knew Max and Nick?"

"He said he'd invested in Jesper's but they'd bought him out and he'd moved on to bigger things. He said he invests a lot in property. I got the impression that he was bragging about his cash."

"Did you take any photos of the party?"

"No, we were working. I got some photos of the house when we were setting up. It's gorgeous. A big pool with a view over the sea."

"Have you got them on your phone?" asked Tristan.

"Hang on," he said, pulling out his phone and scrolling through lots of photos. "Here we go." He turned the phone round so Tristan could see and scrolled through pictures of a huge modern white box house, perched on the edge of a sandy stretch of beach, overlooking the sea.

"This is in the UK?" asked Tristan.

"I know, it looks like somewhere abroad. Max and Nick live right on the end of a long patch of beach, goes on for miles, really desolate. There aren't many other houses around . . . ," he said, scrolling through more photos.

"Is that Max?" asked Tristan when he got to a photo of a stocky man from behind, wearing a baseball cap. He was directing a couple of deliverymen with a trolley filled with drinks.

"Yeah. That's when we were setting up. That's Nick, there," he said, indicating another tall man with his back toward the camera next to a large white canopy set up on the lawn in front of the swimming pool. He was lifting the boxes off the trolley. He had short light-brown hair, and he was well built.

"You got any other photos of them?" asked Tristan.

"Let me see," Bishop said, scrolling through the photos from the inside of the marquee, where a bar was being set up and a huge ice sculpture was being lifted into place.

"I've got photos of the beach. There's a thick patch of dunes in front of the house. That's where Noah wanted to go with me and Sam. He gave us the impression he's been there before, in the dunes."

"How did he react when you said no?"

"I was called away, but Sam told me afterward he wouldn't leave him alone. In the end, he told Noah to f off. Noah flipped up the tray of drinks Sam was carrying and called him all kinds of things."

"What did Max do?"

"I don't know if he was there. By this time, the party was rowdy and loud, so no one really noticed. Max was more worried about people going too far down on the beach."

"Why?"

"I've got a picture I took when we went down to the beach before the party," he said. "Here."

It was a photo of the sun setting over a vast expanse of sandy beach; the tide was far out. To the left was a huge sign planted in the sand dunes that read:

NO CARS, BIKES, MOTORBIKES, OR QUADS

ALLOWED PAST THIS POINT

MAX PENALTY £400 WARNING

WARNING! DO NOT WALK OR DRIVE

ANY KIND OF VEHICLE OUT TO

THE SOFT SAND AND MUD AT LOW TIDE

"Max said that Nick is *obsessed* about the tide on the beach in front of their house—when it's going out, how far it's going out. And when it's going out if there are people still on the beach. There's been so many people who've got stranded out in the mud, and a couple of times their party guests have gotten drunk and wandered out when the tide's low, and they almost got stranded when it came back in," said Bishop.

Tristan peered at the photo. "You can't even see the water's edge."

"Yeah. The tide goes out really far and comes back in fast too. Whenever Nick goes away on business, Max told me that he's always asking him to check the weather to check if there's going to be a storm."

"Is their house at risk of flooding?" asked Tristan.

"I don't think so. Nick just has this weird PTSD about it."

"PTSD? Did he get stuck out on the sand when the tide was coming in?"

"I dunno. But there are always things in the news about people and cars getting stranded out at high tide along that stretch of beach. Max doesn't like to leave him alone there much, cos he can get really worked up about it."

"Has he been officially diagnosed with PTSD?" asked Tristan.

"I don't know. I get the impression they're very reclusive. The only time I've ever heard Max tell me about them going anywhere is when they were in London and went to the cinema and Nick had a full-on panic attack."

"Why?"

"He said they never, ever go out. Nick hates being in crowds, but Max really wanted to see *The Woman in Black* and persuaded him to go out. They only got halfway through the film when Nick started panicking. They had to leave."

"Are Max and Nick married?" asked Tristan.

"I don't think so. They've been together for years."

"Do you know what kind of property development Nick does?"

"Max said something vague about private-equity, high-profile stuff. He's quite a dish. He's tall, like Max, but quite butch, *unlike Max*."

"How old is he?"

"Fiftyish."

Tristan made some notes and checked back over what he'd written.

"Have you heard any stories about the hotel when it was a commune? Has anyone ever come to the hotel who used to live there when it was a commune?"

Bishop shook his head, and then he frowned.

"You say that this guy, David, lived there and then went missing. How?" he asked.

"He didn't show up to his friend's birthday party. This was back in June 1999. He'd been a runaway from home. His friend, Shelley, was concerned and reported him missing to the police," said Tristan. "We were talking about this guy, Noah. Have you ever seen him at Jesper's?"

"No. I've never seen him there. Luckily, he was just some drunken twat at a party. A mean drunk at that," said Bishop. "After he flipped up Sam's tray, he left, and on the way out, he called me a dirty little prick tease."

"Did you tell Max?"

"No. It's part of the job when you work in a bar, dealing with drunken idiots."

24

Kate walked back to her car and was troubled by her meeting with Marnie; her personal interest in Kate made her feel grubby, and her theory that Joanna was just in the wrong place at the wrong time and the victim of a serial killer made her uneasy. So did Bill's link to the asbestos story. She was annoyed they hadn't checked out Bill and his business interests more closely.

Kate sat in the car tapping her foot, unsure what to do. She found Bill's mobile phone number and called him, but it twice went to voice mail. She left a short message asking him to return her call, saying she had an update about the case she wanted to discuss.

She then tried to call Bev, who answered.

"Is Bill there?" asked Kate.

"No. He's away on business," said Bev.

"Do you know when he's back?"

"Friday."

Bev's voice sounded thick, and she was slurring a little. It was only three p.m.

"Are you okay to talk?" asked Kate.

"Course I am. What is it?"

"I really wanted to ask Bill this, but maybe you could help . . ."

"Go on."

"I've been talking to Marnie, Joanna's—"

"I know who Marnie is."

"Yes, of course. She just told me that in the weeks before she went missing, Joanna had been investigating the purchase of an office block, Marco Polo House in Exeter."

"Yes. Jo found out that they were trying to cover up the asbestos problem. That was very awkward. Jo was very good to Bill. She went to him the second she knew about it. I wasn't happy about it when I found out, but Bill had a lot of money tied up in the building, and he swears to me that they were acting on the advice of an expert, who told them that the asbestos didn't need removing as long as they plastered up the walls and sealed it all in tight," said Bev. "You see?"

Kate rolled her eyes. This was nonsense. Everyone knew that asbestos was a huge problem, and environmental agencies took it seriously.

"Okay. But there must have been tension between Bill and Jo?"

"*Of course.* Bill was very worried about it all. And Jo had to do her job, of course."

"According to Marnie—" started Kate.

"According to Marnie!" Bev spat. "What does she know? Last I saw, she was demonstrating toys on her fucking YouTube channel. No doubt thinking she'll get away with working at the same time as claiming benefits off the state."

"Did you and Marnie fall out?"

There was a pause.

"We was good for a time. She helped me a lot. My car got nicked at the same time as Jo went missing, and she was good, running me around, taking me shopping when Bill couldn't. But then she turned nasty. Didn't understand what I'm going through. She got irritated with me wanting to talk about Jo."

"Okay; how did Joanna feel about discovering the story about the asbestos and then finding out Bill was involved?"

"What do you mean?" said Bev, slurring even more.

"Joanna uncovered this juicy story. Didn't she feel cheated that she couldn't print it?"

There was a pause. Bev sighed, exasperated.

"Jo wasn't like that! She *knew* Bill meant everything to me . . . In the end, Bill took it on the chin, and they paid to have the building made safe. Listen. We're paying you to find out what happened to Jo. I don't like this, these questions, Kate. You sound like you think Bill's done something wrong?"

"No. I'm just following up on some leads, and this came up."

"From fucking Marnie. Shit stirrer. Did she ask you for money when you talked to her?"

Kate hesitated, thinking about the book Marnie had asked her to sign. "No. She didn't."

"She was always jealous of Jo making something of herself. Getting out of that estate."

"Bev, if you'd have told me about this in the first place, it wouldn't have taken me by surprise. That's the only reason I'm asking."

She was silent on the end of the phone.

"Oh, I'm sorry," she said.

"Please. Don't be. I can't imagine everything you've been through. This must be so tough."

"My whole bloody life's been tough . . ." Kate heard Bev pouring a drink in the background. "I thought that when me and Bill lived together, we'd see each other so much more, but he's away a lot with 'is work."

"It's a lovely house you've got there."

"It gives me the creeps when I'm 'ere on me own . . . ," said Bev. "I've never lived nowhere so empty. I'm used to having neighbors and people upstairs, downstairs, to the side . . . And the fucking windows. No curtains. And there's all these buttons for things. I tried to turn the outside light on, and the fucking jacuzzi comes on."

"Where's Bill gone away on business?"

"Germany. They're doing a big contract on a new motorway. He has to be there, overseeing. Dusseldwarf . . ." Kate didn't want to correct her. "He's only gone for a couple of days, but still. I miss him . . . Just me and these awful bloody windows, reflecting my ugly mug back at me . . . Do you think you're any closer to finding her? Jo?"

Kate hesitated, feeling her heart sink at the question.

"We're going through a lot of information in the case files. We're talking with everyone who Joanna was friends with," said Kate. She wished she hadn't phoned Bev; it was cruel to phone without having concrete information.

"That's a very political answer."

"I'm going to find her, Bev," said Kate. There was a long silence on the end of the phone.

"I can get Bill to phone you when he's back," said Bev. "He's going to call me later. He won't mind talking to you."

"Thank you."

There was a click, and Bev was gone. When she'd raised her voice on the end of the phone, there had been an echo. Kate thought of Bev, alone at night in Bill's house, staring at her reflection in the huge glass windows. Then she thought back to Marnie, living on the horrible council estate, disabled, and bringing up two small children. Should she have just signed the book? At the stroke of her pen, it would have been worth a couple of thousand pounds. That freaked her out.

Kate had always avoided the merry-go-round of notoriety that accompanied Peter Conway. There had been lucrative opportunities to write books and tell her story to the tabloids, but in Kate's mind, that would be profiting from murder. Singers and actors were famous for their art. Conway was famous for killing, and it was sick to profit from that.

25

Jake phoned Kate to say that the changeover ladies had come to meet him before their first shift at the weekend, and were helping to move the clean bedding from the office down to the storeroom in the surf shop. When Tristan called after meeting with Bishop, Kate asked if they could meet at his flat.

Tristan made them tea, and they sat in his small kitchen, bringing each other up to speed.

"I'm sorry that Marnie was such a freak about the book," said Tristan.

"Part of me feels bad for not signing it. She didn't look like she had a lot of money," said Kate. "It made me understand Joanna a little better. She wanted to escape that housing estate and have a better life. I don't know if Marnie was bitter about that."

Tristan nodded.

"How high were the stakes for Bill, if Joanna had gone ahead and written the asbestos story?" he asked.

"His investment would have gone down the drain. I don't know how much he would have lost, but I get the idea it was significant. Bev sounded defensive on the phone when I brought it up. It must have put her in the middle of things, but she insists that Bill and Joanna sorted it out. She didn't write the story, and his company fixed the problem."

"If they sorted it amicably, then that doesn't necessarily raise a red flag, but it's the same names we keep coming back to. Marco Polo House is now linked to Shelley Morden, Joanna, and Bill. Shelley and David Lamb are linked to Max Jesper's commune, and Noah Huntley is linked to all of them, apart from Bill. We need to talk to Noah Huntley."

"We don't know how deep Joanna dug into his private life, but she had enough to write an exposé on his use of rent boys. We've also got Noah Huntley investing in Jesper's hotel, going to social events at Jesper's house. Who's to say that he didn't regularly drop by the commune?"

"If only we had Joanna's notes and files from that time," said Tristan.

"Joanna's editor, Ashley Harris, told her to drop the whole part of her original story about Noah Huntley and his rent boys. Why? What if Noah Huntley had something to do with David Lamb and Gabe Kemp going missing?" said Kate.

"And George Tomassini—we can't forget him. Ade thinks he went missing mid-2002."

"I've left a message with Alan Hexham, asking if he could pull some strings and find out if David Lamb, Gabe Kemp, and George Tomassini had criminal records," said Kate.

"Do you think he can? Do you think he will?"

"He knows everyone, and he's always said that he'd help us if he can . . ." Kate shrugged and sipped her tea. She didn't feel hopeful. "What about your friend Ade as a backup?"

"I get the impression that Ade left the police force under a cloud. He sued them for an injury he had at work, and his colleagues were called to testify at the tribunal . . . If nothing comes back from Alan, then I can ask," said Tristan.

"It's okay. I get it. I didn't exactly leave the police force brimming with contacts."

"Do you want more tea?" asked Tristan.

"Please." He got up and refilled their mugs from the teapot. "We still need to find Ashley Harris, Joanna's editor at the *West Country News*. He could have known what she was writing about, what she was investigating. That could tell us everything . . ."

"And Famke van Noort—if we could talk to her and be secure in her alibi, then we could rule out Fred," said Tristan, pouring milk in their teas.

"Fuck. I forgot about Fred," said Kate.

The front door opened, and there were loud voices in the hallway, and laughter.

"That's Glenn," said Tristan. Kate could see he wasn't pleased at the disturbance.

"Tris! You in?" came a voice from the hall. Tristan left the kitchen, and Kate could hear them talking. There was a crash as the living room door hit the wall.

"I've got you, keep going straight," said a male voice.

"Shitter, mind the handlebars on the wall," said another. Both voices had West Country accents. Kate was surprised to see two very large hairy guys come into the kitchen, pushing a Harley-Davidson motorbike, which was all gleaming chrome with a huge leather seat.

"This is Kate Marshall, my partner in the agency," said Tristan, appearing at the door behind the two guys. "Kate, this is my housemate, Glenn, and his mate . . ."

"All right, nice to meet you," said Glenn. He took one of his huge, hairy hands covered in rings off the motorbike and held it out. Kate got up and shook his hand. "This is Shitter. I mean, Will. His real name's Will."

Will seemed to be seven feet tall. He had long black hair, and he wore a Guns N' Roses–style bandanna.

"Hi," said Kate.

"Nice to meet you, Kate," he said, smiling amiably. He had two gold front teeth.

"Sorry to interrupt. I'm putting the bike in the backyard," said Glenn, indicating the kitchen door, which led out into the small backyard. Kate got up and flattened herself against the kitchen wall as Glenn squeezed past her in the tiny kitchen and opened the back door.

"Let's go in the living room," said Tristan to Kate. She nodded, picked up their mugs, and squeezed past Glenn.

"How did you end up with the nickname *Shitter*?" asked Kate.

"I'm really good at poker. I've got the best poker face, and I can make people believe any old shit," he said with a grin.

Kate nodded and couldn't help laughing.

"Nice to meet you, boys," she said and went through to the living room. Tristan closed the door. He didn't look happy. There was a crash and a clatter from the kitchen.

"S'all right, Tris. It was only a teaspoon!" shouted Glenn through the closed door.

"Sorry," said Tristan to Kate.

"Don't be. I've got our office full of bedsheets and urinal disinfectant," she said.

"Okay. So how should we approach Noah Huntley?"

"I've got an idea, if you don't mind," said Kate. "I think you should contact him. Your profile picture comes up in your email, doesn't it?"

"Yes."

"I think he might be more forthcoming if he thinks he's going to meet someone as handsome as you, rather than an old trout like me," said Kate.

Tristan laughed. "Okay. What should I say?"

"I think, be honest—just say that we wanted to talk to him about Joanna and what he knows. Emphasize that you need his help with some questions."

Tristan nodded. Then the doorbell rang.

"Bloody hell, what now?" He left the room, and when he opened the door, Kate heard Sarah's voice in the hallway.

"Oh. Hello, Kate," she said coolly when she came into the living room. She had on her work uniform and a huge carrier bag filled with what looked like runner beans. Tristan came back in behind her.

"Me and Kate are just having a meeting," he said.

The guys were still talking in the kitchen. There was a big crash and a tinkle of broken glass, and then Glenn said, "Er, Tris. Can you come here, mate?"

"Jesus, what now?" muttered Tristan under his breath, and he went to the kitchen. They heard muffled voices.

"What's going on there?" asked Sarah. She moved a pile of newspapers and put the bag of runner beans down on the dining table.

"Glenn and his mate, they're trying to put his motorbike in the backyard."

"They brought it inside?"

"Yeah."

"Poor Tristan. I think it's very stressful for him, having a house-mate," she said pointedly. "How's work?"

"We've got plenty of work, and the cold case is going very well," said Kate. Sarah nodded. Tristan came back into the living room and shut the kitchen door. Kate could hear the sound of broken glass being swept up.

"They put the front wheel of the bike through the glass on the back door," he said.

"Did he ask if he could put the bike there?" said Sarah.

"He mentioned it."

The door opened and Glenn stuck his head out.

"Tris, mate, have you got a first aid kit? Shitter's just sliced open his knee on the glass . . . Yerite, Sandra," he added.

"My name's Sarah."

Kate's phone rang, and she saw it was Jake.

"Mum. We've got a bit of a problem. Our changeover ladies have just quit," he said on the other end of the phone.

"Why have they quit?" said Kate.

"They've been poached by Brannigan's Hotel in Ashdean. They'd applied for the job last week."

"Why did they agree to work for us and then go off to work for Brannigan's?"

"It's full-time work at Brannigan's."

"Can you find anyone else? We've got to get eight caravans ready for Saturday morning."

"I'm trying, but everyone is looking right now with the summer season so close," said Jake.

When Kate came off the phone, Sarah was looking at her.

"Trouble at the campsite?" she asked.

Tristan had found the first aid kit and passed it through to the kitchen. "What's happened at the campsite?" he asked. Kate explained.

"I went on a course last week," said Sarah. "To have a successful business, you need a charismatic manager who can inspire their team." She picked up her bag off the table. "I can see this is a bad time. Tris, the runner beans are from Mandy next door. They just need a couple of minutes in salty, boiling water. And remember, you're coming for lunch on Sunday."

There was a triumphant look on Sarah's face as she left the house. Kate had a sudden urge to stick her foot out as she walked by, but she didn't.

"It's okay, Kate," said Tristan when she was gone. "Everything is fixable."

26

Jake didn't find new cleaning staff before the weekend, so he, Kate, and Tristan spent Friday and Saturday getting the caravan-site shop open and the eight caravans ready for guests.

Kate slept in late on Sunday, and just after her swim, she got a call from Alan Hexham, asking her for lunch, saying he had information on David Lamb and Gabe Kemp.

Kate had never been to visit Alan Hexham at home. He lived alone in a large redbrick house in a smart, leafy suburb of Exeter. He was a tall, broad man with a thick, bushy graying beard and a jovial face. Kate often wondered if he used his personality to deflect from all the death and destruction he saw every day as a forensic pathologist.

When he opened the front door, a bouncy Labrador puppy came bundling out, and the delicious smell of something roasting in the oven wafted behind him.

"Hello, hello, do come in," Alan said. "Down, Quincy, down!" he added to the Labrador, who had started to hump Kate's left leg. He pulled the dog away.

Alan's house was eclectic—filled with bookcases and antique wood furniture. He took them through to the kitchen, which to Kate seemed very posh with a bright-green AGA and a vast Welsh dresser filled with willow-patterned plates. Hanging from the ceiling above the work surfaces were all sorts of copper pans and colanders.

"I know you don't drink, but I've just had an awful thought. Are you also a vegetarian?"

"No. I eat meat," said Kate, fending off Quincy, who seemed fixated with her left leg.

"Quincy likes you," he chuckled. "I don't often have the pleasure of good-looking ladies for lunch!" He picked a giant beef knuckle out of a pot on the stove, checked it was cool, and threw it down. They watched Quincy as he grabbed it and retreated to the corner to chew. "I'm roasting a goose, if that sounds good?" said Alan, licking the beef juice off his fingers.

"That sounds divine," said Kate. She'd been living off things on toast for the last couple of days.

Over lunch, Kate filled Alan in on the details of the case and how David Lamb and Gabe Kemp fit into the jigsaw.

After what Kate thought was the most delicious meal she'd had in years, they came through to the sitting room with cups of coffee.

"My contact in CID managed to find criminal records for David Lamb and Gabe Kemp," said Alan, handing her two dog-eared cardboard files. "The most revealing stuff is contained in the witness statements, which give us a gold mine of information about the young guys' backgrounds." He leaned down and scratched Quincy's belly as Kate read the witness statements.

In 1995, when he was sixteen years old, Gabe Kemp had raped a fourteen-year-old girl at a local park and spent eighteen months in a young offenders' institution. The information about his background was from the police report and subsequent police interviews.

Gabe had come from a low-income single-parent family. He'd been born in Bangor in North Wales. His father had left the scene early on and gone to work on construction sites in Saudi Arabia. His mother had been long-term unemployed and died of a drug overdose just after his sixteenth birthday.

Gabe was released from the young offenders' institution in the summer of 1997, and he moved to Exeter and got a job in a gay bar called Peppermintz . . .

Here we go again, thought Kate. *Another clue leads us back to Noah Huntley.* She made a mental note to follow up again on the Peppermintz link and carried on reading.

Peppermintz was raided by the police just before Christmas 1997, and Gabe was arrested for possession of cocaine and ecstasy. He pleaded guilty and got a three-year suspended sentence. It looked like he kept out of trouble, because that was the last entry in the police report, and Kate knew that Gabe had gone missing in April 2002.

Kate turned to the second report for David Lamb. In June 1997, just after his seventeenth birthday, he was arrested at a house in a suburb of Bristol in conjunction with the death of a fifty-five-year-old man called Sidney Newett. Sidney's wife, Mariette, was away on a trip to Venice with the Women's Institute. Sidney Newett was found dead in the back garden of their semidetached house, naked from the waist down. He had a large amount of alcohol in his blood, and cannabis and ketamine. The police released David Lamb after twenty-four hours. The charges of manslaughter were dropped when the postmortem revealed Sidney had died of a heart attack, but David was charged with possessing an illegal substance, and he got a six-month suspended sentence. He also got a formal caution ten months later, in April 1998, for soliciting, but it didn't state exactly what the circumstances were or who the other person was.

"What about George Tomassini?" asked Kate.

"There's no criminal record for George," said Alan, sipping his coffee. "And you say that these young men are now on the missing persons database?"

"David and Gabe are. I think Joanna Duncan was looking into their disappearances, and had perhaps discovered foul play when she went missing. That's the theory we're working on," said Kate. Alan nodded.

"What else do you need?" he asked, seeing Kate was poised to ask a question.

"It's very broad. I'm thinking the bodies of these guys might have been found. They had no dependents, so they may have gone unidentified."

"Did you know, on average, around one hundred and fifty unidentified bodies are found every year in the UK?"

"That's less than I thought. The missing person statistics each year are off the chart."

Alan nodded. "Yes. Some of the bodies found are complete, and sometimes it's just parts. Did you know it tends to be dog walkers, joggers, or *mushroom foragers* who find them?"

"Mushroom foragers? Is that a thing?"

"Of course, especially here in the countryside, outside big cities. You don't find many people doing it in Mayfair or Knightsbridge. The majority of bodies, or body parts, are found in autumn or late winter, when the foliage has died back."

Alan had been scratching Quincy's fluffy belly the whole time he was talking, and the little dog was now snoring.

"Would you be able to do a search for me, from 1998 to 2002, for unidentified remains?" asked Kate. "That would cover the time period when David and Gabe went missing."

"Over that time period could mean over six hundred bodies and remains," said Alan. "I do have an awful lot of work trying to keep up with current deaths and postmortems."

"I know, but what if I could give you very specific criteria within that time frame? The search area would just be the southwest of England. Males, between eighteen and twenty-five. Over six foot tall, with dark hair, who might have been sexually assaulted. Who might have had a criminal record for soliciting or drugs. And good looking. Maybe not that last one. You can't put 'good looking' into a database. It's subjective . . ."

Kate could see that Alan was sitting up in his chair. He got up, went over to the window, and stared out over the garden. He looked troubled.

"I did a postmortem on a young man last Thursday," he said. "Body found dumped in the remains of a recently fallen tree on Dartmoor. He'd only been dead for thirty-six hours. The police identified him from fingerprints . . ." He looked back at Kate. "He matches the description that you've just given me. Matches down to a T, apart from the hair color, which is blond. He had a prior arrest for soliciting."

"How did he die?" asked Kate, her heart thumping in her chest.

"Repeated strangulation. The petechial hemorrhages, which look like a red rash, show that he was strangled and then revived several times. There was Rohypnol found in his blood, along with alcohol, and evidence he'd been bound and sexually assaulted. There was no DNA evidence found on the body."

"What have the police said?" asked Kate.

"Nothing to the media, and as far as I know, they don't have any witnesses or suspects," said Alan.

———

Kate had a call from Tristan when she left Alan's house.

"I managed to find Ashley Harris, Joanna's editor at the *West Country News*," he said.

"Please tell me he's still alive."

Tristan laughed.

"Yes. The reason we couldn't find him is because he got married and he took his wife's name."

"How modern of him."

"I know. His change of name was listed on Companies House. His wife is Juliet Maplethorpe, so he's now Ashley Maplethorpe. They run a company called Frontiers People Ltd."

"What kind of company?"

"They have contracts to run back-to-work schemes for the UK government. They posted a profit of seventy million quid last year."

"So, more lucrative than working for a regional newspaper."

"Yes. I don't know if it's a coincidence, but he quit as editor of the *West Country News* two weeks after Joanna went missing," said Tristan. "I found an old article online from the *West Country News*, dated January 2001, when they announced him as their new editor. He was thirty when he became editor, and he'd been an ambitious journalist. Starting as an apprentice at sixteen, working his way up. He was the youngest person made editor on a regional newspaper—then he gives it all up after Joanna goes missing. What's interesting is that I messaged him this morning, when I found this out, and he's agreed to meet us on Tuesday."

"Good work, Tris."

"That's not all," he said, sounding excited on the phone. "I had a look at Frontiers People's website, and Ashley's bio and photo are on there. I thought I'd seen his face recently. He's in that photo taken at the opening of Jesper's. He's standing next to Noah Huntley with his wife, Juliet, and what looks like Noah Huntley's wife. And when I looked on the Companies House registry, Ashley was also one of the original investors in Jesper's hotel, along with Noah Huntley, Max Jesper and his partner, Nick Lacey, and three other local businessmen."

"Tristan, that's brilliant work! Bloody hell, this is all becoming quite incestuous," said Kate.

"Yes, it will be interesting to ask Ashley about his links to Noah Huntley and Max Jesper."

"I thought you were meant to be going to Sarah's for lunch today?"

"She came down with a bug and canceled."

"Sorry to hear that, but look what you did instead. Brilliant."

"How did lunch go with Alan?" asked Tristan.

Kate went on to tell him about David's and Gabe's criminal records, her theory about searching for missing young men, and the discovery of the body in the fallen tree.

"That's another step closer," said Tristan.

"Yes. He took my theory seriously. I thought I was asking the impossible, but Alan thinks he'll need to do a search on six or seven hundred unidentified deaths, which is still a lot, but not in the thousands."

"How long do you think we'll have to wait for him to come back to us?"

"It will involve a database search, so hopefully he'll come back quite quickly if he finds anything."

27

Kate and Tristan spent Monday in the office, prepping for their meeting with Ashley Maplethorpe. On Monday afternoon, a small article appeared on the BBC Devon and Cornwall website, saying that the body of a young man called Hayden Oakley had been found near the village of Buckfastleigh and that police were making inquiries. There was a picture of the huge fallen tree and a white forensics tent next to the roots at the base, but no other information was released.

On Tuesday morning, Kate and Tristan drove over to meet Ashley at his house, Thornbridge Hall in Yeovil, Somerset, fifty-five miles from Ashdean.

The house was gray stone, and they began to get glimpses of it when they came off the motorway. A mile-long tree-lined driveway wound through fields of sheep grazing, and then the drive opened out into a yard with stables where four big black SUVs were parked. Close up, the house was large with a pillared, grand entrance. The rows of windows looked rather sternly out on the countryside.

"Are we classed as tradespeople? Do we ring the bell or go around the back?" joked Tristan as they looked at a grand set of stone steps leading up to a front terrace and a huge wooden double door.

"We're not going around the back," said Kate. They climbed the steps and arrived a little breathless at the front door. A bell clanged from deep inside. They waited for a minute. Kate was about to ring again, when the door opened.

Ashley Maplethorpe wore denim shorts and a tight black AC/DC T-shirt. His feet were bare. He had short blond hair, was tall, and looked as if he kept himself in shape. Kate was surprised to see Juliet Maplethorpe with him. She was a head shorter, the same height as Kate, and she wore a beautiful aquamarine-colored caftan with a print of large red-and-yellow dragon flowers. Her hair was a rich henna red and was damp and a little wavy. Kate could see the straps of a swimming suit under the caftan. Juliet was also barefoot and had a gold ankle bracelet on her left leg.

"Hello! Do come in!" said Ashley cheerily, as if they were old friends popping over for Sunday lunch. He was very well spoken.

"Hello, welcome to Thornbridge Hall," said Juliet. She spoke with a soft Geordie accent, but her green eyes were sharp and cautious. "Ashley should have told you to text when you got here. The house is so big, it takes a while to get to the front door." Her green eyes ran over Kate and Tristan with precision. *We'll have to watch out for her,* thought Kate.

They went through a long hallway and living room where french doors opened out onto the back garden. It was vast, with a tennis court to the left, a swimming pool with sun loungers and umbrellas, and beyond, at the end of their land, was an ornamental garden with a maze.

There was a green cloth gazebo set up in the center of the lawn, with a table and chairs underneath, and it provided good shade, but Kate could feel the morning heating up as the sun climbed in the sky.

Despite the Maplethorpes' casual summer attire, they had a butler who wore a stiff suit and jacket with tails. Kate was able to watch his progress, laden down with a large tray, as he emerged from the french doors and made his way across the lawn.

"Do you mind if I make notes?" asked Tristan.

"Could we have a copy of your notes, afterward?" asked Juliet. She had produced a small fan and kept up a nervous, rapid fanning of her face. She looked less at ease than her husband.

"Yes, of course," said Tristan.

"We're not journalists," said Kate. "I can assure you whatever you say will be dealt with in strictest confidence."

"I'd still like to take copies of your notes," she said. "My previous experiences of talking to journalists haven't been good." Kate wondered what that meant. Was she worried about incriminating herself?

"Of course," said Kate. "We'll let you have all notes from this meeting."

The butler arrived at the table and placed before them a jug of iced tea, with matching glasses, four espressos with milk jugs, and a plate with delicate petits fours fanned into a circle. The poor guy was sweating in his double-breasted suit, waistcoat, and starched collar.

"Will there be anything else?" he asked. Juliet shook her head. He bowed and left with the huge tray under his arm.

"The whole Joanna Duncan case has troubled me over the years," said Ashley, leaning back in his chair.

"How long were you her editor?" asked Kate.

"It was around a year and a half."

"You quit as editor two weeks after Joanna went missing. Why?"

"There was a conflict of interests," said Juliet, fanning herself with one hand and pouring milk into her espresso with the other. Kate noticed a large pear-shaped diamond ring on her finger. "My company was under fire from the press about the government contracts we'd signed . . ."

"Yes. In 2001, Frontiers People signed contracts with the UK government worth a hundred and twenty-five million pounds," said Tristan, paging back through his notes. "And you took a large dividend shortly after the government paid you. Nine million pounds of public money."

There was an icy silence.

"I started the business in 1989, building it up from nothing. I reinvested millions back into the company in the nineties. I took that dividend of nine million pounds, which I was well within my rights to do after years of barely drawing a salary from the company. The newspapers got hold of this, twisting the story that I was taking taxpayers' money out of the company. It didn't help that I used the money to buy this place from the Thornbridge family, who'd owned it for centuries," she said, indicating the house behind them. "The *Daily Mail* had a field day. A journalist from the *West Country News* wrote a piece on it all. Ashley refused to run the story. He was called up before the board and stood by his decision, and he resigned."

"So when you left the *West Country News*, it was nothing to do with the disappearance of Joanna Duncan, or any story she was working on?" asked Kate.

"No. It was my refusal to make myself the news," he said, and for the first time, the smile left his face briefly.

"It was imperfect, perfect timing. We needed a full-time public relations person," said Juliet.

"In hindsight, it was the best choice I ever made," said Ashley. "In 2002, the internet was really kicking off, so we were able to do so much of our business online. Look at this place. It's paradise!" His face broke into a wide grin, and he laughed, but it seemed a little forced. Juliet smiled thinly and put a hand on his leg.

"Of course, the whole business with Joanna was terrible, wasn't it, Ash?" she said.

"Yes. Yes, of course," he said, his face now earnest.

"Was Joanna working on any controversial stories at the time of her disappearance?" asked Kate.

"What do you mean by *controversial*?" asked Juliet.

"Joanna worked on the Noah Huntley corruption story, which resulted in him losing his seat in Parliament."

"Yes. That was a real scoop," said Ashley, nodding and taking a sip of his iced tea.

"We understand that there were other aspects to this story which you asked her to drop before publication," said Kate, carefully watching Ashley for his reaction. He nodded and swallowed the last of his iced tea.

"Yes. She, er, found out that Noah Huntley was having sex with young men . . . whilst married."

"Was he paying them?" asked Tristan.

"He had paid an escort, yes. He had also had sex with men at bars and clubs."

"Why did you ask Joanna to drop that part of the story?" asked Kate. Ashley sat back and rubbed at his face.

"Joanna had persuaded one of the young men to go on record. Then the young man involved withdrew his statement, and without him, we couldn't verify that part of the story," said Ashley.

"How many young men did Joanna interview?"

Ashley wiped at his face. He was starting to sweat in the heat.

"It was a long time ago, but I believe it was a few young men, but only one of them had actual proof we could use. Huntley was brazen. He'd paid this lad, the escort, with a check! If you can believe it."

"Can you remember the name of the young guy?" asked Kate.

Ashley gave a long pause. There was just the faint wafting sound of Juliet and her fan. Kate could feel the light breeze from it on her damp face.

"Yes. Gabe Kemp."

Kate couldn't disguise her reaction; nor could Tristan.

"Were there any other names you remember?"

"No. As I say, Gabe Kemp was the only rent boy we had concrete proof from that Noah Huntley paid him for sex."

Juliet looked between them. "Why would Ashley remember the names of rent boys after all these years?"

"When did Huntley pay Gabe Kemp for sex?" asked Kate, ignoring Juliet.

"I really can't remember the exact details," said Ashley.

"Did you know that Gabe Kemp went missing in April 2002, a month after Joanna's exposé of Noah Huntley was printed?" said Kate.

"No. I wasn't aware of that," said Ashley.

"Gabe Kemp also served time in a youth detention center. When he was sixteen, he raped a fourteen-year-old girl."

"That's awful. But I wasn't aware of that either," said Ashley.

"Did you authorize Joanna to pay him for his story, or offer him money for his story?" asked Tristan.

"The *West Country News* is a local newspaper—it's not like the tabloids, and we didn't have vast amounts of money to buy stories, but Joanna would have been authorized to pay him two hundred pounds for any expenses, and he would have been paid if the story was picked up by the national newspapers," said Ashley. "But Gabe Kemp withdrew his statement, so we never printed the details of Noah Huntley using rent boys. Anyway, the exposé story was stronger without it."

"When did Gabe withdraw his statement?"

"I think it was a couple of months before Joanna's story was published. Early 2002."

"Why did he withdraw his statement?" asked Kate.

"As far as I can recollect, he didn't want to out himself and risk prosecution. And, hearing that he had a criminal record prior to this, makes all the more sense. He sounds a rather vile young man," said Ashley.

Juliet leaned in, touching Ashley's arm supportively.

"What does this *specifically* have to do with Joanna Duncan going missing?" she asked.

"Of course," said Kate. She went on to explain the petrol station CCTV footage from August 2002, when Joanna met with Noah Huntley. She took out the photos and laid them on the table. "Do you know why she was meeting with Noah Huntley five months after her story was published?"

Ashley and Juliet stared at the photos, and Kate watched them both carefully for their reactions. Again, Ashley looked surprised. Juliet's eyes flicked between her husband and the photos. She was perspiring heavily. Ashley opened his mouth to say something, and she interrupted.

"Oh Lord! I'm so sorry, but could we move our little talk down to the pool? I'm going to pass out with this heat. There's more of a breeze down there, and it would be nice to dip our feet. Ashley, could you help me? I feel a bit faint."

She stood abruptly and set off walking down to the pool.

Tristan looked at Kate.

"It is bloody hot, but she's broken the mood," he said in a low voice. Kate watched Juliet marching out toward the pool with her caftan flapping behind her and Ashley hurrying to join her.

28

The Olympic-size swimming pool at Thornbridge Hall was built on a tiled terrace platform sunk into the hillside at the end of the large gardens. At the far side of the pool, there was a railing where the terrace jutted out over a steep drop, looking down to the sloping hill below. On the terrace next to the deep end of the pool were a barbecue and a small bar, and along the near side were six wooden sun loungers and large umbrellas.

At the shallow end, the tiles sloped down into a paddling area where the water was just a couple of inches deep, before sloping farther down for swimming.

When Kate and Tristan reached the pool, there were a couple of deck chairs placed in this paddling area of the water, along with a huge umbrella.

Juliet was sitting in one of the chairs, fanning herself, with her feet in the water. Ashley was moving two chairs for Kate and Tristan.

"You okay to wade?" he asked.

Kate looked down at her black boots and jeans. Tristan wore shorts and trainers.

"Yes," she said, annoyed that Juliet had caused the interruption, and now she had to take off her shoes and socks and roll up her jeans. *And* she hadn't shaved her legs. On the upside, it was much cooler down by the pool. There was a breeze coming off the hills. Kate took off her shoes and rolled up her jeans as far as she dared, just above the ankle, and waded over to join them.

As much as Kate welcomed the cool, she'd have preferred to keep Juliet and Ashley sweating and agitated.

"We were just talking about these CCTV photos of Noah Huntley when he met with Joanna, two weeks before she went missing," said Kate, steering the subject back to the case. Ashley leaned over and took the photos and looked through them.

"I don't know why she would have been meeting him," said Ashley.

"Would Joanna have had to account for this meeting in her notes?"

"She never had to give a day-by-day outline of her work. She'd only come to me when she'd identified a story she wanted to pursue or if she was close to breaking a story."

"Did you speak to Noah Huntley before or after Joanna's story was published?" asked Tristan.

"I had dealings with his lawyers, of course, in the run-up to, and after, the story was published. I didn't talk to him personally. Joanna gave him the opportunity to comment on the story twenty-four hours before we went to press. He declined."

"Did you ever consider running the story about Noah Huntley paying for sex with rent boys after the fraud story broke?" asked Kate.

"He just told you. Gabe Kemp withdrew his statement," said Juliet. Then she sat back and smiled. "It's perfectly normal for stories to be pulled or killed for various reasons; usually there are legal issues. In this case, obviously, Gabe Kemp was a convicted criminal who didn't want to risk further prosecution."

"Are you friends with Noah Huntley?" asked Tristan.

"Of course not," said Juliet.

"You've never socialized with him or had any dealing with him since?"

"I just told you. No. Never," said Juliet, her eyes narrowing.

Ashley took her hand.

"It's okay, Juliet . . . My wife is very protective of me; she's learned to be after dealings with the press."

Kate saw Tristan look across at her, and she nodded. She took out a copy of the photo from the Jesper's hotel opening ceremony.

"This is both of you pictured with Noah Huntley and his wife," said Kate.

"Well . . . ," blustered Ashley when he saw the photo. "We may have seen him at events."

"So you have socialized with him?"

"That was a very large group of people," said Juliet, wiping sweat from her upper lip. "We're not friends with the Huntleys, but in business terms, we may have crossed paths fleetingly."

"You were also one of the original investors in Jesper's hotel, along with Noah Huntley," said Tristan.

Kate took the Companies House documents from her bag and held them out.

"What the bloody hell is this? A police interview?" Juliet exploded. Ashley stayed calm but didn't say anything.

"Of course not. We're just trying to work out the details of all this," said Kate, managing to look unfazed. "Limited companies legally have to hold shareholder meetings, so Ashley, Noah, and the other company directors must have met. You were a director for five years, along with Noah? That's not fleeting. Do you need to see the paperwork?"

"No! And that doesn't mean Ashley and Noah know each other!" cried Juliet. "And I don't like this mean and underhand way of producing all these photos and documents."

Kate kept the paperwork on her lap.

"We're not suggesting that Ashley has anything to do with Joanna Duncan going missing," she lied. "But your reaction to all this is troubling."

Juliet looked between them all. She was chewing her bottom lip and visibly fuming. She shifted in her chair and brushed her hair away from her face. Ashley looked down at his feet in the water. He seemed much calmer.

"How do you expect me to react?" Kate didn't say anything, nor did Tristan. They let the silence play out. Juliet took a deep breath. She was still sweating, and her face flushed, despite the cool breeze and the water. Kate felt sympathy, wondering if she was suffering from menopause. "Maybe I should let you talk, Ashley," she said pointedly, sitting back and fanning her face.

Ashley blew out his cheeks and wiped away the sweat glistening on his brow. "Yes. I know Noah Huntley. From afar. But I'm no longer a shareholder in Jesper's hotel . . . I've only met him, after Joanna's story, I think, three times. The opening of Jesper's hotel," he said, holding up his hand and counting on his fingers. "Our first shareholder meeting that we held in person . . . In subsequent years we would have shareholder meetings by teleconference—conference call, as they're now known."

"Did you ever visit Jesper's when it was a commune?" asked Tristan.

The question seemed to take Ashley off guard. "No! No way! I mean, no," he said. "Why would I? I wasn't aware of a commune; well, I knew of it from Max when he was given the property, when he claimed squatter's rights—"

"We assumed that Joanna would have gone into detail about the Noah Huntley story with you and the newspaper lawyers?" asked Kate.

"Yes. I've already said that—"

"Was Gabe Kemp ever a resident at the commune? Did this ever come up during the detailed legal discussions which led you to drop the rent-boy part of the Noah Huntley story?" asked Tristan.

"No. I didn't know where Gabe Kemp was registered as residing! That's a detail—"

"Gabe Kemp's address would have been a formality and a detail that Ashley simply didn't deal with," said Juliet, interrupting him. "As the editor, he wouldn't, *couldn't*, micromanage. He was overseeing so many stories on a daily basis."

"When was the third time you saw him?" asked Tristan.

"Who?" asked Ashley.

"Noah Huntley. You said you met him three times after Joanna's story was published."

"Max Jesper's summer party last year," said Juliet. Ashley shot her a look, and then he recovered and smiled.

"Yes. We've had an invite every year, but his annual summer party has always clashed with our summer holiday in France . . . We have a home in Provence. Last year, we didn't go because of renovations, so we went to Max's party." Ashley sat back. "It wasn't an intimate party. There seemed to be hundreds of people there, and it was a masked ball, of all things, so it was rather hard to keep track of who was who. I can't remember seeing Noah Huntley there. Did you?"

"You just said that was the third time you saw Noah," said Kate.

"I mean *meeting*. I can't remember meeting him there. I saw him from afar," he blustered, looking annoyed and stressed.

"We only fleetingly saw Max and Nick, and they were the hosts," said Juliet.

"Why were you invited? If you barely know them?" asked Kate.

"Why not? Past business. The business and commerce world in the West Country is very small," said Ashley.

"These kinds of parties are always a good networking opportunity," said Juliet. "So much of what we do is about networking."

"I spoke to one of the waiters who worked at that party," said Tristan. "He said Noah Huntley offered him money to have sex with him in the sand dunes."

Juliet's eyebrows shot into her hairline.

"Oh dear. I barely know Noah's wife, Helen, but I don't know why she stays with him," she said. "Once a politician, always a politician. I've had to deal with many of them in my line of work, and I've heard so many stories of affairs and adultery. So many of them seem to be gay and yet married."

"Which is a good point, because another reason we were encouraged not to report on the Noah Huntley rent-boy story," said Ashley, "was because of the climate at the time. The Blair government had abolished Section 28; they'd legalized same-sex civil partnerships. 'Outing' people for the sake of news was no longer legal. Without having a rent boy who would go on record, Noah Huntley was just another closeted gay man having consensual sex."

"What does his wife, Helen, do?" asked Tristan.

"She's his secretary, and presumably, she turns a blind eye. I think that Noah invests with Nick's companies."

"Do either of you currently do business with Nick?" asked Kate. They already knew the answer was no, after looking at the Companies House records, but it was worth asking.

"He's a private-equity investor. I'm wary of the stock market. It's my working-class roots," said Juliet. "I prefer to keep my money in property, or in the bank, where I can see it."

Kate nodded and looked at Tristan writing it all down. More spiderwebs were entangling between the same people.

"If we can go back to Joanna Duncan. Would her work have been stored on a central database at the *West Country News*?"

"Only her published work. Back in 2002, we'd only just got internet access for the office a couple of months before. We had a very basic intranet," said Ashley.

"Was there a central hard drive where she kept her work?"

"No. She had a laptop," said Ashley.

"Did she leave it at work?"

Ashley pulled an exasperated face.

"Jesus. That's specific. I don't know? I don't think so."

"The police don't know what happened to Joanna's laptop or her notebooks," said Kate, studying him carefully.

"Nor do I."

There was a long pause. Kate could tell Ashley and Juliet wanted to end the meeting.

"Could we ask you some practical questions?" said Tristan. "Ashley, you were away on Saturday the seventh of September, when Joanna went missing?"

"Yes. That's what I told the police in my statement. I was in London, meeting with a friend from university, who at the time confirmed this," said Ashley.

"Yes. The friend was called Tim Jeckels," said Tristan, looking up from his notebook. "You were staying with him for the weekend in North London, where he had a flat."

"Yes. He was a theatre director, and I went up to see his new play. Tim sadly passed away five years ago."

Kate noticed an awkward moment between Juliet and Ashley. A fleeting look.

"I was at home, here, I think," said Juliet. "The police didn't ask what I was doing, just to confirm that Ashley was away."

"We've been trying to contact Rita Hocking, who worked with Joanna and was at work with her the day she went missing. Are you still in contact with her?" asked Tristan.

"No, I'm not in contact with Rita. She's now in America, yes?" asked Ashley.

"Yes. She works for the *Washington Post*. We've tried to contact her but haven't heard back."

"It's a shame that Minette isn't alive. She ran the copy room with a rod of iron. She knew everything that was going on."

"Was something going on?" asked Kate. Ashley rolled his eyes.

"No, of course not. It's a figure of speech," he said, exasperated. "But she probably knew more about Joanna than I did."

"What was her second name?"

"Zamora. Minette Zamora," said Ashley. "But she died a couple of years ago of lung cancer."

"Did Joanna ever talk to you about a tower block in Exeter, Marco Polo House? She was investigating a group of businessmen who had bought it and were covering up the presence of asbestos during the renovation," said Tristan. Ashley looked genuinely puzzled.

"Erm, no. Marco Polo House, that's an office block, yes?"

"Yes."

"We'll need to wrap this up soon," said Juliet, checking her watch. "My sister is coming with my niece and her friends to go swimming."

"I've just got one more question," said Kate. "What do you think happened to Joanna Duncan?"

Ashley seemed surprised at the question.

"Isn't the thinking that someone snatched her? Some opportune nutter? We'd all warned her against parking in that terrible old car park at Deansgate."

"I've never come across a case where there's so little evidence of someone's vanishing," said Kate.

"Perhaps, sometimes, people just vanish," said Juliet.

29

"Why were they so unprepared for our questions?" asked Kate when they were driving back to Ashdean. "And why lie that they didn't know Noah Huntley?"

"Ashley Maplethorpe's alibi says a lot to me," said Tristan. "Tim Jeckels, *his friend from the theatre?*" He glanced across at Kate and raised an eyebrow.

"I know," said Kate. "There could have been a *Brokeback Mountain* situation going on there, albeit without the whole camping in tents, if Tim lived in London . . . And Juliet's reaction to him explaining his alibi makes me think that it was genuine. She had strong feelings about Tim Jeckels, whoever he was in Ashley's life, but the way they wanted to evade their connection to Noah Huntley is interesting and maddening."

"Yes. The same names keep coming up," said Tristan. "Noah Huntley, Max Jesper . . . Max's husband, Nick Lacey, has come up for the second time. And now Ashley Maplethorpe is linked to them."

"Isn't that a very British thing? You find your clique, your tribe, your friends, and once you're in, you're in for life. Even if you hate them all. It's better to be in a tribe than out?" said Kate.

"And now Gabe Kemp is linked with Noah Huntley. Gabe met with Joanna and was prepared to go on record, and then chickened out."

"The question is, how are David Lamb and Gabe Kemp linked? Joanna wrote down both of their names. If we can link Gabe Kemp to the commune, that gives us the link with David Lamb and Max Jesper . . . If Nick Lacey and Max have been together for years, he may have known David too; presumably he would have visited the commune, being Max's boyfriend, and now we have Ashley as an investor in the hotel. If he's a closeted gay, then what's to say that he didn't visit the commune?"

"Did you see Juliet's face when we brought up him visiting the commune?"

"Yes, and he was denying he even knew about it, but Gabe Kemp was a key source in Joanna's story about Noah Huntley, and Ashley must have had detailed discussions with her about Gabe. It would have been a huge thing to print details of a serving MP paying for rent boys." Tristan shook his head. "It's too fishy."

They were quiet for a moment as they drove over a high bridge and looked out over the cornflower-blue water in an estuary, lined with green reeds swaying in the breeze. The windows were open, and the warm summer breeze smelled sweet with the scent of mowed grass.

"Joanna's friend, Marnie, said the same thing as Ashley," said Kate.

"What?" asked Tristan.

"That Joanna might have been the victim of a random serial killer. There was no planning or motive. Some psycho was in the right place at the right time and saw an opportunity."

"Do you think that?"

"Sometimes. When I wake up in a cold sweat, wondering if we're ever going to find out what happened to her. Ashley Maplethorpe has generated a huge number of questions and suspicions, but he was in London when Joanna went missing."

Kate rummaged in her bag and found a pack of painkillers. The heat and the awkward meeting had given her a headache. She pushed two tablets out of the foil and put them in her mouth, swallowing them dry.

"Yikes! Don't swallow pills dry. I've got some water in the back," he said, rummaging behind his chair and handing her a bottle.

"Thanks," she said, unscrewing the lid and taking a big gulp. "That's better."

The fresh salt air blew into the car and soothed Kate's headache.

An earsplitting ringing sound made them both jump.

"Sorry, that's my hands-free," said Tristan, turning down the radio volume. He pressed a green button next to the steering wheel to answer. "Hello?"

"Oh, you're alive, Miss Marple," said Ade, his voice booming through the car speakers.

"Sorry, things have been busy," said Tristan.

"Yes. I was beginning to think you'd been murdered on the Orient Express, or perhaps you were doing something deliciously evil under someone's son?"

"I'm in the car. With Kate," said Tristan, looking embarrassed.

"Oh. Sorry. Hello, Kate," said Ade, putting on something akin to a telephone voice.

"Hi," Kate replied, grinning. "I like your Agatha Christie puns."

"Thank you. I had Roger Ackroyd on the tip of my tongue . . . But that's enough about what I get up to in my spare time."

Kate laughed.

"I was going to ring you when I got home, Ade," said Tristan, still sounding a bit embarrassed.

"I think you'll want to hear this, Miss Mar—*Tristan*," he said. There was a pause.

"Well, go on, then," said Tristan as they reached a huge roundabout and the first traffic they'd seen all morning. They closed their windows against the stink of exhaust fumes.

"Okay, well, I'd best start from the beginning and give you a bit of background . . . Set the scene," said Ade. Tristan rolled his eyes and mouthed *Sorry* to Kate. Ade went on, "I was walking past the church hall above Ashdean High Street, and there was an old note stuck to the board outside saying that they're hosting an evening tomorrow to meet our local MEP. That means Member of the European Parliament, or Euro MP . . ."

"We know what it means," said Tristan.

"Apparently, this skinny slip of a lass called Caroline Tuset is our local MEP! I was so annoyed that I hadn't even heard *when* the European elections were being held, so I got home and jumped online. Did you know they were last year?"

Tristan pulled out of the traffic and went around the huge round-about, taking the Exeter exit.

"No. But what's this got to do with anything?" said Tristan.

"I'm coming to that, if you'll let me, Miss Mar—Tristan. Oh, fuck off. I'm calling you Miss Marple, I'm sure Kate can cope," said Ade. Kate laughed. "Anyway. I find the EU website, and I discover that I'm not registered to vote, so I do that, and then there's this page where you can look at all the Euro MPs' photos, and I wondered what this Caroline Tuset looks like, and if she's local, cos she sounds a bit French with a name like *Tuset* . . . And there, two rows up, is George Tomassini."

"What?" said Tristan.

"That Spanish guy you've been looking for. The one who I caught in the back of the car with Noah Huntley. He's only gone and become a fucking Euro MP!" said Ade. "The only thing is that he's not George, spelt *G-e-o-r-g-e*. He's George, spelt the Spanish way, *J-o-r-g-e*."

"So that's why we didn't get any hits when we googled him," said Kate.

"Yes. I remember him from when he was a barman. I do admit that I did lust after him. He's filled out nicely, but it's him. He's the right age—all Euro MPs have their date of birth on their little online profiles, and their place of birth, which I remember was Barcelona. You remember the story I told you about Monsterfat Cowbelly . . . who, incidentally, I got back in contact with. He's moved to Orkney, of all

places, and had his stomach stapled. He looks completely different . . .
It even says on Jorge's CV on the European MP site that he *studied in
the United Kingdom*. I know of many things he studied intently, but I
don't think they involved a classroom."

"Ade, is there a number we can get in contact with him?" asked
Kate.

"Yes, I've just emailed a link to Miss Marple. I'm actually really
happy that he isn't dead, and that he's doing very well, by the look of
it. He's been a Euro MP for five years. He got reelected last year to the
Progressive Alliance of Socialists and Democrats, one of the biggest
center-left parties in Brussels," said Ade.

"Ade, that's brilliant. Thank you," said Tristan. "I definitely owe
you a drink."

"Well, mine's a Campari and lime. Phone me later, Miss Marple,
and lovely to meet you, Kate."

Ade hung up.

Tristan glanced across at Kate with a big smile on his face.

"There's a service station coming up in a mile. Do you fancy a cold
drink, and we can try and get in contact with Jorge Tomassini?" said
Tristan.

"Just remember, Jorge Tomassini might not want to talk to us."

"I know, but we've found him."

"Yes, we have, Miss Marple," said Kate.

"You should hear what he calls you."

"What?"

"Hercule Poirot."

30

The petrol station café was hot and crowded, so they bought iced coffee and sandwiches and came back to the car. It was like a hotbox when they opened the doors, so they waited a couple of minutes for it to cool down before they got back in.

Tristan found the email from Ade, and they compared the photo of Jorge Tomassini on the European Parliament website with the photo from Ade of Jorge at the fancy-dress party as Freddie Mercury. His hair was short, and he wore a shirt and tie, but it was the same person.

"It's great that he's alive, but we've been basing our investigation on Jorge, David, and Gabe going missing," said Kate, suddenly seeing this might not be the breakthrough they were hoping for.

"If he was there at the time, he might have known David and Gabe. What do you think we should do? Email or phone him?" asked Tristan.

"Let's see how far we get phoning the switchboard. I'm sure we'll have to leave a message," said Kate.

She dialed the number and listened to a long recorded message in Spanish and then English. She was surprised when the phone was answered after a few rings and a voice said, "Tomassini."

"Hello. Jorge Tomassini?" asked Kate, saying his name as she thought correct—with a *j*.

"*Yorge*. The *j* is pronounced as a *y*," he said, speaking clear English with a Spanish accent. It threw Kate for a moment.

"Hi. My name is Kate Marshall. I'm calling from the UK. I run a detective agency based in Ashdean, near Exeter. I'm trying to track down a couple of guys called David Lamb and Gabe Kemp. I think you knew them, and I just need your help."

There was a long silence.

"Can I call you back?" he said and hung up. A minute passed, and then five.

"Do you think he freaked out?" asked Tristan.

"Maybe."

Five more minutes passed.

"I'm going to call him back," said Kate, but there was no answer, and this time the recorded message went straight to voice mail.

"We've spooked him," said Tristan. He started the engine, but just as they got to the motorway ramp, Kate's phone rang again. She answered and put it on speakerphone.

"Hello. Kate? I'm sorry," Jorge said. "I prefer to speak on my private mobile phone, and it takes quite a while to get outside the building. I'm at the European Parliament in Strasbourg."

They could hear the sound of traffic and people in the background.

"I thought I'd scared you off," said Kate.

"No, I just avoid discussing personal matters on my business phone," he said.

Kate briefly outlined everything to do with the Joanna Duncan case, and she explained that everyone she'd spoken to thought he had gone missing, along with David Lamb and Gabe Kemp.

"People seriously thought I'd gone missing?" he said, sounding shocked.

"Yes."

He hesitated.

"I just had enough one day, and I left the UK. I came back home to Barcelona. I didn't really tell anyone in Exeter, and back then I didn't have any social media or email. Thank God! It was a much freer time."

"Did you ever live at the commune on Walpole Street in Exeter run by Max Jesper?"

"Yes, for a couple of months, when I first got to England—I think it was back in early 1996. It was very cold."

"Do you remember Max Jesper?"

Jorge laughed. "Yes, I do. A wily queen if ever I've met one, but he was kind and welcoming."

"Why was he wily?"

"He never seemed to pay for anything. That old dump was falling to pieces. He drilled into the electric meter to stop the disc going around, he said he never paid for electricity."

"Did you have to pay to stay at the commune?"

"Yes, but it was pennies. I forget how much. I think I paid five pounds a week or something silly like that. Max had various friends who used to give him food, and we shared a lot of stuff. He used to boast that he'd been on state benefits whilst three prime ministers were in office."

Kate told him about Max Jesper's reversal in fortunes with the hotel.

"You're kidding. A boutique hotel? It is a long time since I was there. He always said he wanted to claim squatter's rights."

"Did Max Jesper have a boyfriend?" asked Kate.

"*Boyfriends* I think is the better description. I think most of the young guys who passed through there might have had a night or two with Max. He did have one guy who was a constant in his life. Nick," said Jorge.

Kate and Tristan exchanged a glance.

"Nick Lacey?"

"Yes, that sounds right. Nick Lacey was Max's boyfriend: a tall, well-built guy with thick brownish hair. He'd come for a night or two each week, sometimes a weekend. And he'd often bring Max food and give him money, and I think some of the other guys would join them in their bedroom . . . Listen. I hope this is going to remain confidential?"

"Of course," said Kate.

"I'm part of a progressive socialist party in Parliament, and I'm lucky to live in Europe, but none of my past life is on the internet. No one knows me now from that time in the UK. I'd like to keep it that way. In fact, how did you get hold of my name?"

Kate explained about Ade, and the case files, and the box with David Lamb's and Gabe Kemp's names written on the inside lid.

"There was also a phone number with the names," said Kate. "Hang on . . ." She rummaged around in her bag and found the printout. "Does the number *07980 746029* mean anything?"

There was a pause. Kate wondered for a moment if she'd embarrassed him, talking about his past as a promiscuous barman, but then he said, "That was my mobile phone number."

"Are you sure?"

"Yes. It was my first mobile phone number."

"Joanna Duncan, the journalist who went missing, wrote your number down on the box lid. Did you meet her?"

"Yeah. She wanted to talk about *someone* . . ." He sighed. "There was a guy, kind of high profile, who I'd been involved with."

"What was his name?" asked Kate. Tristan glanced across at her.

"Noah Huntley. He was an MP."

"Did you have a relationship with him?"

"Sort of," he said, his voice suddenly small and quiet.

"Did you know he was married?"

"Yes. I did. I take it you know this already?"

"His name has come up repeatedly in our investigation. We know that he's married but he's been cheating on his wife for years with young men. There are also allegations that he used rent boys."

"I was never a—I never did that," said Jorge.

"Where did you meet Noah Huntley?" asked Kate.

"He was a regular visitor to the commune, and after I moved out, I used to see him around in gay bars. He was very handsome, quite funny. He obviously liked young guys, and he liked to show them a good time."

"Did you sleep with him when you lived at the commune?"

"Yes."

"Was he ever violent?"

Jorge sighed again on the end of the phone. "In life, no. But he could get carried away in bed."

"How?"

"Once, when we were having sex, he tried to choke me," he said quietly. "It happened a couple of times, when he got drunk. He always pulled back from the brink. But those were small incidents in what was, for a while, fun."

"Did you visit the commune after you moved out?"

"Yes, a few times, for parties. I lived in the area for quite a few years."

"Jorge, I really appreciate you talking about this. You are one of the first concrete leads that we have on this case . . . What about the other guys at the commune? Do you remember a guy called Gabe Kemp?"

"Er, no; some of the guys had nicknames. Some just used first names."

"Did you know a David Lamb?"

"Yeah. I knew David. He was there at the commune just after I was."

"Do you know if he ever slept with Noah Huntley?"

"Yes, David did."

"Did David ever talk to you about Noah Huntley's violent tendencies?"

"The choking? Yeah. David was very beautiful, handsome, and he had a personality to match. He could have done anything with his life, but he got mixed up with too many drugs and too many guys."

"Jorge, did Joanna Duncan talk to you about the story she wanted to write?" asked Kate.

"Yeah. She came to my bedsit, got my address from someone I worked with."

"When exactly was this, can you remember?"

"Yes, it was right before I left the UK and came back home, which would have made it . . . end of August 2002."

Kate and Tristan exchanged a look. This felt like a real breakthrough.

"What did you talk about with Joanna when you met?" asked Kate.

"She said she was working on a story about Noah Huntley. She said that he'd been using rent boys for many years, and the commune had come up in conversation with more than one of the young guys he'd slept with there. She said that she was following up on a story that he'd used his parliamentary expenses account to pay for rent boys and the hotels where he entertained them . . . I got the impression that she wanted to sell a big story. She said she needed to get as many guys on the record as possible so her editor wouldn't kill the story. She was ambitious. She also stole negatives from me."

"Negatives?"

"Photo negatives. I think she went through photos I kept in a box under my bed, when I was in the kitchen . . . When I was packing up the next week to leave, every single set of negatives in my photos was gone. No one else had been round."

"How many sets of photos?"

"Quite a few. It was *all* the negatives from *all* my photos. They were in those paper packets of twenty-four you used to get when you had film processed."

"Do you still have the photos?"

He laughed.

"I've no idea. I'd have to check. It was a very long time ago," he said.

"What were the photos of?"

"All the time I'd spent in the UK, friends, places I'd been, my time in the commune. I lived in the UK from early 1996 to end of August 2002."

Kate and Tristan exchanged a glance.

"Is there any way you could find these photos for us?" she asked.

"Listen, I'm very busy . . ." He sighed. "I'll have a think where they are."

"Thank you. Why did you leave England?"

"At this point, I was done with England. I'd been there for too long and fallen into being this promiscuous party boy, and everyone I hung around with thought that of me. It gave me a low opinion of myself. I wanted to do more with my life, and I missed home. I booked myself a flight back to Barcelona. I didn't tell anyone I was going. No one knew my address. I got rid of my phone. I came back to my parents' house in the country and spent a few months being normal, and then I enrolled in university and studied politics. I graduated in 2007. I worked for a European lobby group for a year and then ran as a European member of Parliament. I was as shocked as anyone that I got elected, but I love it . . ."

"Congratulations," said Kate. "We're just so happy to know that you're not . . ."

"Dead?"

"Yes. Did you know that Joanna Duncan went missing a few weeks after you left to go home?" asked Kate.

"Yeah, I saw something a few years later, but the media presented it as an abduction."

"Do you think Noah Huntley was capable of making Joanna disappear?" Kate was annoyed at herself for asking such a leading question, but she was worried his window of candor might close and he'd hang up.

"Of abducting her?"

"Yes. If Noah Huntley *had* been found guilty of misusing his parliamentary privilege, then he could have gone to prison."

"Do you want to know my honest, off-the-record opinion?" asked Jorge.

"Yes," said Kate.

"Noah Huntley was too good looking to have to pay for sex, and he was smart enough to fiddle his way around parliamentary expenses. Do you know how many young guys threw themselves at him back in the day? Lots. He was in his midthirties, he had money, and he was very good in bed. One of the reasons I didn't take Joanna Duncan seriously was that I thought she had an ax to grind. She wanted to bring him down, and this was after her story had been in the newspaper and he lost his seat. It felt vindictive."

"Thank you for talking to us," said Kate. "Please can you let me know if you find those photos? They could really help our investigation, and we'd keep your name confidential."

"I will have a look. But you need to understand, I want to keep this part of my life in the past," he said, and then abruptly, he hung up.

31

When Kate and Tristan turned the corner onto Kate's road, the sun was high in the sky above the sea, and the temperature was nudging eighty-two degrees.

Kate felt hot and thirsty after their journey. Jake was coming down the stairs from the campsite, leading a group of five young women and two young men. Jake was shirtless and wore a pair of board shorts. He'd caught the sun, and with his long hair and beard, he looked like a carefree hippie. The two other young guys wore shorts and sleeveless T-shirts, and the girls had short dresses on over lurid fluorescent pink and yellow bikinis. They were a good-looking bunch and reminded Kate of those reality shows where sexy young people are all sent to a far-flung island. Tristan slowed the car and pulled up next to Jake.

"Hey, how's it going?" asked Jake. "You two look hot and bothered."

"Tristan's car doesn't have aircon," said Kate, waving a copy of *GQ* magazine in front of her face.

"She should pay me more, don't you think, Jake?" said Tristan.

"I should be first in the queue for a pay rise," said Jake with a grin. "We should form a union!"

Tristan laughed. The group of young guys and girls had stopped on the other side of the road, waiting for Jake.

"I'm just taking this lot out on the boat. I'll be back at five," he said, and patted the car door. "The old dude, Derek, came and put the new window in the Airstream . . . Does he always do that thing with his false teeth?"

"Yes," said Kate. "How much was it?"

"Two hundred and fifty. I paid him cash from the kitty."

"I've asked him to come and fix the glass in my back kitchen door," said Tristan.

"Be prepared for his long pauses," said Jake. "At one point, he left such a big pause in a sentence, I thought he'd died."

"My housemate, Glenn, will have the pleasure of dealing with him," said Tristan with a smile.

"Oh, a courier just delivered a letter addressed to you both. It's on the desk in the office," said Jake. He patted the car door again and went to leave.

"Thanks, love. Be careful diving," said Kate.

"I will. I think it's going to be stunning out there," said Jake, shielding his eyes from the sun and staring out over the glittering sea. Kate wished that she could go with them. She'd love to just jump in the sea and cool off for a carefree afternoon of diving.

"See you later, mate," said Tristan. Jake waved, and they carried on up the road to the office.

A cardboard DHL envelope was waiting on the desk. Jake had propped it up against a pile of case files. Kate picked it up. The sender's address was a law firm in Utrecht, Netherlands—Van Biezen Attorneys. She tore it open, and there was a thick envelope inside.

"It's an official letter from Famke van Noort, care of her lawyer," said Kate, unfolding the thick, heavy stock paper. Tristan came over to join her.

"'I'm writing with regards to your email query care of Nordberg apartments. My client, Famke van Noort, spoke to Devon and Cornwall police on September tenth, 2002, with regards to the missing persons investigation for Joanna Duncan,'" said Kate, reading. "'I enclose a copy of the official signed statement she gave to the police, where her UK solicitor, Martin Samuels of Samuels and Johnson, Exeter, was present. Ms. Van Noort has no further comment.' . . . It's signed by the lawyer."

Kate found the second page. Tristan took it from her.

"This is a copy of the statement we already have. She was with Fred between two p.m. and four p.m. on Saturday, September seventh. She went to visit him on foot, using the footpath running along the bottom of the plots of land from the doctor's house to his," he said.

Kate sighed and took two cold cans of Coke from the minifridge in the corner of the office. She handed one to Tristan and put the other against her forehead to try and cool down.

"We're getting closer to the truth," said Tristan, opening his can and taking a long drink.

"Are we?" said Kate, enjoying the feeling of the cold metal against her hot forehead. "Famke won't talk to us."

"I don't think Fred had anything to do with Joanna going missing."

"*I don't think* isn't helpful . . . Ashley and Juliet Maplethorpe are slippery . . . I don't know if there's something just out of reach that we're not seeing. One of our potential victims has turned out to be alive . . ."

"Jorge gave us a gold mine of information," said Tristan.

"He confirmed what we knew or guessed at, but he left the country a couple of weeks before Joanna went missing."

"I really hope he finds those photos. Why would Joanna have taken the negatives? There must have been something important in them."

———

The weather was hot for the rest of the week. Tristan had to go into work at the university on Wednesday and Thursday for the last two days before the semester ended for the summer. Kate wrote up reports on their investigation so far and tried to find more information about the body that had been found on the moor, but the police had issued little to the public. The task of finding staff for the campsite changeovers drained a lot of Thursday and Friday, taking her away from the case. By Friday evening, Kate and Tristan had spent most of the day calling agencies and other contacts from Myra's old records, but they couldn't find anyone.

So, on Saturday morning, Kate, Tristan, and Jake had to clean and change the beds in eight caravans and ready the site for new guests. Kate was halfway through cleaning the toilet and shower block. It was a grotty, depressing job, but she'd volunteered to do it, knowing how much Sarah disapproved of Tristan having to work on the campsite.

Kate was trying to fix the toilet seat in one of the stalls when her phone rang in her pocket. When she slipped off one of her rubber gloves and looked at her phone, she saw it was Alan Hexham.

"Kate, do you have a minute?" he asked.

"Of course," she said, wiping the sweat off her brow with her forearm. She came out of the toilet block, glad of the cool sea breeze blowing across the caravan site.

"I've had some luck with those names you gave me," said Alan. Kate hurried over to the caravan next to the road, and she knocked on the window where Tristan was changing the beds. He put his head through the window, still holding a duvet.

It's Alan Hexham, she mouthed. "I'm just putting you on speakerphone, Alan. I'm here with Tristan."

"Hi, Alan," said Tristan, putting down the duvet and kneeling on the bed.

"Hello, Tristan," said Alan, his voice booming through the speakerphone. "As we discussed a few days ago, I asked one of my research assistants to look at postmortem examinations conducted on unidentified bodies of young men aged eighteen to twenty-five, over six foot tall, with muscular, athletic builds and dark or blond hair, where hair color could still be determined. We also investigated the type of death recorded during postmortem, concentrating on signs of sexual assault, if the wrists or ankles were bound, and if their cause of death was asphyxiation. We identified four postmortems with these traits."

"Four?" said Kate, looking up at Tristan.

"Yes. If I may explain," said Alan. "The first case we found was of a body washed up off the west coast close to Bideford on April twenty-first, 2002. The body was never identified because it was badly decayed. The unidentified male was over six feet tall, and there were lacerations to the wrists. The body was found tangled in a net, and it had been washed up during a storm, so much of the skin and soft tissue were decayed by the water. After a postmortem, and after all stages of trying to identify the body were exhausted, the poor chap was cremated. However, dental imprints were taken from the body. I was able to request dental imprints for David Lamb and Gabe Kemp. The decayed body found washed up on the beach in late April 2002 was Gabe Kemp."

"Jesus," said Kate, leaning against the side of the caravan. Tristan took the phone and put it on the windowsill. "Gabe Kemp was reported missing in the first week of April 2002."

"Yes, and that would account for the decay—the body could have been in the water for two weeks . . . I have more," said Alan. "We matched a second body from your suggested criteria. It was found on Dartmoor, on Mercer Tor, and it was found by a dog walker in the early spring of 2000, wedged between two rocks. Much of the face had been eaten away. There had been heavy snowfall over the winter, but looking at the rate of decay, the body had been dumped five or six months before it froze . . ."

"Which would make it April or May 1999," finished Kate.

"Yes. This young chap was found wearing full walking gear with a backpack . . . So this, coupled with the decay, meant that the police couldn't rule foul play. At the time, dental impressions were taken, but they were only compared with the records of two other walkers who'd been reported missing on Dartmoor, and they didn't match. On comparison with David Lamb's dental records, it was a match."

"David Lamb wasn't a hiker," said Tristan.

"Yes. The police were confused as to why the body was found wearing all this brand-new walking gear, but no money, no identification," said Alan.

"You said there were two more victims?" asked Kate, who was already reeling from the news that the bodies of Gabe Kemp and David Lamb had been found.

"Yes, the bodies of two other unidentified men matched your criteria. The first was found next to the M5 near Taunton Deane, in November 1998, in a storm drain. Postmortem results showed that the body had been dumped within the previous twenty-four hours. The body had all the same hallmarks as the death of Hayden Oakley last week. He'd been tied up, sexually assaulted, and asphyxiated. The second young man's body was found in a landfill site in Bristol in a black plastic bag in November 2000. The body was decayed—it had been there for a week to ten days—but the postmortem showed he'd been tied up and asphyxiated."

"Why didn't the police link these murders?" asked Kate.

"I don't have the answer for that."

They were silent for a moment.

"From 1998 to 2002, four bodies were found," said Tristan. "This is a serial killer."

"Are you able to open out the search? I only specified from 1998 to 2002. There could be other unidentified bodies," said Kate.

"Thanks to your information, the police are now looking at these four murders in connection with the death of Hayden Oakley, and they'll be opening up the investigation to look at unidentified deaths before 1998," said Alan. "I'm afraid, though, that these are no longer cold cases, and I can't share any of the case files with you. They are now active police investigations. I was given permission to call you by the police officer who will be taking charge of this, a DCI Faye Stubbs. She asked me for your details, and she'll be in touch. Well done, you two."

"That's incredible," said Tristan when they came off the phone call. "We've helped find David and Gabe; Jorge is alive . . . We weren't imagining things. Joanna Duncan wrote down their names for a reason. Do you think she knew that there was a multiple murderer doing this?"

"I wish we could find out. We don't have her computer or any of her notes from work," said Kate.

"This means we're going in the right direction," said Tristan.

"But now the results of our hard work are being handed over to the police."

Kate's phone rang again. It was an Exeter landline number. When she answered, a woman introduced herself as DCI Faye Stubbs.

"I got your number from Alan Hexham, our regional coroner. I understand you're a private detective?" she said.

"Yes, we've just spoken to him," said Kate.

"We?"

"Myself and my associate, Tristan Harper. I've got you on speakerphone."

"Hi," said Tristan.

Faye ignored him and carried on talking. "I understand that you've been given access to case files from the Joanna Duncan case?" she asked. Her voice was now a little less friendly.

Shit, mouthed Tristan.

"Yes, that's correct," said Kate.

"*Right.* Are you aware that these case files are property of the Devon and Cornwall police? And that we keep records for a reason?"

Kate felt the floor drop underneath her.

"Of course. We understood that we were allowed access to them."

"And who in Devon and Cornwall police told you that?"

"I didn't get the case files from the police. Our client was given access to them by a senior police officer, Superintendent Allen Cowen. I have a signed letter from Superintendent Allen Cowen stating this. We were told that we could view the cold case materials, as the Joanna Duncan case is now dormant."

"Well, things are changing fast," said Faye.

"Are you reopening the case?"

"No. I didn't say that. Okay, your client is Bill Norris, yes?"

"Yes."

"He tells me that you have the original case files in your possession. Is that correct?"

"Yes," said Kate. The tone of DCI Stubbs's voice was making her feel like a naughty schoolgirl.

"Did you make copies?"

Shit, mouthed Kate to herself. This was a gray area. A private detective could operate within this gray area, but crossing the line to breaking the law wasn't something that she was prepared to do. *Shit*, she mouthed again.

"Paper copies?" asked Tristan.

"That's what copies usually are," said Faye.

"No. We just have the original paper files."

"Right, I'll need to arrange to come and collect them from you."

"Listen, Faye—may I call you Faye?" asked Kate.

"Of course."

"I'm an ex–police officer, and I understood that we were operating within the law. Of course we'll cooperate fully with you."

Faye's tone grew lighter.

"Kate, I'm not phoning you to give you a bollocking. You've given us a breakthrough on a murder case and three other unsolved murders. But considering this, things have changed. I have to follow procedure now that this has become active."

"Are you also reopening the Joanna Duncan case?"

Faye sighed. "It looks like it, yes. When can I arrange to collect the case file materials? Is first thing tomorrow morning acceptable?"

Kate looked at Tristan. He rolled his eyes and nodded. She went to rub her eyes with her free hand, then saw she still had on the dirty rubber glove.

"Of course, yes. I'll give you the address of our office," she said.

32

DCI Faye Stubbs arrived at the office at eight thirty the next morning. Her short black hair had gray at the roots and was scraped back from her face in a tiny ponytail. Her face was pale and devoid of makeup. Kate wondered if they were a similar age, midforties. In another life, Kate had hoped to reach the DCI rank before she hit forty, and she wondered how long Faye had been a DCI.

Faye arrived with her colleague Detective Constable Mona Lim, a petite, dark-haired officer with doll-like features who looked no more than a teenager.

"So, this is your little detective agency?" asked Faye, looking around the office, where cleaning products and bedding for the campsite were piled up against one wall. She had a bright, patronizing tone in her voice. Kate and Tristan had discussed how they would play it at this meeting, and Kate thought it might be a good idea to let the police think they were amateurs, but having Faye in her space made Kate feel the need to compete and prove herself.

"Yes, we opened our doors nine months ago," said Kate.

"And how are you finding it? It must be tough trying to start something new all the way out here," said Faye, moving to the window and looking out over the bay. Mona nodded and joined her at the window.

"Yes, it's been challenging," said Tristan. "But here we are, giving the police the breakthrough they need."

Kate smiled at Faye. *Nice one, Tristan,* she thought. Faye returned the smile.

"So, Kate. You were once, long ago, a WPC?" she asked.

"I was a detective constable in the Met."

"Yes. That ended rather badly, didn't it?"

Kate had a sudden childish urge to grab Faye by her ponytail and yank hard.

"Would you like a coffee, perhaps a doughnut?" asked Tristan, indicating a box he'd picked up from Tesco on his way over.

"How lovely that you have time for morning coffee," said Faye. "But go on, I didn't have any breakfast." She moved over to the box and flipped up the lid, picking up a doughnut. She indicated to Mona, who joined her and peered inside with a serious look on her face, as if it were also evidence in the Joanna Duncan case. She picked up a doughnut.

Tristan went to the coffee machine and quickly made them each an espresso. He came back with the cups, and they all sat down at the table.

"Is that all the files, and the box?" asked Faye through a mouthful. Indicating the blue box at the front of the pile of case file boxes stacked neatly by the door.

"Yes, the names all came from an indentation of Joanna's writing on the lid. David Lamb and Gabe Kemp are the two victims, and there's also a phone number we traced to Jorge Tomassini. Jorge was a barman who had slept with Noah Huntley, and he knew David Lamb. Joanna wanted to interview Jorge," said Kate.

"She was preparing to write a tell-all piece about Noah Huntley. How he hired rent boys and used his parliamentary expense account to pay for them and buy them gifts. One of the young men, Gabe Kemp, had been willing to go on the record about sleeping with Noah Huntley, back in early 2002, but he withdrew his statement and it never went to print. Gabe went missing shortly after the story went to press, and his body was found a few weeks later," said Tristan.

"We tracked down Jorge Tomassini last week. He says that he had a sexual relationship with Noah Huntley, who had, on occasion, displayed violent tendencies to him and to David Lamb when they had sex," said Kate.

"Did this Jorge Tomassini say why he never went on record for Joanna Duncan's story?" asked Faye.

"He didn't want to be part of a tabloid sex scandal, which is what Joanna wanted to write. He says he was planning to leave the country, and this hastened his exit. He's Spanish, and he decided to go home."

"Do you think he's a reliable source?" asked Faye.

"He's now a Euro MP in Strasbourg. He wasn't keen to delve into his former life here in the UK. We've made some additional notes in the case, and his details are in there if you'd like to follow it up. There's a plastic file with everything we've been working on," said Kate.

"You'll see that we've spoken to lots of the people in Joanna's life and gone back over their original statements. We do think that there are a lot of unanswered questions surrounding Noah Huntley," said Tristan.

"Joanna met with Noah Huntley two weeks before she went missing, at a petrol station close to where she lived. The meeting was caught on CCTV," said Kate.

Faye was nodding along as she swallowed the remains of her second doughnut, downed the last of her coffee, and got up, slapping her legs.

"Right. Thank you for everything you've done on advancing this case, and thank you for the refreshments."

Mona popped the last bite of her doughnut in her mouth and wiped off the sugar. She stood up.

"Is that it?" asked Kate. She'd expected Faye to ask some more questions about their findings.

"Did you expect more? You've been a huge, *huge* help. You've saved us time and resources, and I'll make sure that your little agency is mentioned in one of our press releases. Do you have a website?" asked Faye.

"Yes."

"Text it to me," said Faye. "Tony, would you give us a hand with the boxes?"

"It's Tristan."

"Of course, sorry. Tristan," said Faye. She picked up three of the boxes.

"Will you be contacting Bev Ellis, Joanna's mother?" asked Kate.

"At some point we will. Both of the investigations will probably merge very soon."

"Can I just ask, When will Hayden Oakley be buried? Have you released the body yet?" asked Tristan.

"Next week. Hayden didn't have any dependents. No family has asked for the body. Looks like it will be a council funeral," said Faye.

"The pub where he was last seen is organizing a memorial," said Mona.

"Which pub?" asked Kate.

"The Brewer's Arms in Torquay."

When Faye and Mona had taken all the boxes, Kate and Tristan came back up to the office. Kate made two more cups of coffee, and Tristan took a pile of linen for the campsite off the printer and scanner.

"I was worried when I said *paper copies* to her that she'd want to know if we'd scanned any of the case files digitally," said Tristan. "Do you think DCI Stubbs is a bit thick?"

"I'm hoping she's just overworked. She asked us to hand over the printed case files, and that's what we did. If she'd have asked us to delete the digital scans, then we'd be in trouble," said Kate.

"So this is a gray area?"

Kate nodded. "We've cooperated and shared everything we know. We have one advantage over the police. This is our only case, and I'm not giving up on finding out what happened to Joanna Duncan, or who killed those young men."

33

Kate and Tristan spent the rest of the weekend in the office, planning their next steps with the investigation. They were due to meet Bev and Bill on Wednesday, which marked three weeks since they'd started working on the case. They spent some time composing an email to Noah Huntley and then sent it from Tristan's account, requesting a general interview, hoping that the prospect of a meeting with a handsome young man might entice him to take the bait.

On Monday morning, they drove over to the Brewer's Arms in Torquay, where Hayden had been seen for the last time. Torquay was less than an hour's drive from Ashdean. It was another hot day, and they took Kate's car and had the air-conditioning on full blast.

When they reached the outskirts of the town, they had to drive round the ring road a couple of times before they found the turnoff toward the canal and the sloping road down to the Brewer's Arms.

They parked on a piece of scrubby, litter-strewn grass and walked up to the pub's entrance, which was under the first arch in a line of brick arches running along the water's edge. The canal shimmered in the heat, and there was a strong smell coming off the stagnant water, which was a soup of discarded rubbish and a half-submerged shopping trolley.

"Why do shopping trolleys always end up in canals?" asked Tristan.

"It's mostly homeless people who use them for all their belongings, and they're thrown in, or fall in along with their owners," said Kate, remembering from her time in the police.

A tall, stringy young man with terrible acne emerged from the front entrance with a bucket. He wore old ripped jeans, and he was shirtless. He emptied the bucket in the grass.

"Hello, do you work here?" asked Kate.

"Do I look like I'm doing this for my health?" he snapped.

"We're private detectives looking at the death of Hayden Oakley."

"Des!" shouted the young man over his shoulder. "Someone here to see you!"

Without saying more, he walked off around the side of the building.

"I wonder if he was hired for his customer service," said Tristan. Kate smiled, and they went in through the narrow entrance. The inside was lit with bright fluorescent strip lights, and it smelled of stale beer and vomit. An older man with thinning hair and grimy glasses was behind the bar, refilling a small fridge with brightly colored alcopops.

"What can I do you for?" he asked, pushing his glasses up his greasy nose.

Kate explained who they were and asked if he'd been working on the night Hayden Oakley went missing.

"I'm here every night, for my sins," he said with a smile that reminded Kate of the keys on an old piano. "I pretty much see everyone and everything. I knew that Hayden could go either way in life when he started coming here."

"How do you mean?" asked Kate.

"He was good looking. Athletic. And I'll make no bones. This pub is a dodgy pickup joint . . . but dodgy pickup joints can be lucrative. We don't have to worry about stocking fine wines or making cheese and olive platters. People come here to find sex . . . Hayden was popular with the regulars. Sometimes you see these lads work their way through these older blokes, find someone rich, and then strike out and start a business or move away. And sometimes they hang around for too long, get old, and start looking a little used up and worn out."

"Who are your regulars?"

"I want to say suave divorcés and local intellectuals, but it's mainly dirty old men," he said without blinking.

"Has what happened to Hayden affected your business?" asked Kate.

He thought for a moment.

"Not that I've noticed. A lot of the gay bars round here have Facebook groups, and they've been putting out warnings to young lads about a potential killer on the loose, but we were packed over the weekend, as usual. I think it's that attitude people have: it won't happen to me . . . Can I get you a cuppa or a coffee?" he added, indicating a grimy plastic tray with mugs, an old kettle, and a kilo bag of granulated sugar covered in tea stains.

"No, thank you," said Kate. "I presume these older men come here because you get young, attractive guys here?"

"Well, they don't come for the decor," he said. "The police asked me if I get a lot of rent boys coming in. Hayden was, according to rumor, a rent boy, and I'll say to you what I told the police. I just serve the drinks and provide the seats, and as long as no one does anything illegal in these four walls, live and let live."

"Hayden went missing after he left here?" asked Tristan.

"Yes. It was the last time he was seen."

"Did he leave with someone?" asked Tristan.

"He did. He was a big fella. Long dark hair and a baseball cap. Looked a bit like a country and western singer. Well, he did under the dance floor lights. I'm sure if I'd had these daytime lights on, he would have looked a bit more like a local who enjoys line dancing in his spare time."

"Did they leave on foot or in a car?" asked Kate.

"We're off the beaten track here, so everyone arrives in a taxi, or they come in a car. The police think that they left in a car, but no one saw the make or model, and there were no taxis waiting outside who saw them either. It was a Monday night, so it was a bit quiet."

"Do you remember what this guy looked like, his facial features?" asked Kate.

"The police sent over one of them artists, who worked with me to put together a picture of the fella Hayden left with . . . Hang on— Kenny! *KENNY?*" he shouted behind him. A moment later, the young man with the acne came through from the back. "Are you going deaf?"

"What is it, Des? I'm down doing barrels."

"Have you got that picture on your phone, of the police sketch?"

Kenny pulled a smartphone out of his pocket, swiped the screen, and found a photo. He handed it to Des, who peered at it over the top of his glasses and handed it to Kate. Tristan moved closer to see the screen.

Photofit images gave Kate the creeps, and this was no different. The face was a composite of different pieces—eyes, nose, mouth, lips, hair—but they came together to make a freakish, menacing image. The eyes were an intense brown and spaced a little far apart. The nose was straight and looked unremarkable, but the teeth were slightly bucked. The hairline was low and dark on the wide forehead, and the baseball cap was set quite far back on his head.

"Can you text this to me?" asked Kate.

"I'm on pay-as-you-go," said Kenny.

"Oh, for God's sake, I'll give you the twelve pence," said Des. "Go on, love," he said. Kate typed in her number and texted the message to herself, then handed the phone to Kenny, who stomped back off downstairs.

"Did his hairline look odd?" asked Kate, now staring at the E-FIT photo on her own phone.

"Yes. I thought that, well, not too much at the time cos we get all sorts in here, but when I think back, his hair did look like a wig. A decent wig, cos the hairline would have been glued down."

"False teeth too?" asked Tristan, tilting his head to look at the photo.

"I don't know, maybe. Or he was just unlucky," said Des.

"Have the police questioned any of the other regulars?" asked Kate.

"Yes, I had a few young lads come in. One of them is convinced that things were the other way around and that Hayden was planning to slip something in this bloke's drink and rob him. He says that Hayden's done this before."

"Had anyone reported Hayden to the police? Did he have a record?" asked Tristan.

"No, and no. Most of the blokes this kind of thing happens to are too embarrassed to phone the police. They're often married, and they don't want the wife to find out," said Des.

"Did you know much else about Hayden?"

"He was in care for most of his childhood. We get a lot of young lads in here who I have to chuck out for being underage. I'm very strict about that. Hayden had been coming here every Monday for about five months."

"He was raped and strangled. His body was found dumped on the moor near Buckfastleigh," said Kate. Des looked horrified. He shook his head and tutted.

"The sad thing is that we've lost quite a few young men from the community. Drug overdoses, beaten up by a punter. A lot of it goes under the radar. This is the first time anyone from the police has sent a sketch artist," said Des.

"Are a lot of your regulars violent men?"

"A lot of men are violent; add unhappiness and alcohol into the mix, and you've got flames," said Des.

"This guy has killed before," said Kate.

"Like a serial killer?"

"Yes. Could we show you some photos and ask if you've seen any of these people come in here in the last few weeks?"

"Of course."

Kate was ready with some printouts, and she put them on the bar. The first photo was of Max Jesper.

"Nope, never seen him," said Des, peering at it and adjusting his glasses. Kate then showed a picture of Ashley Maplethorpe, taken from his LinkedIn page.

"Nope. Too classy for this place."

Des also said no to photos of Fred Duncan and Bill that they'd included as a control group. The last photo was of Noah Huntley.

"Oh, I recognize him," said Des. Kate and Tristan exchanged a glance.

"You've seen him in here?" asked Kate.

"Sorry, no. I meant I know who he is. He was our local MP. I wrote to him about getting the canal bank outside cleaned up. He wrote back to me. It never got cleaned, but he wrote back to me; that's something, isn't it?"

"You're absolutely sure he hasn't been in here?" asked Tristan.

"Absolutely sure," said Des. "Why would he come to a shithole like this?"

34

From the bar in Torquay, Kate and Tristan drove back to Ashdean for a Skype call with Rita Hocking. She'd returned Kate's third email, apologizing that she'd been away in India reporting on their election. She said that she'd be happy to talk about her time working at the *West Country News* with Joanna.

When they got back to the office, they had lunch, and Tristan printed off the photofit image and pinned it to the wall next to A4 photos of Noah Huntley, Ashley Maplethorpe, and Max Jesper. There was also a photo of Nick Lacey, which Tristan had got from Bishop, but it was a photo of him from behind. Tristan had drawn a big question mark over it in black ballpoint pen.

"Our photofit man doesn't look like any of them," said Tristan.

"The noses all match. They all have quite strong Roman noses, but we need more than just a nose," said Kate.

"We need a photo of Nick Lacey. He's been bubbling away in the background of all this."

Underneath the line of photos were pictures of David Lamb and Gabe Kemp. They'd also added two pieces of paper for the unidentified bodies found in 1998 in the storm drain and in 2000 on the landfill site. Kate and Tristan stared at them all for a minute.

"If this guy is wearing a disguise to abduct his victims, it's made it easier for him to get away with it for a long time," said Kate, staring at the cold brown eyes, which seemed to dominate the room, watching them from the noticeboard.

"The E-FIT at the bar portrayed him as an older man, fifties. He could have been doing this for more than five years. There could be more bodies that he's tucked away and haven't been found," said Tristan.

"There's something Des said about Hayden. He'd been going to the Brewer's Arms pub for five months, and one of the other lads who drank there was convinced that things were the other way around and that Hayden was planning to slip something into his abductor's drink and rob him . . ."

"Yes. He said that Hayden's 'done this before,'" said Tristan.

"So they could have met before. Hayden had already scoped him out as someone with money who was worth robbing."

"You think our man isn't just abducting guys randomly? He's getting to know them first?"

"And he travels around the West Country. Hayden was abducted in Torquay, David Lamb lived in Exeter, Gabe Kemp lived and worked in a gay pub near Plymouth," said Kate.

"Shit. He could be using other disguises."

———

On the dot of three p.m., which was ten a.m. in Washington, they called Rita Hocking on Skype. Rita looked like a stereotypical journalist. She had long gray hair tied up in a bun with two pencils, heavy makeup and red lipstick on her craggy features, and a pair of bright-red-framed glasses that magnified her brown eyes. Behind her were bookshelves and a slice of an office window. The tip of the Washington Monument's tall needle appeared above a row of redbrick buildings.

"Hi there," she said, her British accent only slightly muddied with a transatlantic twang.

When the pleasantries were over, Kate said, "Thank you for talking to us. We appreciate your time."

"Not a problem," she said, picking up a huge takeaway iced coffee and sipping through the straw. "So, Joanna Duncan, eh?"

"How long were you colleagues for?" asked Tristan.

"The *West Country News* was my first gig out of university. I was twenty-five, and it was the year 2000. I stayed there three years until I was twenty-eight . . . Looks like I've given away the fact I'm forty," she said, smiling and taking another big gulp of her drink.

"Well, you look amazing," said Tristan.

"I wasn't asking for your comment on how I looked," she said, her smiling attitude turning on a sixpence. "Why do men think it's okay to pass comment? How old are you?"

"I'm twenty-five," said Tristan. "Sorry. I didn't mean to offend you."

"You didn't *offend* me. I don't know you," she said.

"Joanna Duncan must have started at the newspaper a year before you," said Kate, steering the conversation back.

"Yeah. And she loved hierarchies, Joanna did."

"How do you mean?"

"She was always at pains to say she was more senior, that she had more experience," said Rita. "And she hated the fact that I was privately educated, like it mattered . . ." Kate didn't dare glance over at Tristan. *Of course it matters,* she thought. Rita went on, "We'd often cover these personal-interest pieces about kids who fell through the cracks. There was one story about kids who lived in a high-rise, and their mothers were all screwing this drug dealer; when he was arrested, six of the women committed suicide, and the kids were packed off to a home. I remember her saying to our editor that she should cover the story because she had more working-class authenticity. She played on people's emotions. Manipulated them." She took another sip of the enormous coffee.

"The editor was Ashley Harris?"

"Yeah. He was a good editor. He had her worked out early on."

"How do you mean?"

"A journalist needs empathy. Not that we use it all the time. It's not the most empathetic profession. Often, you're writing a story to expose or unmask a facet of someone's life, but you need to be able to put yourself in the other person's shoes. You need empathy, and you need to know when to deploy it in your work. You also need to be one step ahead. Like a chess match. You need to know when to hold back, because someone can become a source and valuable to you more than once. If it's someone powerful, you might hold back on writing about their infidelity or petty crime because you know you can keep them in the fold and tap them for more juicy leaks and information," she said.

"And Joanna didn't do that?" asked Kate.

"The big story was that Noah Huntley took bribes for government contracts whilst he was an MP. It's a good story. It appealed to a broad range of readers, and it created waves, but when Joanna didn't get the glory for the story when the national newspapers picked it up, she lost sight of her journalistic instincts. Instead of going out there to find another great story, of which there were many, she chose to grub around in the dirt and go after Noah Huntley and his gay affairs. She was like a dog with a bone, looking up all these young guys who he'd screwed. She wanted one of them to wear a wire! Remember, this was a regional newspaper. Joanna didn't have the balls to quit and try her luck in London—she just hung around and got bitter and vindictive."

"Had you ever met Noah Huntley?" asked Kate.

"Yes. I'd spent time with him on the campaign trail for the 2001 general election. He won his seat by a huge majority. Both him and his wife, Helen, were fun to be around. Noah is a bit of a charming fool, but a lovable one. People think she's this long-suffering doormat, but no one has ever bothered to look beyond her standing next to him in official photos. They met at Cambridge. He's gay, she's a lesbian. The deal was that they would marry for security and companionship. He became the more high-profile partner in the couple, so his love of cock, if you excuse my bluntness, was good gossip, but I wouldn't have spent so much time chasing that story."

"We spoke to your editor a few days ago, and he said that he'd told Joanna to drop the whole rent-boy angle of the original story?" said Kate.

"Yes. You can't just 'out' people for sport. There was no proof that Noah used his parliamentary expenses account to solicit said cock."

"He wrote a check to one of the rent boys," said Tristan.

"Yes, but he could have been paying for freelance research or secretarial admin work. Unlikely, yes, but so many MPs hire secretaries and researchers. That check wouldn't have stood up in court if the young lad involved had refused to be interviewed."

"Did you know that Joanna met with Noah Huntley two weeks before she went missing?" asked Kate.

"No. I didn't know that."

"Were you working in the office on the day that Joanna went missing?"

"I worked in the morning. I left around lunchtime."

"Did you notice anything odd about Joanna that day?"

"Define *odd*."

"Was she stressed about anything? Acting out of character?"

Rita sat back and thought for a moment.

"God, it was so long ago. I do remember her being nice to me . . ." She chuckled. "Things had been rather frosty between us, but she bought me a coffee; she seemed upbeat, excited even. She'd just got a load of photos back from Boots. You remember that, when we used to get our photos processed?"

"Holiday photos?" asked Kate, sharing a glance with Tristan.

"No, I don't think so. She asked me for an expense claim form. I remember because it was the last thing she ever said to me," said Rita.

"What happened next?" asked Kate.

"Nothing. I stayed for another ten minutes or so, and I left to meet my boyfriend for lunch."

"Was it a lot of photos?" asked Kate.

"I know she had a stack of those envelopes they used to give you back for your processed photos. It wasn't unusual back then for journalists to work with photos, films, et cetera. We were still a few years away from going digital."

"Can you remember how many of these photo envelopes she had?" asked Kate.

"It was a long time ago. It was a pile of, I don't know, fifteen, twenty?"

"If Joanna wanted to use a hard-copy photo in a news story, would she scan it herself?" asked Tristan.

"No. It would have been sent down to the copy room via the picture desk," said Rita.

"Did you work on laptops or desktop computers at the *West Country News*?" asked Kate.

"I had a laptop. Most of us had laptops, so we could work at home."

"Did people leave their laptops at work?"

"No. Joanna never left her laptop at work. She would have taken it with her. She was ferociously competitive. She was a good journalist in the sense that she was out of the office as much as she was in."

"Did the police come and talk to the staff at the *West Country News*?" asked Kate.

"Yes. We all gave them what little information we had. It was shocking," said Rita, her face clouding over. "I've been honest what I thought about Joanna, but it was a difficult time, when one of your own becomes the story. I wrote most of the copy on the first days of Joanna going missing."

"Do you know what happened to the photos?" asked Tristan.

Rita shook her head. "No."

"What do you think happened to her?" asked Kate.

"I think it was either someone who knew her very well or a stranger."

"Noah Huntley sticks out as a possible suspect because of their history, and the fact that Joanna had this clandestine meeting with him, at night, in a petrol station car park. And she could have had some kind of compromising information about him."

There was a pause. Rita thought about it for a moment and then shook her head.

"I always thought Noah Huntley was a bit of a buffoon. He came across as disorganized; he drank too much on the campaign trail. Of course, back then, there weren't any camera phones, and it was easier for him to get away with being drunk. Also, I don't think Joanna was a good enough journalist to have information on him that was so explosive. His fondness for younger men was an open secret, and he'd already lost his seat, so anything to do with his misuse of parliamentary funds wasn't a story either. Do you really think Noah was bumping off these guys?"

"It's a theory," said Kate.

Rita snorted and shook her head. "Do you have any other leads or suspects? Any clue where her body could be?"

Kate and Tristan looked at each other.

"No," said Kate.

"I know one thing for sure. Joanna didn't run away. She was far too ambitious to do that. She wanted fame and glory in her own name," said Rita.

———

"Wow. The photos Joanna was having processed, that's a big lead," said Tristan when they came off the Skype call.

Kate picked up her coffee cup and saw it was empty. She got up to make herself another. "Jorge says Joanna came to his flat at the end of August 2002. A week later, the day Joanna goes missing, she gets a stack of photos processed. The police can't have seized them, because there was nothing in the case files. We need to get those photos from Jorge. I've already sent him a text about them. I'll send him another and impress upon him the urgency." Kate took her phone out and it pinged. With a text message. "It's from Faye Stubbs," she said, looking at the screen. "She says to switch on the BBC News channel."

Tristan grabbed the remote and turned on the small TV in the corner of the office.

"Which is the BBC News channel?" he asked, flicking through. "Ah, here it is."

A news report was just starting, showing an image of the fallen tree on Dartmoor where Hayden's body had been found.

BODY ON MOOR LINKED TO FOUR UNSOLVED MURDERS was the headline at the bottom of the screen.

"Police today are appealing for witnesses to help them trace the last movements of Hayden Oakley, a twenty-one-year-old from Torquay. He was last seen on the night of Monday, the eleventh of May, at the Brewer's Arms pub in the town . . ."

A photo of the pub flashed up on screen, and then three blurred images taken from a security camera in the back of a taxi: Hayden lit from above in the back seat, and then him leaning across to pay the driver, and then him getting out of the cab.

"Police believe the murder is linked to four other unsolved murders: David Lamb, who went missing in June 1999; Gabe Kemp, who vanished in April 2002; and two other, as yet unidentified, young men . . ." The pictures of David and Gabe from the UK missing persons website flashed up on the screen. "Police also think these unsolved murders have a link to the disappearance of Exeter journalist Joanna Duncan in September 2002. A local private detective, Kathy Marshall, got in contact with the police with compelling evidence to show that Joanna Duncan was investigating the disappearance of David Lamb and Gabe Kemp when she went missing. There have been several appeals over the years, and her disappearance was featured in the BBC *Crimewatch* program in January 2003, but her body has never been found."

Joanna's photo flashed up on-screen, and then they showed footage from the *Crimewatch* reconstruction of an actress who looked like Joanna walking up Exeter High Street to the Deansgate car park. "Devon and Cornwall police have set up a dedicated help line, and they ask for any witnesses to call this number."

"*Kathy* Marshall," said Kate, looking over at Tristan as the help line number flashed up on-screen, but he was looking at a message on his phone.

"Noah Huntley took the bait," he said with a grin. "He's agreed to meet us tomorrow."

35

Tom's feeling of godlike power had evaporated when Hayden's body was found. He'd been convinced that the rain and mud would fill the hole left by the tree and that the council would chop up the dead tree, haul it away, and fill in the rest of the hole, entombing Hayden in a muddy grave.

At first, he was relieved to see that the discovery of Hayden's body had made only a small splash on the local news. He'd been careful to clean away all DNA evidence, and he was sure he'd been alone on the moor. No one had seen him.

Late on Monday afternoon, he was driving down the motorway toward Exeter with the radio on and the windows down, when he heard on the news that the police had linked the death of Hayden with four other bodies that had previously been unidentified. David Lamb and Gabe Kemp were mentioned. He swerved the car, narrowly avoiding a large lorry, and then he pulled off the road into a lay-by.

He sat for a few minutes, sweating, with the engine ticking over in the heat. The news finished, and a song started to play. He switched off the radio and looked on his phone. The story was now on the main BBC News website, and it said that the police believed the deaths of these young men were linked to the Joanna Duncan missing-journalist case from 2002 and that they would be reopening her case. There was a recap of all the details and a hotline number for anyone who wanted to report information to the police.

"Hotline number. Fuck," he said out loud.

Tom had feared that this could happen. That one day the police would make the link. He took some deep breaths. The bodies of those young men may have been linked, but he was certain that there was no DNA evidence to trace their demise back to him . . .

And Joanna Duncan.

Joanna's body was tucked away nicely, and he was certain she would never be found. However, the police needed a suspect for their investigations, someone that they could go big and wide with and blame.

A lorry went roaring past, shaking the sides of his car. Tom turned the rearview mirror to face him and stared at his reflection.

"You need to stay calm. Don't lose your shit," he said to his reflection in the mirror. He sounded weak and pathetic. "Peter Sutcliffe . . . They only caught the Yorkshire Ripper by a fluke, when the police stopped him for a traffic violation. Ted Bundy, the same. The police have fuck all. They know nothing. And anyway . . . you're not like them, you're not . . . like them."

He reached up and stroked his face, feeling the contours of his nose and mouth, his lips, and tracing the line of his forehead as it rose to his hairline.

"You're the innocent one. You should know that . . . Those young men, they might look like something on the outside, but they have problems, serious mental problems. They used their looks to manipulate and hurt other people. You stopped them from hurting others. Like you were hurt. But you survived the bullies, and you have a purpose."

Tom closed his eyes against the blazing sun, and for a moment, he was thirteen and back in that hospital bed again. The attack in the school showers had left him with a broken jaw, a fractured eye socket, and broken ribs. He'd been trampled on so viciously that he had internal bleeding on his kidney, which meant the bag connected to the catheter at the end of his bed had filled up with pink urine for two weeks.

Three of the boys involved were expelled from school, but none of the other boys there that day had given evidence to support him. They had all joined together and said they saw nothing. Even the teacher, Mr. Pike, told the police that he'd found Tom afterward, lying in the showers, bleeding.

He'd made a full recovery, but never having the answer to the question *why* had driven his anger and fear ever since. He'd also had bad experiences in his early twenties. The men he'd slept with, or tried to sleep with, had been cruel, and he'd been used, abused, and beaten up. It was only by paying for sex that he was able to find acceptance. If you were paying, they didn't have the right to complain. And then he decided to be someone different. He decided he needed to be the one in control. That was when Tom's paying for sex took on a darker tone.

Movement outside the car window brought him back to the present. There was now a large lorry pulled up on the hard shoulder behind, and cars were whipping past. He looked down and saw that he was hitting the steering wheel over and over with the palm of his hand. The man outside the car was short and portly, with sweat glistening off the top of his bald head. Tom stopped and had to catch his breath.

"Are you okay there, mate?" asked the man. He looked concerned—a little frightened, even.

Tom wound up his window and started the engine. He pulled out of the lay-by with a squeal of rubber and glanced back as the bewildered-looking man receded in the mirror, hoping he wouldn't remember his face.

36

Sarah rang Tristan's phone as he was driving along Ashdean seafront.

"I need to talk to you," she said. Her tone of voice was sharp, and he immediately thought he'd done something wrong.

"You make me nervous when you sound like that," he said, seeing a parking spot up ahead outside his flat and guiding the car into it.

"It's quite serious," she said. "Your application for a mortgage hasn't been accepted."

Tristan switched off the engine and immediately began to sweat.

"You told me it was approved."

"Gary thought that, as the bank manager, he was able to override the system . . . Someone at head office then reviewed the approved mortgage application, and you don't earn enough—on paper, that is," said Sarah.

"What do you mean? I earn money."

"They can't count the agency because it's a new business. They need to see a year's tax returns before they can count it as income."

"Okay, so what do I do?"

"Now don't panic. It means that this month your mortgage will revert to the general APR, which luckily isn't a great deal more."

"How much more?"

"A hundred and fifty pounds."

"That's a lot," said Tristan, running through the amounts in his head. Money was already tight, and if the police reopened the Joanna Duncan case, then Bev might not need them anymore.

"We've got a month to get this sorted out, and we will sort it. Do you need any help with money?" asked Sarah.

"No. Thank you."

"It just makes me wish that you didn't have to invite some stranger to live with you . . ." There was a muffled noise as she put the phone down, and he heard her throwing up.

"Sarah?"

"Oh. Sorry about that," she said.

"Are you still ill?"

Sarah let out a long breath.

"Tris, I have something to tell you . . . I'm pregnant."

"Wow. That's brilliant news," said Tristan, feeling genuinely excited for his sister. "I thought you wanted to be married for a bit before . . ."

"Yes. This has come as a big shock. I literally just found out. Just now did the test," said Sarah.

"Where's Gary?"

"He's at work. You're the first person I'm telling . . ." Her voice sounded melancholy and far away.

"This is great news. You're married to someone you love. You have jobs, a home. You've got that spare room," said Tristan.

"I know. I am happy. I will be happy. I'm just worried; it all seems so grown up. Do I know enough about my own life to be responsible for another one?"

"Sarah. You've been just as much a mum to me as a sister. You're going to be the best mother. The best. That's one lucky kid."

He could hear Sarah was beginning to cry.

"And you're going to be the most fun and wonderful uncle."

"I didn't think of that," said Tristan, feeling the tears in his eyes. "You bet. Do you think it's a boy or a girl?"

Sarah laughed. "It's just a blue line on a pregnancy-testing kit. I can't be more than a couple of weeks gone."

There was a pause. They were both sobbing.

"This is good news! You have to tell Gary, right now. Phone him now," said Tristan.

He heard her sniff and blow her nose.

"Okay. I will. I love you. And we're going to sort out your mortgage, you hear?"

"Okay. Love you too."

When Tristan came off the phone, he went indoors. The house was empty, and he saw that the back window had been mended in the kitchen. He looked at himself in the bathroom mirror. Sarah was pregnant. She was having a baby. It made him think about his own life. He was happy at work. Very happy, but what about his personal life? There wasn't even a significant other on the horizon. And what about kids? He'd always wanted children, but now he didn't know how it would happen, and that made him feel sad and lonely.

He changed into his running gear. It was a warm evening, and he ran along the seafront and across the beach to the lighthouse and back. Running made him feel better and made his thoughts and worries fall off his shoulders. The weather would be good for the next few months. He would have to buy Sarah and Gary something. Did you give pregnancy gifts? Money was a worry. What if Bev and Bill decided not to keep them on after the first month, when they were getting closer with the investigation? He was now on reduced hours at the university over the summer. He could cancel his gym membership, which was sixty pounds a month, and his habit of buying an expensive pair of trainers every month could stop, or he could start taking sandwiches to the office—that would save him a fortune. It would give him the extra money for the mortgage if things didn't work out. His birthday was coming up, and he could ask for free weights.

When he reached the seafront, he was dripping with sweat, and he took off his T-shirt and mopped his face and chest and stopped at the water fountain by the pier and had a long drink. When he stood up, Ade was coming out of the chip shop on the pier with a big cone full of chips and a battered sausage. He looked at Tristan's torso.

"Bloody hell, I hate you," he said with a smile.

"Why?" said Tristan. "Hello, and nice to see you too."

"Look at your body! Oh my God," said Ade, pulling out the battered sausage and fanning himself with it. "And here I am about to guzzle three thousand calories." He bit the top off the sausage and offered him a chip. Tristan took one and chewed.

"Thanks."

"What's up? You look a bit down. Well, you look hot, but your face seems a bit down," said Ade.

"Money worries . . . and my sister's pregnant."

"Are you the father?"

"No!"

"Then what are you worrying about?" cried Ade, taking another bite out of the sausage.

"At some point, before . . . before I was gay, I thought I might have children. That's probably not going to happen now."

"Why not? You can go online and buy an egg . . . Find a nice fag hag with childbearing hips, inseminate her with a turkey baster. Or you could adopt. Or you could do both and become the Mia Farrow of Ashdean!"

"Ade. Be serious," said Tristan.

"I don't know how it works. I've never wanted kids . . . Come on, let's go and sit on the pier. I feel rather common, eating chips on the pavement."

They found an empty bench looking out to sea.

"This case is getting to me. Hearing about these four young men whose bodies were found, raped and strangled. Noah Huntley is gay but got married so he wouldn't be lonely . . . My sister loves me, but I know she's scared I'm going to end up alone, that I won't find happiness . . . And you said something a few weeks ago, at the pub, that you've lost plenty of friends to parenthood. I just don't know where I fit in. What my life is going to be like."

Ade put his hand on Tristan's.

"Tris. You don't have to *fit in*, you know. There are plenty of straight people who don't want children or can't have children. And that's fine. Life isn't all about having children. Yes, there are plenty of gays and lesbians who have children or adopt. And then there are rancid old queens like me, who are quite happy to live alone . . . I love my own space. I cherish living alone, but I'm not lonely."

"Don't you wish you had a boyfriend?"

"Sometimes. But I've been there, done that, got the T-shirt. I'm a very good friend, but I don't think I'm a good boyfriend. Tris, you're what? Twenty-five?"

"Yeah."

"You know who you are, and you know what you want to do with your life. I believe you are going to be a successful private detective, with a successful business. Think how lucky you are in comparison to David Lamb and—what was his name?"

"Gabe Kemp."

"They didn't have the choices or the advantages you do, and they no longer have the luxury of life. And you get to be the person to catch who killed them. Yes?" said Ade. He was now looking serious.

"Yes, but the police want to reopen the Joanna Duncan case, now we've found the link. We're worried Joanna's mother won't want us to continue," said Tristan.

"Yes. I saw the news earlier. *Kathy* Marshall."

"I know. Kate wasn't happy about that. The police said they would credit the agency, but they got her name wrong. It was thanks to us that they're able to link the investigations."

"Then don't give up! If you and Kate want your business to succeed, make it happen!"

"Thank you. You're right," said Tristan, wiping his eyes and pulling his T-shirt back on.

"Good, that's settled, then," said Ade. "What are you doing tonight? Do you fancy a couple of bevvies at the Boar's Head? There's that Canadian Cilla Black impersonator who sings 'What's It All Aboot, Alfie.'"

Tristan smiled and nodded. "Okay. Just a couple. We're meeting Noah Huntley tomorrow, and I need to prepare."

37

After Tristan left to go home, Kate made dinner for Jake, and they ate, watching the TV. The story came up again on the evening news, showing the photos of David and Gabe and part of the *Crimewatch* reconstruction.

When they'd finished and Jake was clearing away the dishes, Kate had a craving to smoke, so she found the pack of cigarettes she kept on a shelf on the back porch.

It was a balmy night, and the sounds of the wind and the waves were muffled by the dunes as she climbed down the cliff. At the bottom she found the two rusting deck chairs that she and Myra had sat in many times to talk and have a cigarette. One of the chairs lay on its side. Kate picked it up, and dusted off the sand, and placed it next to the first. She sat down, tipped her head back, and looked up at the stars, brilliant against the black sky. Tiredness and worry overwhelmed her, and she closed her eyes.

———

Kate heard a rasping cough and opened her eyes. Her friend Myra was slowly making her way down through the dunes, her shoulders rounded and hunched over. She wore a long dark coat, which was open, and underneath, an old gray tracksuit and bare feet. Her white hair was luminous, even in the darkness, and her skin glowed.

"Evening, Kate," she said. "Good Lord. The dunes have shifted, haven't they? It's been a while since I've been here."

She sat next to her. The deck chair creaked. The tide was far out, and the wet sand glistened in the moonlight. It was the strangest feeling. Kate knew that she was asleep and dreaming. How else would her dead friend be sitting here on the beach, talking to her?

"Hello," said Kate.

Myra smiled and took a bottle of Jack Daniel's out of her coat pocket and set it down on the sand between their feet. Kate stared at it as Myra rummaged in her other coat pocket and found a pack of cigarettes. She opened it, teased one out, and put it between her creased lips. The flickering glow of the lighter illuminated the old woman's face, making the pupils contract rapidly in her large brown eyes.

"Do you fancy a drink?" asked Myra, indicating the bottle of Jack Daniel's on the sand. "I'm dead, and this is a dream, so I think you can have a drink."

It was tempting, but even in her dream, Kate knew the stakes. What would happen if she ever drank again. She shook her head.

"No."

"Good girl," said Myra, smiling and exhaling smoke through her teeth.

"I miss you," said Kate, feeling a surge of sadness for her departed friend. "I put flowers on your grave every month." She reached out, and Myra took her hand. It felt real—soft and warm. Myra chuckled.

"Nice ones they are too. None of that shit from the petrol station forecourt."

"I'm making a mess of everything," said Kate. "My first big case with the agency is going to slip through our fingers . . . Tristan's given up a good job, and I don't know how long I can keep paying him . . . I'm relying on Jake running the surf shop and caravan site . . . I don't know what I'm going to do at the end of the summer."

Myra took a last drag on her cigarette and flicked it away. The red ember sailed through the air, landed on the wet sand, and vanished.

"Well. I'd better be going," she said, patting Kate on the hand and heaving herself up out of the deck chair.

"Is that it?" said Kate.

Myra pulled her coat around her. "Kate. Think of all you've been through in your life. Jake is finally living with you. You're finally doing what you dreamed of with your own detective agency. The police have linked four unexplained murders. Those lads would have remained in unmarked graves if it wasn't for you. You're even refusing to drink this Jack Daniel's in your dream. And here you are, wallowing and getting in a state about the small shit. Cash-flow problems. Work problems." Myra leaned down and picked up the bottle of Jack Daniel's. She tapped her hand on Kate's shoulder and pointed with her finger. "You're back from the wilderness, my girl. Don't throw it away." She started to walk slowly back up the cliff. Kate watched her turn and vanish through the sand dunes.

———

Kate woke up, sitting in the deck chair on the beach. The chair next to her was empty. A warm breeze was blowing, and her phone was ringing in her pocket. She took it out and answered just before it stopped ringing. It was Tristan.

"Sorry to call late. Everything okay?" he asked. "You sound groggy."

"Yeah. I dozed off. What is it?"

"Noah Huntley. I'm sitting here working out what we should ask him, or should I say, how we should go about asking him tough questions, and I don't know where to start. It's not like he's going to tell us if he's been going around killing and raping young guys."

"I've been thinking about this," said Kate. "We won't ask him about that. We'll concentrate on working out what his relationship was with Joanna. That's the key."

38

In the early hours of the next morning, Tom parked in a quiet residential street on the outskirts of Exeter. He dressed head to toe in black. It was a hot night, but he pulled on black gloves and a black balaclava with eyeholes. From beside him on the seat, he picked up a plastic bag that contained the underwear belonging to Hayden. He placed it in a black rucksack and got out of his car.

The street of finely appointed terraced houses was still and quiet, and the only sound came from the buzz of moths hovering in the orange glare of the streetlamps. Keeping to the shadows, he walked two streets over and came to a black SUV in the shadows of a tall tree. The windows of the surrounding houses were all dark. He reached into his pocket and found the car lock immobilizer. It had been an expensive purchase online, but worth it. Standing next to the SUV, and preparing to move fast if it didn't work, he pressed the button on the device. With a slick whir and a flash of headlights, the SUV's central locking opened, and the locks popped up.

Bracing for a car alarm, he opened the passenger door and waited, but nothing happened. There was beautiful silence. Taking care not to touch anything, Tom took out a pair of long metal tongs, pulled Hayden's underwear from the plastic bag in his rucksack, and wiped the fabric all over the passenger seat, dashboard, and steering wheel. He then shoved the underwear under the passenger seat of the car.

He straightened up, put the tongs back in his rucksack, and closed the passenger door of the SUV. He pressed the button of the immobilizer, and the car locked itself, and the headlights flashed once.

It had taken less than a minute. Tom melted away, back into the shadows to his car.

He made one stop on the way back home, to an old red phone box on a country lane, where he phoned the police hotline and left urgent information about the Hayden Oakley murder investigation.

39

On Tuesday morning, Kate and Tristan found themselves in a Starbucks close to the university campus in Exeter. Perched on a hill, it was in a busy row of shops and looked out over the estuary. It was close to where Noah lived with his wife.

Tristan thought it was odd to see him arrive, in person, after weeks of staring at pictures of him on CCTV, with Joanna, and hearing all the stories and conflicting opinions about him.

He was a tall, broad man, much taller than he'd looked in photos. He'd also filled out a little more since the early 2000s. He was dressed like an off-duty actor, in slightly creased white chinos and a blue linen shirt with a thin scarf knotted loosely at his neck.

He came up to them at the table, and there was a moment where Tristan didn't know what to say.

"Hello," he said, getting up and offering his hand. "I'm Tristan Harper, and this is my associate, Kate Marshall."

"Lovely to meet you both." He smiled, taking Tristan's hands in both of his when they shook. Tristan noticed he clasped Kate's hand a little less warmly, just using his left hand.

"Thank you for making time to meet us," said Kate. "I'm just going up. Can I get you a coffee?"

"I could murder a latte, large, and a scone if there's one up for grabs," said Noah. He was very confident, but underneath was a tinge of nerves, thought Tristan. Kate went off to the counter, and Noah seemed to look him over.

"Where is your detective agency, exactly?" he asked.

"We're in Thurlow Bay. It's about five miles outside Ashdean."

"Ashdean, such a quaint place. I used to go there for weekends as a young boy. I had an aunt who owned a house up on the cliff. Aunt Marie. She was a lot of fun, liked the gin, if you know what I mean . . ." He made a drinking motion with his hand.

"Right," said Tristan. There was an awkward silence, and he looked to see how Kate was getting on. She'd given her order and was waiting to collect the drinks.

Noah drummed his fingers on the table. "So . . . I'm here to talk to you about Joanna Duncan, yes?" He raised his eyebrows. "Painful time that was, losing my seat. Great deal of embarrassment all round . . . Although"—and at this point he laughed—"there are plenty of other MPs, right now, who still have their seats, doing far worse."

Tristan was glad to see Kate collecting their order, and a moment later she came back to the table with their coffee and a scone for Noah.

"Lovely, thank you," he said.

"Tristan here was starting to grill me about Joanna Duncan," said Noah. "I've told him that I'm a big boy, and I don't hold grudges, all water under the bridge."

Tristan thought how confident Noah was and cursed himself for feeling shy. Why should he feel shy? It was crazy, but well-spoken people always made him feel like he was a country bumpkin.

Kate had bought herself a scone and was opening the little pack of butter. She glanced at Tristan. They'd agreed that he would lead with the questioning.

"We've been trying to find Joanna Duncan," started Tristan.

"Yes, you've said that," said Noah, his eyes down, buttering his scone.

"Yes, and there's a large amount of information about the last few days before she went missing. We understand you met with her two weeks before she vanished, on the twenty-third of August, 2002. You met her that evening at a petrol station near the village where she lived, Upton Pyne."

"There's never enough bloody butter in these little packets," he said, holding up the empty container. "Would you mind awfully getting me another one? Tristan?"

Tristan saw Kate give the tiniest roll of her eyes.

"I can go," she said.

"No. Tristan, you can go. Your associate here has already made one trip up to the till." He looked up at Tristan, and there was a mocking look in his eyes.

"Of course."

Tristan got up and went over to the barista station and asked if he could have more butter.

"Sure, just a sec," said the barista, who was spraying cream onto a large coffee. Tristan looked back and saw that Kate was talking to Noah, and he felt foolish. He hadn't got anywhere with his questions. He had to go back to the table and start again. There was no reason to feel intimidated. The Starbucks was busy—most of the tables were full—and as he looked across, he saw Detective Mona Lim sitting at a table by the window. She was dressed in jeans and a woolen jumper, with headphones in her ears. She had the paraphernalia of a student in front of her: a large textbook open in front of a laptop. They locked eyes, and Mona looked a little panicked. Tristan saw through the window behind her a delivery truck outside on the pavement. Sitting inside was a courier who was looking into the Starbucks and talking into a radio. Across the street was a blue car, and sitting inside that, on the phone, was DCI Faye Stubbs.

He looked back to Mona, who was staring him down.

"Shit, he's under police surveillance," said Tristan to himself.

Abruptly, Mona got up out of her seat and reached into her coat hung on the back. Faye was getting out of her car, and two police cars screeched to a halt outside the Starbucks. And then it all happened very quickly. Four police officers in uniforms rushed into the coffee shop and over to the table where Kate was sitting with Noah. Mona reached the table just before Tristan and held up her police card and ID.

"Noah Huntley, I'm arresting you for the murders of David Lamb, Gabe Kemp, and Hayden Oakley . . ."

Noah looked up, holding half a buttered scone, and Kate sat back in her chair, looking at the officers.

"You can't be serious," he said, biting into the scone.

"You do not have to say anything. But it may harm your defense if you do not mention when questioned something which you later rely on in court. Anything you do say may be given in evidence," said Mona. Faye reached the table, and one of the police officers had a pair of handcuffs open.

"Could you stand up, please, sir?" he said.

"This is—you can't be serious!" said Noah. "Is this what you wanted?" he said to Kate. "You lure me to a public place and make a big scene!"

"There doesn't need to be a scene," said Faye.

"Who the fuck are you?" shouted Noah, his face suddenly red with rage.

"DCI Faye—"

"Show me your fucking police ID card," he spat, spraying the table with bits of chewed-up scone. Faye already had her card ready and held it up.

"I'm DCI Faye Stubbs. This is DC Mona Lim, and . . ."

"I don't want to know all your fucking names!" shouted Noah. "Why do you have to do this here? You could have waited until I'd finished my fucking scone!"

"Cuff him," said Faye.

Noah's face was almost purple, and Tristan thought he was going to have a heart attack. Noah stood up, kicking his chair back into the wall, and allowed himself to be handcuffed.

"This way, sir," said the two uniformed police officers as they led him out of the Starbucks, which had fallen dead silent. Everyone was staring.

"What are you looking at?" Noah shouted at a woman with a stroller. "I want to speak to my wife and my solicitor. There's no need to guide me, I can see the fucking door!" he shouted as he was bundled toward the exit of the Starbucks.

"That's one to add to my list of last requests before arrest: *let me finish my scone*," said Faye.

"Has new evidence come to light?" asked Kate.

Faye nodded. "Come on. Let's go outside."

Tristan and Kate followed her out onto the street, where Noah was being put into a police car.

"You don't need to touch my head. I'm not a moron. I have got into the back of a car before!" he was shouting. There was a group of people watching from the Starbucks window as he was driven away.

Farther up the road, Tristan could see they'd cordoned off a black SUV, and a couple of forensics officers in white suits were working on the car.

"We had a tip-off on the help line," said Faye. "This person implicated Noah Huntley, saying he saw a large black SUV with Hayden inside. Whilst you were in the coffee shop with Noah, we found garments reportedly belonging to Hayden in his car," said Faye. "This, coupled with the evidence you provided us, has made us confident to make an arrest so we can question him further."

A voice started calling Faye on her radio.

"I have to go. Good work, you two. We had no idea you were who he was meeting. We've only had him under surveillance since early this morning."

Faye and Mona crossed the road and got into the blue car and drove away with the remaining police car.

"I only noticed Mona sitting by the window when I went to get him his bloody butter," said Tristan. "Shit. I didn't get anything out of him. I'm sorry."

"You did better than me. I should have seen her there. Not that it would have made any difference," said Kate.

"Did he tell you anything whilst I was gone?"

"No. He was bitching about the little pot of jam being too small."

"I feel like I fucked that up," said Tristan. He felt Kate touch his shoulder, and he looked at her.

"No. You didn't. And he's been arrested. He's been our main suspect since the beginning," said Kate. He could see she felt cheated that they weren't able to question him.

40

The next day was three weeks since they'd started their investigation, and Kate and Tristan drove over to see Bill and Bev in Salcombe to give them an update.

It was a hot morning, and they left early, arriving at Bill's villa just before ten a.m. The sea and sky were in unison, a perfect blue. A group of sailing boats moved across the flat surface of the bay, and a yacht was moored farther out to sea next to a Jet Ski carving its wake in a large circle.

Bev and Bill's garden had burst into life since their first visit and was filled with sweet-scented summer flowers and the lazy hum of bees. When they reached the front door, Bev was waiting for them. Kate was alarmed to see she was crying, but as they drew closer, she smiled and launched herself at Kate, grasping her in a hug.

"Thank you, thank you so much," she said. She reached out a hand and pulled Tristan into the embrace. Bev smelled of cigarettes and stale alcohol mingled with peppermints. "It's been on the news; the police have arrested Noah Huntley . . . Bill recorded it for me. I've already watched the news report back twice. Come on in."

They followed Bev in through the front door into the vast marble living area. It was as empty and neat as before, and just like the first time, Kate thought how out of place Bev looked, padding across the elegant white-and-gold marble in a beat-up pair of pink Crocs. Bill was sitting at the huge breakfast bar with his laptop. A flat-screen television was mounted on one of the walls in the kitchen.

"Hello, Kate; hello, Tristan," said Bill, with a smile just as wide as Bev's. They all shook hands.

"This is Noah Huntley's house," said Bev, grabbing the TV remote. The frozen image on the TV screen was the outside of a house on a leafy suburban street where a row of police cars were parked. The sun was low in the sky, casting its beam almost horizontally and flashing gold on the surrounding windows, which made Kate wonder how early or late they'd arrived at his house. Bev pressed "Play," and the camera switched angles to show where neighbors were watching from their doors on either side of the street as a team of forensics officers emerged from the front door carrying items of clothing in clear plastic evidence bags.

"Police obtained a warrant to enter the home of the ex–Member of Parliament for Devon and Cornwall Noah Huntley," said the news reporter's voice. "He was arrested at the same time." It then cut to Noah Huntley as he was escorted to the front steps of Exeter police station, with his hands cuffed in front of him. There was a crush of journalists outside, waiting with cameras and smartphones, and he kept his head down as the police guided him through the crowd.

"Noah Huntley lost his seat in a 2002 by-election after he was accused of taking bribes to award council-run contracts. Police are now arresting him in conjunction with the body of a twenty-one-year-old man found in the West Country. They also wish to question him in relation to four other unsolved murders dating back to the time he was an MP, and the disappearance of Joanna Duncan, a local journalist from the *West Country News* who was investigating Noah Huntley shortly before she went missing," said the news reporter. The photo of Joanna smiling on the beach with the coconut cocktail in her hand flashed up on the screen.

"Oh, my darling," said Bev, taking out a tissue and putting it to her face. "They've got him. They've got the bastard," she said, moving closer to the screen and talking up to the photo of Joanna. Tristan glanced across at Kate. Bev's grief was so raw that it felt almost intrusive to be standing next to her.

"It looks like the news reporters were tipped off about Noah Huntley being arrested," said Tristan.

"Is that a good thing? That must be a good thing . . . They'll be looking for Joanna. Is there anything more about her? Have they said that they're reopening Joanna's case?" said Bev, turning to face them.

Bill remained sitting at the breakfast bar with his laptop. "It's still very early days; I presume they only have a few days to question Noah before they have to charge him or let him go," he said. Bev moved around and nudged Bill out of the way. She put her fingers on the touch pad and scrolled down to the photo of Joanna.

"I told you that we'd find out who did this to you," she said, to the photo. Bill looked up at Kate and Tristan, almost apologetically. "I know it was that nasty politician. You found him out, and he didn't like it, did he?"

Kate understood that Bev was mired in guilt, but the way she was talking to the photo of Joanna was uncomfortable.

"Could we talk to you both and give you our update on the case so far?"

Bev was still talking to the photo on the screen, oblivious to Kate and Tristan. "We're now going to question that awful man, and he's going to tell us where you are, do you hear me, Jo?"

"Why don't you go and have a seat out on the terrace? There's an umbrella and table. I'll make us some coffee, and we'll join you," said Bill, indicating that he would deal with Bev.

Kate nodded, and she and Tristan moved over to the glass doors and outside. The terrace ran the width of the house, and it was equally deep as it was wide—to Kate it looked huge. It was empty of furniture, apart from a wooden table and four chairs under a white umbrella. She and Tristan sat down.

"The police must be confident, to move so quickly and arrest Huntley?" said Tristan.

"They have potential DNA evidence; if that comes through and links him to Hayden or any of the other young men, then they'll have a strong case to charge him," said Kate.

Bill emerged from the glass doors with Bev, who was clinging on to his arm. She looked frail in the sunshine, her skin pale. They came and sat at the table.

Kate gave them an update on everything they'd discovered over the past three weeks: how the names David Lamb and Gabe Kemp printed on the lid of Joanna's cardboard box had led them to Shelley Morden, who knew David Lamb, who in turn led them to Max Jesper.

"We've thrown a wide net with the investigation over the past few weeks," finished Kate. "But we'd like to continue and focus in on Max Jesper's commune and the people who went there. So many of the people we've investigated have been linked to the commune."

"I've never heard of this place. Have you, Bill?" asked Bev.

Bill rubbed his face. He looked serious after Kate's recap.

"I've heard of Max Jesper, just because of the squatter's rights story. That building is now worth a fortune. I've had a couple of business meetings there in the past. Some of my clients like to meet in nice restaurants."

"And you think that Jo was onto Noah Huntley because he used to go to the commune and carry on with these young lads?" asked Bev.

"We think that it could be Noah Huntley, and that for whatever reason, he or someone killed these young men and dumped their bodies," said Kate.

"The police might think they have their man in Noah Huntley, but that's down to our investigation," said Tristan. "It was Kate who linked the deaths of Hayden Oakley with David Lamb and Gabe Kemp and two potential other victims, and at that point we had to hand over our findings and Joanna's case files to the police."

"The police will have to find a definitive link between the deaths of all the young men. At present the evidence is compelling, but in a court of law, this could be seen as circumstantial without DNA evidence to link all the dead men," said Kate. "The bodies were found badly decayed, and they've since been cremated."

Bill and Bev were quiet. Kate couldn't work out what they were thinking.

"So Noah Huntley could go free?" said Bill.

"If the police don't have any DNA to link the young men, they're going to find it hard to build a case."

"We believe that Joanna is the link," said Tristan. "You asked us to find Joanna, and we want to continue."

"What about the police reopening Jo's case?" asked Bev.

"We would cooperate with them, of course, but we would be able to devote all our time to finding out what happened to her."

Bev was nodding along and dabbing at her eyes. Bill was close to her, gripping her free hand. Kate thought how desperate they both looked. Kate and Tristan still had concerns about some of the conflicting information they'd heard about Bill. They had discussed whether to ask him questions about his business dealings and about the asbestos-contamination story Joanna was looking into about Marco Polo House, but they thought it was best to confirm whether he wanted to continue their investigation. Once Bill had agreed to them continuing, then they would speak to him alone and ask him questions. However, he looked so torn and caught up in Bev's grief.

"It's all right, darlin'," he was saying. He put his arms around her, and she sobbed into his chest.

"Do you want us to give you a minute?" asked Kate.

"No," said Bev, composing herself and wiping her eyes. "You've come all this way, and you've found out more than the police ever did . . . I'd like them to keep looking for Joanna," she added, looking at Bill. "I don't want to put my trust in the police again and wait around for them."

Bill looked serious. He nodded and paused for a moment, thinking. "Okay. Let's do another month, and this time, if you could keep me up to speed every few days on the phone?"

"We'd be happy to carry on with our investigations," said Kate, feeling a little zing of happiness that they could continue.

Bill was called away to answer a phone call in his office, and Bev seemed to go off into another world, staring out to sea.

"We'll get going," said Kate, indicating to Tristan.

"All right, do you want a sandwich or anything?" asked Bev.

"No. Thank you."

Bev came back inside with them, and on the way out, Bill poked his head out of his office at the end of the corridor with his hand covering his phone.

"I'll get your payment sorted and be in touch," he said, with a wave.

Bev walked with them out to the car.

"Are you okay?" asked Tristan, as she leaned with her hand against the wall to catch her breath.

"Yes, love, too many cigs," she said. "I like your car. Is it new?"

"Yes, I got it a few months ago," said Tristan.

"It's nice. I haven't driven since my car got nicked, years ago," said Bev. "I wouldn't have the confidence. It got nicked the night Jo went missing too . . . Talk about a kick in the gut. I know I've moaned about moving here, but I'm glad I don't have to live on that horrible estate anymore. Have you got a wheel lock?"

"Yes."

"Good. The police thought that someone jimmied the lock and hot-wired it, got clean away with it. Wheel locks are good, cos the bastards can't turn the steering wheel without breaking the glass on the windscreen."

"Did they ever find your car?"

"Gawd, no. The police told me they find less than half of cars. They end up being resprayed and plated and sold on, or they're burnt out on some wasteland or dumped in the water. I doubt I'd have the confidence now, to drive. Thank you again, for everything. You've given me the first rays of hope in years. You'll keep in touch? The second you have anything new?"

"Yes, of course," said Kate. Bev waved them off, and Kate saw her, lonely and forlorn, in the rearview mirror.

"I'm so pleased they want us to continue," said Tristan. Kate could see he also looked relieved that there would be money coming into the agency for another month. "Did you think Bill was hesitant to keep us on?"

Kate nodded.

"I don't know if he would rather the police take over the investigation." They were now driving up the winding roads toward the motorway at the top of the hill. "Let's pay another visit to Jesper's. I want to try and meet with Nick Lacey."

41

Tristan parked the car opposite the pavement terrace outside Jesper's. It was busy with the lunchtime rush, and the tables were full. There were even two groups of people waiting on the street with menus, which was something Kate had never seen in Exeter.

They got out of the car and ran into Bishop at the main entrance. He was carrying a tray of drinks.

"Hey, Tristan," he said. "Do you want lunch? Cos I might be able to squeeze you in just after one . . ."

"No. Thank you. We wanted to talk to Max," said Tristan.

"He's not here—he's on holiday. Gone to visit his sister in Spain," said Bishop.

"Do you know how long he'll be away?"

"He's back next Thursday, the fourth."

"Is Nick Lacey here?" asked Kate.

Bishop pulled a face.

"No. Nick's never here . . ." A gray-haired man in glasses was raising his hand. Bishop smiled and indicated the tray of drinks. "I'd better go. Are you sure you don't want lunch? It's my last shift."

"No, thank you," said Tristan. They came back to the car, and he felt deflated. Max Jesper's timing wasn't great. "What do you want to do?" he asked Kate.

"A week is too long to wait. We've got Max Jesper's home address from the Companies House records, haven't we? What about we drive up and have a look. Perhaps Nick Lacey is there," said Kate.

"Okay. Let's put it in my GPS," said Tristan, tapping it into his phone. "Burnham-on-Sea is an hour away, not too bad."

———

They drove up on the M5 motorway for most of the journey north. Neither of them had been to Somerset before. When they came off the motorway, it was a short journey into Burnham-on-Sea, which had a long stretch of coastline. They passed through the touristy area, where the beaches and promenade were busy with people sunbathing and eating ice creams. A warm burst of song from a Salvation Army brass band floated on the air, and the smell of fish and chips and candy floss mingled in the sunny breeze. Farther along the seafront, a crowd of children and parents sat in front of a Punch-and-Judy show close to an amusement arcade.

Then the crowds started to thin out as the promenade turned into an ordinary road, and the beach grew wilder. They came to a fork, and Tristan's GPS instructed them to take the road on the right. This led away from the seafront; the pavement disappeared, and a row of detached houses sprang up between them and the beach. They passed the houses, which were big, with huge plots of land. The road seemed very quiet, and then they saw why. It came to a dead end with a tall metal gate and a high wall. A sign on the gate said LANDSCOMBE GATED COMMUNITY.

"In five hundred meters, you'll reach your destination," said the GPS in the clipped, slightly surprised-sounding female voice.

There was an intercom next to the gate, and beyond, they could see a row of luxurious-looking houses on the seafront.

"Shall I ring the intercom?" asked Tristan. Kate looked around and turned to look back through the rearview mirror.

"Let's go back to that fork in the road. It looks like that road leads to the beach. See if we can get closer to their house on foot," said Kate.

Tristan put the car in reverse and turned round in front of the gate. The GPS voice started telling them to turn around, and Tristan muted it. When they got back to the fork, he took the left turn.

The road ran alongside a wild, rugged beach lined with sand dunes and marram grass. They now passed the row of houses from the beach side, and they were all perched elegantly on a hill and set back from the beach.

"It should be just up here," said Tristan, peering at the map on the GPS as they passed a large, crumbling gray house with a pillared entrance. It was the only house with an overgrown front lawn.

Just after this house, the tarmac road ended, and Tristan's car bounced along an unmade road of sand and grass. It ended at a small parking area for three or four cars and a low metal barrier where a footpath led onto the beach.

"Those houses there must be in the gated community," said Tristan, indicating the footpath. A group of four houses spaced far apart sat up on a hill a hundred meters from the beach.

As Kate and Tristan got out of the car, the sun disappeared behind a thick layer of silvery clouds, and it was colder than it had been in Exeter. Directly in front of the car were the dunes and a vast, empty expanse of burnt-orange-colored sand. The wind was blowing this fine sand into undulating ridges. The sand beyond the dunes was darker and looked wet, but it seemed to stretch out for a mile or more. Kate couldn't judge the exact distance, but she couldn't see the water's edge. The wet expanse of sand was flat and dotted with pools of seawater. A group of gulls hovered above a large pool of water and were cawing as they dove down to pick at shells. A thin mist was rolling off the water, and it suddenly felt more like autumn than early summer.

It was an eerie, deserted spot, thought Kate. The patch of beach in Thurlow Bay was cut off from Ashdean, but it never felt lonely. She thought back to Jake's visits when he was small and how he used to love wading and exploring the rock pools at low tide. This patch of beach, in comparison, felt hostile.

Kate crossed her arms, feeling chills in just her thin jeans and T-shirt. She took a sweater out of the car and pulled it on, and Tristan did the same.

They followed the footpath, which ran between the beach and a strip of ferns and weeds, for a hundred yards. They came to a big metal sign planted in the sand. Tristan had seen it before in one of the pictures Bishop had shown him.

"Warning, do not walk or drive any kind of vehicle out to the soft sand and mud at low tide," said Kate, reading the sign. "Do you think that's low tide? It's really far out."

"Looks like it," said Tristan. He turned and pointed out a large LA-style white box with a paved terrace and landscaped gardens. "And that looks like Max Jesper's house."

There was one more house beyond, a small redbrick bungalow that was dwarfed in comparison. Max's house was surrounded by a tall wall with white cladding. A steep sand track ran up alongside the sidewall, perpendicular with the seafront. It was wide enough for a car, and the sand was churned up from footfall. There was a metal bollard in the middle of the track with a sign on it that read **NO ACCESS. DEAD END.**

"I bet that leads up to the house and the private road on top," said Kate.

They started to walk up the track alongside the wall bordering the property. It was almost two meters in height, so they couldn't see into the back garden.

"It's hard going in the sand," said Kate, panting. She was wearing a thin pair of trainers.

"Good for the leg muscles," said Tristan. At the top, there was another bollard, and the track opened out onto the private road. There was a large garage door in the wall, which was closed, and next to it a small front door, made of steel. There was no number, and no handle— just a keyhole. There was a small intercom to the side, and Kate was about to press it when the steel door opened.

An elderly lady wearing a pleated tartan skirt and a woolen fleece and Wellington boots came out. She had a carrier bag filled with fruit, and a key in her hand. She looked up and saw them.

"Oh! You made me jump," she said. "Can I help you?" She had a soft Scottish accent, and she looked at Kate and Tristan suspiciously.

"Hi. We were just about to ring the bell for Nick," said Kate, thinking quickly. "We're friends from Exeter passing through. Is he in?"

"Yes. Hello," said Tristan, smiling.

"No, he's not in," she said.

"Oh. We knew that Max is in Spain to see his sister . . . He's back next week, on the fourth, isn't he?" said Kate, thanking God that they'd run into Bishop at Jesper's.

The elderly lady relaxed a little.

"You're their neighbor, aren't you? It's . . ." Kate hesitated.

"Elspeth," she said. She came out of the doorway and closed the door.

"Of course, hello. I'm Maureen, and this is John."

"Hi," said Tristan, looking at Kate.

She was thinking on her feet, and these were the only two names that had popped in her head at short notice.

"Nice to meet you. Nick's away until Monday . . . Whenever they're away, they ask me to pop in and water the plants, check the post. Feed the fish. They've got lots of fish in their pond," said Elspeth.

"Do you live close by?" asked Kate.

"I'm next door, the wee bungalow next to this huge compound . . . They do have me over often, and I swim in their pool a couple of mornings a week, so I can't complain. They're lovely lads . . . How do you know them from Exeter?" she asked inquisitively, peering up at them.

"We go to Jesper's often, their bar. They're always saying that we must pop in when we're in the area," said Tristan. "We've been in Birmingham for the day."

Elspeth locked the door and pocketed the key. "Can I leave them a message? Although I probably won't talk to them on the phone," she said. She started to walk back down the track toward the beach. Kate and Tristan followed.

"No. It's fine. I'll send them an email. I'll probably run into Max when he's back next week," said Kate.

"Righto. Is that you parked down there?"

"Yes. The beach is so different here than it is further down with the promenade," said Kate. "The tide goes so far out."

Elspeth followed Kate's gaze down to the beach.

"The tide isn't fully out. People think that's it, but it goes out way further. Burnham-on-Sea has the second-highest tidal range in the world. The tides range eleven meters from high to low. We're second only to the Bay of Fundy in Canada," she said.

"How far out can you walk?" asked Tristan.

"I wouldn't go much further out than you can see there," said Elspeth. "And even then, you must keep an eye out because it comes in very fast, and there are patches of sinking mud out on the flats. There are patrols down the coast in the high season . . . Nick, bless him, gets very concerned when he sees people out walking when the tide's low . . . I've often seen him go and start shouting at people to come back. Has he told you about his hovercraft?"

"No."

"He's got this wee hovercraft, the same one as the lifeboat people use. It's the only thing you can take far out on the mudflats because it hovers."

"How much does a hovercraft cost?" asked Kate.

"I don't know. Probably more than I get in a whole year for my pension," Elspeth chuckled. "He helped pull a wee doggy out last summer. Even when the mud is shallow, it's thick like porridge, and you can get into trouble, like this woman did with her basset hound . . . You must have seen the reports on the local news?"

"The story of a basset hound getting stuck made the news?" asked Tristan. They'd now reached the bottom of the track.

"Of course not," said Elspeth, flashing Tristan a flirtatious smile. "I meant people getting stuck in the sand, it often makes the local news . . . There isn't a summer that goes by without a person or some foolish picnickers who drive out on the sand and then have to abandon their cars when they get stuck and the tide comes roaring back in."

"Are they here often, Nick and Max?"

"A few days a week. They both have busy jobs . . . How well do you know them?" she said, shielding her eyes from the sun, which had just come out from behind a cloud.

"They seem to travel around so much—I'm used to seeing them in Exeter," said Kate.

"You must come to their summer parties?"

"Yes, we enjoyed the masked ball last August, with the ice sculpture . . . I don't remember seeing you there?" said Tristan.

"I'm too old for all that. I prefer to see the boys for morning coffee. Although Nick seems to always be away; I never get to see them together . . . Right. I'd better be off. Nice to meet you."

"Lovely to meet you, bye," said Kate. Elspeth gave them a nod and started along the sandy footpath to her bungalow.

As Kate and Tristan walked down to the car, Kate watched Elspeth picking her way along the footpath, and was pleased to see she didn't turn to look back at them.

"I don't know if I overdid it."

"Where did you get Maureen and John?" asked Tristan.

"I don't know."

"Good thinking on your feet, though. It sounds like she's a good friend of theirs."

"Or is she just a nosy old biddy to keep an eye on their house whilst they're away? I wonder why she was leaving with a bag of fruit. She was probably nicking it. Let's go," she said, shivering. They got in the car.

"It's like the end of the earth," said Tristan. He started the engine and turned on the heater. He turned the car around in the small parking area and then drove back down the sandy track. Thick cotton wool–like clumps of mist came drifting in front of the car, breaking away from the mist on the sand.

"We need to come back on Monday. I'm determined to talk to Nick Lacey," said Kate.

42

Kate and Tristan spent the journey home discussing their next move. The traffic was bad along the M5, so they didn't get back until five, and by that time, they were both tired and hungry.

"Let's get a good night's sleep and meet tomorrow," said Kate when Tristan dropped her home.

She texted Jake to find out where he was, and he said he was coming back from a diving trip and would be home at seven.

Kate decided to make dinner for a change, rather than heating things up or ordering in. She could cook only a couple of things, and one of them was Jake's favorite, chili con carne. Kate had the things she needed, and she set to work, glad of a distraction from the case. When Jake came in just before seven, she was happy to see his face light up with a smile.

"Chili con carne? Sweet!" he said. "You need a hand?"

"No. It'll be ready in ten minutes; I'm just making the rice," she said. "Do you want to eat outside? It's lovely and warm."

"Cool," said Jake. He went to the fridge and got himself a beer and Kate an iced tea, and then he went out and sat on the porch.

When she came outside with two bowls of steaming chili, Jake was sitting in one of the chairs, looking out at a beautiful sunset.

"This smells goooood," he said, taking the bowl of chili and a fork.

Kate sat in the chair opposite, and they started eating.

"How was the diving trip?" she asked.

"It was nice, just me and this girl, Becca. She's the blonde-haired girl you saw the other day when you were in the car. She's staying at the site with her mates."

"She's pretty."

"She is, and she looks really good in a bikini," said Jake. He put another forkful of chili in his mouth and smiled. "This is the second time she's asked me to take her diving."

"That's cool. How old is she?"

Jake shrugged. "Twenty, I think. She's in her third year at uni."

"Is it serious?"

"No. She's leaving on Saturday morning. It's just been nice, casual."

"Are you being careful?" said Kate, hating to ask the question but needing to make sure.

"Mum, Jesus, I'm eating," he said, going red.

"Just tell me yes or no, and then we can change the subject."

"Yes, I'm being careful . . . I'm the one who fills up the condom machine in the men's shower block so there's no shortage."

Kate started to laugh. "Okay, I'm your mother—I don't need to hear that much detail."

"You're my mother and my father, so I have to talk about everything with you," he said.

Kate's phone rang. She didn't recognize the number and answered.

"Hi. Kate. It's Marnie. Jo's friend."

Kate swallowed a mouthful of chili.

"Hi," she said cautiously. There was a long pause.

"Listen. I'm sorry if I put you on the spot the other day, about signing the book . . . It's just that I'm on disability benefits, and they've recently been cut by the government. The kids' dad doesn't give me much support. It's hard trying to bring up two kids on piss-poor money, and I can't work. If I could work full time, I would."

Kate felt a sinking feeling in her stomach. Jake mouthed, *Who is it?* Kate shook her head.

"Marnie. I'm sorry. I'm really sorry, but I feel the same as before. I don't want to sign that book. I don't want to be part of this whole ghoulish exploitation," said Kate.

Marnie went silent on the end of the phone. Kate expected her to unleash a barrage of swearing, but Marnie just said, "Okay. Well, there you go. I thought it was worth a try."

There was a click, and the line went dead. Kate stared at her phone for a moment, feeling sick.

"What was that about?" asked Jake. Kate told him about Marnie and the copy of *No Son of Mine* that had already been signed by Peter and Enid.

"I think you should sign it, Mum," he said.

"But that's exploiting . . ." Kate couldn't finish the sentence; she was too shocked. She hadn't expected him to say that.

"Mum. It's all in the past. Peter did what he did. So did Enid. The book is written. It's out there. All this awful stuff that happened to you, to all those poor women. You can make good out of it. You can help this Marnie out just by signing your name. You say she'll get two grand for the book?"

"Yes."

"And she's got young kids?"

"Yes," said Kate.

"Just sign it, Mum. Two grand will probably go a long way for her," he said. Chewing the last of his food, he got up. "Thanks for the chili, it was awesome." He kissed her on top of the head. "Oh, sorry. I just got chili mince in your hair," he said, wiping his mouth.

Kate reached up and felt the lump of chewed mince sitting in her parting. He picked it off and flicked it into the dunes.

"What a lovely way to say thank you," she laughed.

"Yuck, sorry, Mum." Jake's phone rang, and he picked it up. "Yeah. I can see you; I'll be down in a sec," he said into the phone and hung up. "I'm meeting the guys on the beach. Thanks again for dinner."

Before Kate could say anything, Jake was gone, climbing down the sandy cliffside between the dunes. She could see that the group of young guys and girls from the campsite, including Becca, were on the beach. The boys were building a fire, and two of the girls were sitting on the edge of a giant piece of driftwood.

Kate watched as Jake hurried down the last part of the cliff and ran through the dunes. He slowed when he emerged on the other side.

"How did you turn into such a good kid, Jake?" she said to herself. When Jake reached the group on the beach, Becca got up and gave him a hug and a kiss. "If you tell me I'm going to be a grandma, I'll kill you."

She pulled a tiny piece of stray mince from her hair, picked up the bowls, and went indoors to the kitchen; then she phoned Marnie.

43

Kate was up early the next morning. It was already warm at six thirty a.m., and she saw the remnants of the fire when she walked down to the beach. She was pleased to see that there was no litter—just the smoldering remains of the fire surrounded by a rough ring of rocks. She'd heard Jake come in at two twenty a.m., so she'd left him sleeping.

The water was beautiful, and it was getting warmer by the day. After she ate breakfast, showered, and dressed, she texted Tristan to say she'd be a bit late back to the office, and then she drove over to the Moor Side Estate.

The car park was empty. The burned-out cars still there, like pieces of modern art. Kate met Marnie at the entrance to the building—she was moving slowly and leaning on her crutch.

"I'm just back from dropping the kids at school," she said, not wanting to meet Kate's eye. The journey up the stairs looked slow and painful for Marnie, and she was out of breath when they reached the front door.

"Would you like a cuppa?" she asked as they went inside.

"Yes, thank you," said Kate, regretting her answer as soon as it was out of her mouth. She just wanted to sign the book and go.

The door to the living room was closed, and there was the same oppressive smell of stale cigarettes and air freshener. When they got to the kitchen, the book was waiting on the table with a blue ballpoint pen next to it.

Kate sat at the table as Marnie filled the kettle. She pulled the book toward her. It was the hardback edition, and the dustcover was a little yellowed at the edges. The title was in bold black letters over the cover image.

NO SON OF MINE
ENID CONWAY

The cover image was a split-pane photograph. On the right was a picture of a sixteen-year-old Enid Conway cradling baby Peter. The picture was blurred in a nostalgic way, and baby Peter's eyes were wide and staring at the camera, while Enid looked down at him adoringly. Enid was a hard-faced young woman with a shock of long dark hair. She wore a long flowing dress, and behind her was the sign AULDEARN UNMARRIED MOTHERS' HOME. Through a window behind Enid and Peter was the blurred image of a nun, in full penguin habit, staring out at them.

The other half of the cover was a police mug shot of Peter Conway, which was taken on the day he gave evidence at his preliminary trial. In this photo, his hands were cuffed, and he was smirking at the camera. His eyes were wild and pupils dilated. This was before he'd started on the cocktail of drugs to deal with his schizophrenia and dissociative identity disorder.

"Is it hard to look at, the book cover?" asked Marnie. Kate didn't know she'd been staring at it for so long. Marnie had made two mugs of tea and was putting one on the table in front of her.

"Yes. You see in the mug shot, Peter has stitches above his left eyebrow?" said Kate, tapping her finger on the photo. "That's where I hit him with a lamp when he was attacking me . . ." Kate stood up and lifted her T-shirt to show Marnie the six-inch scar on her abdomen, which curved close to her belly button. "And that's where he sliced me open. I was four months pregnant with Jake; I didn't know that at the time. The doctor said the knife missed him by millimeters. It was a miracle he wasn't killed . . ." Marnie was nodding with her mouth slightly open in shock. "So, when I said no about signing this book, I had my reasons, don't you think?"

"Yes," said Marnie softly. "What made you change your mind?"

"Jake did. He's my little miracle. It made me think about your kids, and how you need help."

Kate took a deep breath, opened the book, and found the title page. She signed her name between Enid's and Peter's names. She blew on the ink to make sure it was dry and wouldn't smudge, and she closed the book.

"Thank you," said Marnie.

"You should ask for two and a half grand. I had a look last night, and there's a bloke in America who sold this book with just Peter's signature for three thousand dollars on eBay," said Kate.

Marnie nodded. They sipped their tea in silence for a moment.

"I saw on the news about that lad and Noah Huntley. They mentioned Jo too. Do you think they'll reopen the investigation?" asked Marnie.

"I hope so. We're still working on the case . . . I think that the commune on Walpole Street is the answer. The missing guys that Joanna was investigating lived there. Quite a few of the men we're looking at visited the commune and then invested in the hotel, but the owner, Max Jesper, and his partner, Nick Lacey, seem to be evading us."

Marnie frowned and sat back in her chair.

"What?" asked Kate.

"Nick Lacey?"

"Yes. Didn't I mention him before?"

"No."

"Do you know him?"

"No, but the name sticks in my mind."

"Why?"

"You know I told you that the day after Jo went missing, I backed into that brand-new BMW? The guy who owned it was called Nick Lacey."

"There's probably more than one Nick Lacey," said Kate, trying not to get too excited. "What did he look like?"

Marnie shrugged.

"I don't know. I left my details under his windscreen wiper. And then I only heard from his solicitor . . . I don't know what possessed me to own up. I should have just driven off. It cost me a fortune to claim on my insurance and his. I lost my no-claims bonus," she said.

"Do you remember Nick Lacey's address?" asked Kate, her mind moving fast. *If it was the same Nick Lacey, why would he have been parked outside the morning after Joanna went missing?*

"No, but I keep stuff. I might still have the claim forms," said Marnie. She got up and went to a drawer in the kitchen. It was full of paperwork, and she started to dig around. Marnie then went out into the corridor and down to the living room, where she opened the door. Kate heard her opening drawers and cupboards; she came back a few minutes later with a piece of paper.

"Here, this is it. The insurance claim papers," said Marnie, handing the sheet of paper to Kate. "He's local, Nick Lacey. He's got a Devon and Cornwall address."

44

Tristan had just arrived at the office and was making coffee when Kate burst in holding a piece of paper. She went straight to her laptop, opened it, and started typing.

"Morning?" said Tristan.

"Sorry! Morning," said Kate. He joined her at her laptop. "Look at this," she added, handing him a piece of paper.

"It's a car insurance claim form between Marnie Prince and *Nick Lacey*?" he said, reading it. He watched as Kate logged on to the UK Companies House website, where you could check the details of people who are limited company directors. She found the entry for Nick Lacey. There was a list of confirmation statements going back to 1997.

"What are confirmation statements?" asked Tristan.

"Every year, company directors have to either confirm their details are the same, or they have to update any changes," said Kate. "What's his address on the form?"

"Thirteen Maple Terrace, Exeter, EX14," said Tristan. He looked up. Kate had the same address on the screen.

"Jesus. It's the same Nick Lacey," said Kate.

"What's happened?"

Kate told him about visiting Marnie and finding out that Nick Lacey owned the car that Marnie had reversed into the morning after Joanna went missing.

"Nick Lacey owned a top-of-the-range BMW. Maple Terrace is miles away. It's a posh area of Exeter. Why would he be parking his car on the Moor Side Estate?" asked Kate. "And Marnie said she backed into Nick Lacey's car early in the morning, the day after Joanna went missing, so he could have parked there the night before."

"Bev said her car was stolen from the same place on the night Joanna went missing," said Tristan.

"It's too much of a coincidence. Nick Lacey is linked to the commune, which links to David Lamb and, potentially, Gabe Kemp, and their deaths are linked to Hayden Oakley."

Kate called up the case files on the computer.

"What are you looking for?" asked Tristan.

"I want to get it straight in my head where everyone was on the night Joanna went missing. Can we print off everyone's statements?"

"We don't have a statement from Nick."

"No, I want to see the details of where Fred, Bev, and Bill were, and Marnie . . . There's something bothering me—an idea."

Kate got up from the chair, and Tristan sat down. He pulled up the police statements from Fred, Bev, Marnie, and Bill and printed them off.

Kate went to the whiteboard and wiped it clean.

"Okay. Let's start with Joanna. She was at work on Saturday, September seventh, 2002. How did she get to work?"

"Fred said she took their car, which was a blue Ford. She left around eight thirty in the morning, and we know she was at work all day. She left work at five thirty p.m. and walked up to the Deansgate multistory car park. She was photographed close to the bus stop at five forty-one p.m., and that's the last known sighting of her."

"Okay, on to Fred. He's at home all day. Having it away with Famke in the afternoon. He's expecting Joanna home at six, but she doesn't show up. He tries Joanna's phone a few times after six p.m., and it's switched off. He then phones Bev, who is at home in her flat on the Moor Side Estate . . ."

"Then they—" started Tristan.

"Hang on, let's deal with where Bill and Bev were up to that point," said Kate.

Tristan flicked through the statements until he found Bev's. "Okay. Bill and Bev went to Killerton House in Devon on Saturday the seventh. It's a National Trust house twenty miles outside Exeter. They left at nine a.m. . . ."

"How did they get there?" asked Kate.

"By car. Bev picked up Bill in her car, and then they drove to Killerton House, arriving just after ten a.m. They spent the day there until four p.m., when they came back because Bill was called into work."

"Where?"

Tristan could see Kate was getting impatient.

"Do you want to switch? I'll write on the board?" he said.

"No. Sorry, I'm not annoyed with you. I've just got this niggling thing in my head. You know when you know something, but it's just out of your grasp?"

"Bill's work was an office block they had under construction, Teybridge House. It's quite close to where Bev lived on the Moor Side Estate. They left Killerton House at four p.m., and drove over to Teybridge House in Bev's car . . . Bev then walked home from Teybridge House to her flat on the Moor Side Estate, leaving her car with Bill. He says in his statement that he stayed at Teybridge House until eight thirty, then drove Bev's car back to her flat."

"So around eight forty-five or nine p.m. on Saturday night, Bev's car was back parked on the road at the Moor Side Estate?" asked Kate.

"According to Bill's statement. Yes."

"But at eight p.m., Bev was no longer at her flat."

"Yes. Fred had phoned Bev at seven p.m., asking if Joanna was with her, saying she hadn't come home from work. Bev tries ringing Bill a few times, but his phone is also off. Bev asks Fred to come and get her in his car so they can go out and look for Joanna," said Tristan.

"Fred leaves home at seven thirty p.m. and shows up at the Moor Side Estate in his car around seven forty-five p.m. He picks up Bev, and they drive back into Exeter and go to the multistory car park, where they find Joanna's car with her phone underneath. Bev calls the police. They say that Joanna can't be classed as missing until twenty-four hours have passed, so Bev and Fred start driving around the local hospitals to try and find her," said Kate.

"Bev tries calling her flat at a quarter to nine, using a phone box, as neither her or Fred owned a mobile phone. Bill answers the landline, and says he just got in and tells her his phone battery died. Bev tells him that Joanna is missing. He agrees to stay at Bev's flat in case Joanna shows up there. Fred and Bev continue driving around the local hospitals, but they have no luck finding Joanna. Fred drops Bev back at her flat just before midnight. Fred drives home in case Joanna has showed up there but confirms to Bev half an hour later that she didn't," said Tristan. There was a long silence as they looked at the timeline Kate had written on the whiteboard.

"At some point that night, or early morning, Nick Lacey parks his BMW outside the Moor Side Estate," said Kate. "What if Nick and Bill know each other? Bill was on his own at the flat from eight forty-five p.m. until midnight, when Fred dropped Bev back at the flat. They could have met?"

"Bill also has the time from when he went to work at four forty-five p.m. until he got back to the flat at eight forty-five p.m., and then between eight forty-five and midnight," said Tristan.

"He answered the landline at Bev's house at eight forty-five," said Kate.

"Okay, Bev says in her statement that she phoned him again at ten thirty and he answered," said Tristan, reading from the case file.

Kate came over to the computer and searched through the case file folders.

"Two of the construction site workers at Teybridge House gave Bill his alibi to say that he arrived at the site just after four forty-five p.m. on Saturday, September seventh, and stayed for around four hours, leaving just before eight forty p.m. Where are they? Here. Raj Bilal and Malik Hopkirk are the two witnesses who worked there . . ."

Tristan watched as Kate scrolled through the scanned statements.

"They're both signed, I checked," he said.

"The two people willing to go on the record and give Bill an alibi are both construction workers, working for him, and presumably on a low-income wage. Could they have been lying for him?" said Kate.

"Isn't the bigger question why Nick Lacey was also parked outside Bev's flat on the same night?" asked Tristan.

"Yes. Why would you park a top-of-the-range BMW on that dodgy estate overnight?"

"What if Nick had a lover? A bit of rough on the council estate?" asked Tristan.

"We seem to constantly be asking 'what if' and 'who is he' questions about Nick Lacey. But are we asking the right questions? So far, we've heard that he's a highly successful, rather ruthless businessman. His neighbor Elspeth says he's a lovely man. He was around when Max had the commune, which means he could have met David Lamb, Gabe Kemp, and Jorge Tomassini."

Kate's phone rang.

"Speaking of. It's Jorge Tomassini," she said, answering the call and putting it on speakerphone.

"Hi, Kate," said Jorge. "Listen, I had a look in my attic, and I found my photos from when I was living in England. There are eight packets of twenty-four photos. I scanned them all."

Tristan clenched his fists and mouthed, *Yes!*

"That's very kind of you, thank you," said Kate.

"I scanned them in groups of eight on the scanner at work. It saved time. You'll have to zoom in on the photos."

"As long as they're clear images, that's brilliant," said Kate.

"There's quite a few from the commune, when I went to a couple of parties there. There's one of me and my boyfriend at the time with Noah Huntley, a couple of Max, and one of me sitting on the sofa in the commune with Max and his boyfriend, Nick Lacey."

"This is so helpful, thank you," said Kate.

"Okay. I'll get my assistant to email them over," he said.

Ten minutes later, the photos came through, spread in two emails. Kate and Tristan went to their laptops. Each JPEG image in the folders contained a scan of eight photos. They downloaded the images and started to scroll through. There was a photo of an intoxicated-looking Noah Huntley, red-faced, with his arm draped over Jorge and a muscular blond-haired youth.

"Jesus Christ," said Kate, when she came to the photo of Jorge and Max sitting on a sofa with a third man. "Tristan, come and look at this."

Tristan got up and came round to look at her computer screen. "Jesus Christ, indeed," he said. "That's Nick Lacey?"

"Yes . . . ," said Kate, shaking with shock. "Oh my God. That photo is it. The key that makes this all fall into place."

45

Late on Saturday night, Nick Lacey was driving through Southampton on his way back from a business trip.

Whenever he visited Southampton, his route home went through its own unofficial red-light district. The street was brightly lit by the lights from the busy dockside, and over the years, attempts had been made to clean it up and banish the curb crawlers. It was one of those streets in Britain that reinvents itself every hundred meters, moving from run-down to residential and then back again.

He'd circled the block twice, passing the same brightly lit gay pub, checking if there were any street cameras or CCTV.

A hundred meters from the pub, in the shadows of a broken streetlamp, he noticed a young guy hanging around. Tall and athletic with a strong jaw. On his third pass around the block, Nick slowed by the streetlamp and wound down his window.

"Hi," he said.

"Hi," said the young guy, looking him up and down. "Nice car." He wore skinny blue jeans; expensive, new-looking white trainers; and a thin V-neck T-shirt. Nick could see he had broad, muscly shoulders and developed leg muscles.

"What you up to tonight?" asked Nick.

"What do you think?" he said, moving closer to the window and looking through the gap. He had an affected aggression that made Nick laugh. Like he was performing.

"I think you're a dirty fucking whore, and that's just what I'm looking for," said Nick.

The young lad's face showed a flash of hurt, and Nick drank it in. Suddenly, he was desperate to pick this young guy up. He kept eye contact to see if the young guy would look away. He didn't.

"What's your name?" asked Nick.

"Mario."

"What's your *real* name? I'll pay you more if I can use your real name . . ."

There was a long pause, and a blast of wind blew around the car, stirring up the leaves and rubbish by the curb and blowing his brown hair. He looked down at his feet, and Nick wondered what he needed the money for. To live? To buy drugs? To buy more of those white trainers?

"It's Paul."

"Hi, Paul. How much for the whole night?"

"Three hundred cash, up front."

Paul smelled of aftershave and soap.

"Come round to the passenger side," said Nick and closed the window. He watched Paul walk behind the car and wondered why he was in such a rough area on the street. The good-looking ones were moving over to using the phone apps. It was easier, and safer to a degree, and of course there was a digital trail of bread crumbs should the police get involved.

A police car appeared up ahead, and Paul must have noticed it, because he carried on past behind Nick's car and crossed the street and started off down the road in the other direction.

Nick opened the console between the front seats and looked down at the neatly stocked champagne and Coke bottles in the minifridge. He slammed it shut.

It was then that he came to his senses and realized he'd been on autopilot. He'd come so close to picking up Paul. He never picked up young men as himself. The first few times, he'd done it as Nick Lacey, but that was years ago, and the more he got away with it, the more there was to lose. So he'd started using different names and disguises, small alterations to his appearance to make him look different. Steve, Graham, Frank, and Tom, his most recent alter ego when he'd picked up Hayden Oakley.

He'd been checking the news every day to see if the police had charged Noah Huntley. They were questioning him, and no doubt waiting for the DNA results to come back from the underwear that Nick had planted in his car.

It put him in a bind. If Noah Huntley went to trial and was convicted for the murders of David Lamb, Gabe Kemp, and those two other men whose names now escaped him, he was off the hook. It would also mean that he'd have to change his methods if he wished to carry on.

The police car reached the end of the long road and turned off to the right.

Paul came walking out of the side road where he'd been waiting, and Nick saw him coming back.

He gripped the wheel of the car. The desire to capture and torture this young buck into submission and death was overwhelming.

He mentally wrenched himself away, and with the smell of Paul's aftershave still in the air, he put the car in gear and pulled out, heading back to Burnham-on-Sea.

46

Kate could see Tristan was scared as they drove up to Burnham-on-Sea early Monday morning to confront Nick Lacey. She felt apprehensive, too, at the prospect of them coming face-to-face. They'd spent the past day tracking down additional witnesses and verifying details.

It had been sunny and warm when they left Ashdean, but the weather deteriorated as they drove on the M5, and it was cloudy and overcast in Burnham-on-Sea. They parked in the same spot as before. The wind was roaring across the vast, empty beach, blowing the sand in drifts toward them.

"Are you ready for this?" Kate asked Tristan.

"No," said Tristan. "Have you got the photo?"

Kate nodded.

He locked the car, and they started walking up the sandy track toward Nick Lacey's house. Part of Kate was hoping that Nick wouldn't be back from his business trip, but as they were halfway up the track, Elspeth appeared from the house, walking toward them, swinging her stick.

"Good morning!" she said cheerily. She wore a thick headscarf and sunglasses.

Kate and Tristan wished her a good morning and went to carry on walking.

"We seem to get the brunt of the wind screaming across the Bristol Channel," she said. "But we do get a few nice days too!" The wind had strengthened, and she had to shout the last part. To their right was the field of ferns and weeds, and the sand made a crackling sound as it blew up from the beach and hit the leaves. "Are you looking for Nick?" she shouted after them.

"Yes," said Kate.

"He's in. I've just come from there for my regular early-morning coffee," shouted Elspeth. She staggered a little as she was buffeted by the wind. "This wind doesn't seem to be letting up," she said, and with a wave, she put her head down and carried on walking toward the beach.

"She doesn't know, does she?" said Tristan.

"Course not," said Kate.

It was an easier walk with the wind at her back. They reached the front door, far too quickly for Kate's liking.

"The important thing is to keep him talking," she said. "I have my Mace."

"Do you think you'll need it? It could backfire on us if you use it . . . It's not legal to carry."

"It's an absolute last resort."

Tristan nodded and swallowed. "Do you think he knows we're coming?"

"We're John and Maureen, remember?" said Kate, trying to make a joke, but neither of them laughed. "Okay?"

Tristan nodded.

"Okay."

Kate leaned over and rang the bell. A moment passed, and then another. The wind seemed to scream up from the beach.

What if he refuses to answer the door? thought Kate. *What if that neighbor told him we'd been here last week and he started to put things together?*

Kate and Tristan jumped when there was the crack of a bolt being shot home, and then the door opened slowly.

Bill was standing in front of them, carrying a washing basket filled with laundry.

There was a moment where they all froze. The 1998 photo taken at the party in the commune had shown Jorge sitting on a sofa with Max and Bill on either side of him. They'd spoken to Jorge again, and he'd confirmed, again, that the person sitting with him and Max was Nick Lacey. It had been a shock to discover that Bill and Nick Lacey were the same person. It was a bigger shock to see it confirmed by Bill opening the door of the house he shared with Max Jesper.

Bill looked between them and opened and closed his mouth. He then seemed to compose himself and smiled. It was an off-kilter smile. His eyes were slightly crazed and bright.

"Hello," he said.

"Hello, Bill," said Kate. "Or should we call you Nick?"

Behind Bill was a long, airy hallway with a wide table under a mirror. On the table, Kate could see a selection of personal photos in gold and silver frames. Bill saw where Kate was looking and moved into the gap made by the door.

She took the photo out of her pocket.

"Do you remember this party, Bill? Back in 1998 at the commune on Walpole Street?"

In the photo of Max and Bill sitting on the sofa with Jorge Tomassini, Bill was raising his hand to cover his face, but he hadn't been quick enough. It was very clear who was in the photo.

"Jorge Tomassini sent us this photo late yesterday afternoon. He also identified you as Nick Lacey. Max Jesper's boyfriend," said Tristan.

Bill stood very still, blocking the doorway. Tristan put out his hand and shoved the door open again. Kate pushed past him and into the hall.

"Hang on!" said Bill. He tried to grab Kate's arm, but she twisted out of his grip. Tristan remained on his other side, blocking the door.

Kate went to the hall table and picked up one of the photos in a silver frame. It was a picture of Bill and Max Jesper sitting in a rubber dinghy against a backdrop that looked like the Grand Canyon. Bill had his arm around Max's shoulder. She put the photo down and picked up the second, which was in a gold frame. The picture was taken of Bill and Max in a garden. They both wore suits and bow ties; Max had his arm around Bill, and they were smiling.

"You didn't answer me. What should we call you? Bill or Nick?" said Kate. "Which came first, Bill or Nick?"

All the color had drained from Bill's face, and he took a step back and leaned on the wall. His shoulders sagged, and he dropped the washing basket. Tristan stepped into the hallway and closed the front door behind him. He moved past Bill to the table of photographs.

It was a surreal moment. None of them spoke.

"You don't understand," said Bill quietly. He swallowed and seemed to compose himself.

"How long have you been Bill and Nick?" asked Tristan.

"Too long," he said. "Bill is my birth name. Nick came later."

He eyed the landline phone sitting on the hall table, and then he ran for it, pushing past Kate and Tristan and running deeper into the house, vanishing around the corner.

"Don't let him go," said Kate. They moved down the hallway, which opened out into a large kitchen and living room area with floor-to-ceiling windows looking over the garden with a pool and terrace and the beach beyond. There were back doors leading out, but they were closed.

"Upstairs," said Tristan, pointing to a staircase. Kate and Tristan climbed the steps two at a time. On the second floor was a long corridor with a skylight, and rooms leading off it. They could hear sounds coming from the second room along the landing. Kate put her hand in her bag and found the can of Mace. Tristan went first.

The second door was open. It was an office, similar in style to the office in Bill's house in Salcombe. But there was a glass-fronted cabinet with a row of gleaming black-and-silver break-action shotguns. One of the glass doors was open, and Bill was holding one of the guns. The desk beside him was empty, and on the polished surface sat two shotgun shells.

Kate tried to ignore the feeling of panic as her heart started to race. She was not going to lose it. Tristan reached out and grabbed her arm, stopping her in the doorway.

Bill looked up at them, and he had a strange, vacant look in his eyes. He opened the shotgun. Tristan lunged into the room and swept the shells off the desk. They landed with a clink on the tiled floor and rolled out of sight. Tristan was now standing on the other side of the desk. Bill kept hold of the gun.

"Put the gun down," said Kate, following Tristan into the office.

"You flatter yourself," said Bill to Kate.

"Bill. Give me the gun," said Tristan, holding out his hand.

"And you can fuck off. You're not going to bully me. I HAVE THE GUN!" Bill screamed the last part, and Kate flinched. Bill and Tristan were nearly a match in height and were both well built. Tristan stayed close, with the desk between them. Bill remained standing with the shotgun open in his hand.

Kate put her hand in her bag and felt the can of Mace again. *We have to keep him talking.*

"What about Bev? Does she know that you lead a double life? And that your other life is with a man?"

Bill laughed and shook his head.

"Does Max know?"

"You leave Max out of this! He doesn't know anything. NOTHING!"

"So Max is the one you love. Where does that leave Bev in all this?"

"I love Bev, but . . ."

"But what?" asked Kate.

"I don't have to justify and explain myself to you!" cried Bill.

"You're going to have to justify yourself to the police," said Tristan. "You've been meticulous in crafting these two identities, and presumably other identities when you picked up your victims, but you made one big mistake. Nick Lacey parked his BMW on Bev's road the night that Joanna went missing. But Bill told the police he'd parked Bev's car on the same street that same night. Nick had a top-of-the-range BMW. Bev had an old Renault, but for some reason, this 'thief' chose to steal Bev's car."

Bill laughed at this. "That means nothing. Cars get nicked for all sorts of reasons. Low-level drug dealers nick cars, and they don't want nothing flashy."

Kate nodded. "Yes, true. We went back over your statement for the day Joanna went missing. You were out with Bev at Killerton House and then got a phone call just before four p.m. calling you to work at a construction project at Teybridge House. You drove to Teybridge House with Bev, and she walked home and left her car with you. Two construction site workers, Raj Bilal and Malik Hopkirk, gave you an alibi saying you arrived at four forty-five p.m. and stayed for around four hours."

"Yes," said Bill.

"We've spent the past couple of days tracking them down," said Kate. "Malik Hopkirk died of lung cancer six years ago, but Raj Bilal is alive. We explained our theory to him, and the jail time for lying to the police, and now he's not so sure that you *did* stay at the Teybridge House construction site for four hours. He says you paid him to lie."

"Where's the proof?" said Bill. "It's circumstantial."

"If Bill wasn't at Teybridge House between four forty-five and eight forty p.m. on the evening of September seventh, what did he do for almost four hours?"

Bill stared at them, both hands on the gun. His stare reminded Kate of a dog—a scared dog deciding if it was going to attack or run away. Her hand was sweaty on the can of Mace inside her bag.

"Joanna was trying to get dirt on Noah Huntley, wasn't she? Trying to dig up any dirt she could about Noah hiring rent boys and cheating on his wife," said Kate. "She heard through one of these young guys that Noah Huntley liked to visit Max Jesper's commune on Walpole Street. What she didn't know is that you, Nick Lacey, also liked to visit the commune. Did Max always know you as Nick?"

"Shut up! I told you, he has nothing to do . . ." Bill stopped himself and carried on staring at them. Kate saw Tristan inching closer to Bill, his eyes on the gun.

"The phone call you got at four p.m.—it wasn't from work, was it? It was from Joanna. We think that's when she made the discovery that you and Nick were the same person. And Nick had killed those young men."

Bill gripped the gun, taking deep breaths. "You can't prove any of this. There's no body. No car," he said, almost chanting it like a mantra. "Bev's car got nicked from outside her flat. You can't prove otherwise."

"Then how did Nick's BMW end up outside Bev's flat that night?"

"I'd parked on the road already," said Bill with a triumphant smile.

"Why? On the morning of Saturday, September seventh, Bev picked you up from your flat on the other side of Exeter."

"Okay, I'd parked it there the day before. There was no CCTV on that road," he said.

"You got the call from Joanna. She'd worked out you were Bill and Nick . . ."

"You're fishing. You can't prove it!" he shouted.

"This photo proves it, Bill," said Kate, holding up the photo taken in the commune. "We got this photo from Jorge Tomassini. Joanna had interviewed him about David Lamb, and he'd shown her some photos of the commune. And she'd taken the negatives without asking him. On the day Joanna went missing, one of her colleagues at the newspaper, Rita Hocking, said Joanna picked up some photos that she'd had developed that day, from negatives she'd stolen from Jorge Tomassini.

This photo was amongst the photos that were developed. Jorge said that you had a thing about having your photo taken. This was the only photo in the pack where someone caught you by surprise and managed to get a photo of your face."

"It was Joanna who phoned you that afternoon, wasn't it?" said Tristan. "We know from Raj Bilal that the Teybridge House construction site was closed that day. Joanna saw this photo, worked it out, and phoned you. You asked to meet her, to try and explain yourself before she called the police. After you parted ways with Bev at Teybridge House, you drove to Exeter to meet Joanna at the Deansgate multistory car park. You knew it would be deserted. That's where you grabbed Joanna and killed her, and you used Bev's car to dump her body."

Bill laughed and lifted the gun again.

"I say bollocks. And that's what a jury will say too."

"You were close to Joanna, weren't you?" said Kate.

Bill's face softened a little.

"Of course . . . I wouldn't have hurt one hair on her head!" he said, raising his voice. He slammed the gun down on the table.

"That's why it must have been tough to kill her," said Kate.

"I did not! I did not kill her! You fucking shut your mouth!"

"You did. You abducted her and killed her because she had information about you and your double life. She knew you were responsible for the deaths of David Lamb, Gabe Kemp, and other young men," said Kate. "You put her in Bev's car and drove her here, didn't you, Bill? You drove her up to this house. No one who knew Bill knew of this place. We've spoken to people who came to your summer parties, and we've spoken to your neighbor. They've all talked about Nick's fear of people going down there on the sand when the tide's out. We thought, at first, that you were a Good Samaritan, so scared of people drowning that you have a hovercraft to go patrolling the sand when the tide is low. But that's not the case, is it? You're scared that one day the tide will shift the sand and it will uncover where you've hidden Joanna's body. You drove up here in Bev's car with Joanna's body in the back. You waited until it was dark, and you drove the car far out onto the mudflats, further than most people dare to go out, where you knew it would sink down and hide her body and the car. Afterward, you needed to get back to Exeter and meet Bev, so you drove Nick's BMW back and parked it outside the Moor Side Estate. Bev's car was never stolen. It never made it back that night because it's buried out there in the sand with Joanna's body inside."

Bill was staring at her, and the blood had drained from his face.

"How many years have you been holding on to this terrible secret?" asked Kate. "You've kept it from Max. You kept it from Bev."

"You have no proof. This is just you telling me what you think!" he cried. Bill picked up the gun, closed his eyes, and clutched it to his chest. Tears were running down his cheeks. He was quiet and still. Kate took a step closer, and so did Tristan, but Bill opened his eyes.

"Who are we talking to now: Bill or Nick?" asked Kate.

"It's not like that," said Bill, looking up at her. His voice was calm. "Nick was just a name I used when I met guys. I didn't think about it back then. I didn't want those guys to know my real name. It got out of control, and my two identities took on a life of their own."

"Did Bill kill Joanna? Or did Nick kill her, like he did those young men?" asked Kate.

"Stop!" he shouted.

"I know it must have been frightening," said Kate. "Out there in the dark. Sinking in the sand. With the tide rushing in . . . It plays on your mind, doesn't it? That after all these years, Bev's rusted car, with Joanna inside, will be exposed on the beach."

"Why did you hire us to find Joanna?" asked Tristan.

"Bev," he said quietly. "For Bev. I wanted closure. I thought you'd find nothing and we could draw a line under it all. I needed Bev to give up on Joanna. And leave it be."

"Bev must know, deep down, that you killed Joanna," said Tristan.

"You shut your mouth!" shouted Bill, slamming the gun repeatedly on the desk. "You can't prove it. You can't prove it!" he cried in a child-like singsong voice. His face was red and he was shaking.

"When we're done here with you, Bill, I'm going to make sure the police search every inch of that fucking beach. They will find the car, and they will find Joanna's body inside," said Kate.

Her heart was now pounding, and her mouth was dry. Bill moved fast. He picked up one of the shells from the floor and loaded it into the gun. For a moment, Kate thought he was going to aim it at them and fire, but he closed the shotgun, turned it around in his hands, and put the barreled end in his mouth.

Tristan got around the desk just in time, knocking the gun from Bill's mouth just as he pulled the trigger. The glass exploded in one of the cabinet doors behind Kate.

Bill and Tristan wrestled with the gun. They were the same height, but Tristan was stronger. Kate felt pain in her right arm, just below the shoulder, and she looked down and could see a spot of red expanding on the sleeve of her T-shirt.

Bill got the upper hand and shoved Tristan. He fell back against the bookshelves. Bill grabbed the other shell from the floor and ran out of the office with the gun. Tristan got up and saw Kate with the blood spreading from her arm.

"Kate. You've been hit!"

The pain was like a hot knife, but when she rolled up her sleeve, she could see there was a deep graze in her upper arm. "It's a flesh wound," she said, pressing her hand to it. "Go after him. Don't let him use that bullet!" she shouted. "Go!" Tristan nodded and ran off after Bill.

Kate winced and reached into her bag. She found a thin black scarf and quickly tied it around the wound on her arm. She took some deep breaths and then grabbed her phone and called the police.

47

Tristan felt a huge gust of wind as sand blew into the hallway through the open door. He reached the door a moment later and ran outside. Bill was running barefoot down the sandy track toward the beach holding the shotgun.

Tristan started running after him. At the bottom of the track, Bill jumped over the low barrier where they'd parked the car and hit the sand, stumbling, but then he righted himself and carried on running.

Tristan gained on him and a moment later vaulted the low barrier. Bill was now running out across the sand toward the sea.

What is he doing? thought Tristan, as his feet hit the damp sand. It was harder to run on the sandy surface in his heavy trainers, but Bill was moving faster in bare feet. The wind was now screaming off the shore and blowing a layer of sand along the beach. It whipped around Tristan's head, getting in his eyes and stinging his skin.

"Bill! Stop!" he shouted, but the wind took the words out of his mouth, and he choked on the sand. Bill ran toward a flock of seagulls huddled in a group, and they took flight, soaring above Tristan, cawing and screaming into the sky.

The farther out they ran, the wetter the sand became. Bill was holding the shotgun in both hands and pumping it side to side to give him momentum. Tristan could now see where the waves were breaking on the wet sand far in the distance, and when he glanced back, the houses were far behind. He was alone in this no-man's-land with Bill, a gun, and one shell.

Bill glanced back and looked like he was slowing down. The sand was growing wetter and ridged in places with pools of seawater. Tristan's shoes were wet and were sinking a couple of inches into the sand with each step he took.

Tristan gained on him further, narrowing the gap between them to a few meters. Bill turned back, but as he did, he tripped and went crashing down on the sand. The shotgun flew out of his hands. Tristan crashed into him and tripped, and they both ended up lying on the sand. Tristan knew he'd got himself into a stupid situation. Bill was either going to kill himself or try to kill Tristan, or they were going to drown in the sinking sand.

Tristan was still lying on his front, but before he could get up, Bill grabbed him and rolled him over onto his back. Bill was on top of him, pinning him down, and he felt Bill's hands around his throat.

"You think you can bully me? You think you can push me around?" Bill shouted, his face red and eyes crazed. Tristan could feel Bill's hands tighten on his throat, and he lifted his legs, trying to get leverage to push Bill off him.

The wet sand underneath started to give as Bill pushed down on his neck. The sounds of the wind and surf were muffled as the back of his head and his ears sank into the wet, sludgy sand. It flooded over his face, enveloping his head in darkness, going into his nose. He felt Bill above, pushing. His grip was loosening on Tristan's neck, but Bill was going to push him deep into the wet sand and drown him.

Tristan tried to move his arms and legs, but he was now half-submerged in the wet sand. He felt the air being pushed out of his lungs. He was going to drown.

———

Kate ran as fast as she could across the beach. She could make out the shape of Bill crouching on the sand. Her arm was in pain with the scarf tied around the flesh wound, but it had slowed the flow of blood. As she got closer, she could see Bill pushing Tristan down into the soft sand. The whole of his head and upper body were submerged, and Bill's hands were under the sandy sludge. Tristan's feet were kicking in the air.

Bill's face was transfixed on Tristan drowning in the sand; the veins stood out on his arms, and he was sweating and shaking with the effort.

Kate saw the shotgun lying on the sand. She ran to it, picked it up by the barrel, and swung the handle at Bill, hitting him across the back of his head. There was a crack as it made contact, and he cried out and let go of Tristan, landing on his side, dazed.

"Tristan!" Kate cried. She reached down into where he was submerged and found his torso. She knelt down, hooked her arms under him, and with a huge heave, she leaned back onto her heels, pulling. At first, he wouldn't budge, and she thought they were both going to sink down deeper, but with a soft sucking sound, Tristan emerged from the sand, and they fell back together.

"It's okay," she said, wiping the sand from his face. He spat and heaved, and his body was covered in a thick layer of brown. Finally, he took a deep, rattling breath.

"Where is he? I can't see," said Tristan. Bill was lying still on his side.

"I hit him with the gun," said Kate. She went to one of the pools of clear seawater, scooped it up, and came back to Tristan and used it to clean his face. Then she saw Bill's head twitch, and he moved across the sand, grabbed the shotgun, and rolled over. He pointed the gun at Kate and pulled the trigger, but there was a click as the hammer struck the empty barrel. He pulled the trigger again, and Kate cried out, but it clicked again.

"No, no, no!" cried Bill, searching for the single shell he'd brought with him. Kate saw it just behind him, and she ran to it and grabbed it, stuffing it in her pocket.

She was glad to hear shouts coming from the shore, and a group of police officers were running across the sand toward them.

A moment later, the police reached them and arrested Bill, putting handcuffs on his wrists.

"Bill Norris, Nick Lacey. You are under arrest on suspicion of murder," said the police officer fixing on the cuffs. "You do not have to say anything, but it may harm your defense if you do not mention when questioned something which you later rely on in court. Anything you do say may be given in evidence."

Kate went to Tristan, who was now lying on the sand catching his breath.

"I thought that was me done for," said Tristan, spitting out more sand. "Jesus."

Three police officers were leading Bill away toward the houses.

"We need to move, quickly," said another of the officers, coming over to Kate and touching her on the shoulder. "The tide's coming in, and it can move faster than we can walk."

Far ahead, Kate saw a foamy carpet of water creeping toward them.

"Are you okay?" she said, helping Tristan to his feet.

"No, but I will be," he said. "What about you? You need to get your arm seen to."

Kate nodded, but she didn't feel any pain. She just felt euphoria. They'd got him. They'd solved the case. She took Tristan's arm, and they started back across the sand toward the safety of the shore.

48

Four days later, at four o'clock on Friday morning, Kate and Tristan arrived back at Max and Bill's house in Burnham-on-Sea.

It was still dark, and they'd seen the floodlit forensics tent from a couple of miles off, casting its spectral glow into the darkness. The parking spot near the house was filled with two police vans and a black forensics van, so Kate pulled past and parked up at the end of the sandy track.

The past four days had felt like a lifetime. When Bill had been taken into custody, he'd been in an emotional state, and Kate had naively presumed that he would repeat what he'd told her and Tristan. He'd been taken to Exeter police station, and he'd used his one phone call to contact Bev. Who in turn had called in a solicitor. Bill had refused to answer any questions, so now the pressure was on to find Joanna Duncan's remains in the sand.

Kate had called Bev, but rather than being grateful for the breakthrough in the case, Bev had blamed Kate for everything. She refused to accept that Bill had been living another life, and even more steadfastly, she refused to believe that Bill had killed Joanna. A part of Kate understood the denial. After all those years of her crying on Bill's shoulder and having his support, it would be hard to believe.

The police had been in contact with Max Jesper, and he had reacted in a similar way to Bev. He had remained in Spain, missing his flight home. Kate wondered how long Max would delay coming back.

DCI Faye Stubbs had kept in contact with Kate and Tristan, and things were now very tense. They had just a few hours to recover the car and charge Bill, before their time ran out and they had to release him. Noah Huntley had already been released, pending the investigation into Bill.

"Oh my Lord. The thought of going back on that beach," said Tristan when Kate switched off the engine. It was pitch black outside, and the wind was rocking the car. Kate took his hand and squeezed it.

"You can stay in the car if it's too much," she said.

"Are you crazy? I want to see this through until the end," he said with a laugh. They got out of the car and pulled on their warm coats and gloves. They walked down toward the beach and went to the police van, where Faye emerged from the side door.

"Morning," she said. "Do you want a cuppa? We're waiting for low tide, which should be in the next twenty minutes," she said, checking her watch. "I just need to go and speak to the forensics team and the Coastguard. They're setting up on the beach."

Faye climbed over the barrier next to the track and headed off onto the beach. Kate and Tristan went into the warmth of the van, where two police officers sat with Styrofoam cups of tea. They said hello, and Tristan went to the small table with a kettle and cups and started to make tea for them both.

This was the third morning that Kate and Tristan had joined the search team on the beach. The police had guessed the trajectory Bill could have driven the car down the hill from the house. And they predicted it had left the track and gone straight out across the beach and into the sea. Even if Bill had been intending to drive in a straight line, the radius of his drive was wide. The police search team had used ground-penetrating radar to scour the area. A small transponder had been dragged toward the edge of the breakers on the back of a hovercraft borrowed from the Coastguard, and yesterday the radar had detected a large mass out at the very edge of the tide reach. There had only been time to drive in a metal pile to mark the spot before the tide came back in and made it impossible for a recovery operation. Today, they were hoping to return to the same spot and find something.

Kate and Tristan drank their tea standing outside the van with two police officers.

"I heard that you were the guys who searched the house?" said Kate to the officers.

"Yeah, I'm Keir, and this is Doug," said one of the officers. "Forensics have been working on the master bedroom and bathroom. They've recently been cleaned with bleach and ammonia. We've found some fibers in his car, and some hair, blood, and bodily fluids."

They heard an engine, and a police car came down the track and stopped next to Kate's car. The beach was now bathed in a dim dawning light, but they couldn't make out who was inside the car until the police officer driving opened his door and the interior light came on. Kate caught a glimpse of Bev Ellis sitting in the passenger seat looking drawn and haggard. The police officer got out and ducked his head back inside to speak to her.

"Jesus Christ. I don't know what I'd do if I was in her shoes," said Doug.

"I'd want to be here," said Kate. "However difficult it was. Bev needs the closure of finding Joanna, even if it's unbearably painful."

Part of Kate wanted to go over to the car and talk to Bev, but she thought it was best to leave her. There was nothing else she could say right now. They watched as the police officer left Bev in the car and came up to the van.

"Is the kettle on? I think she needs a strong cup of tea," he said.

"If I were Bev, I'd need something stronger than tea," said Kate. She looked back to the car, where Bev sat, staring trancelike out at the beach bathed in dawn shadows.

Thirty minutes later, the sun had risen, casting the sand in a blue-silver glow. The wind had dropped, but it was still cold. When Kate and Tristan climbed over the barrier to join Faye and watch the recovery, they saw that the Coastguard's hovercraft was already moving down the beach toward the water, with five men sitting inside. A green tractor with oversize tires followed at a distance. Three forensics officers in Tyvex suits and waders were walking toward the recovery area, where Kate could see the long, thin pile poking out of the sand.

"We have less than an hour to do this, before the tide turns," said Faye.

"Won't that tractor sink in the sand?" asked Tristan. The hovercraft had stopped a few feet from where the pile was driven into the sand, and the tractor was a hundred feet behind it, still moving, slowly inching forward.

"The tractor's fitted with special extra-wide flotation tires with the air pressure lowered, which should give it the best possible traction. He's going to get as close as he can," said Faye.

Kate and Tristan followed Faye out across the sand to get closer to the action. They watched as the tractor slowed, and came to a stop around fifty feet from the hovercraft. A moment later, they heard a shout from the driver and he waved his hand. He couldn't go out any farther.

It felt tense as Kate and Tristan stood with Faye, watching the Coastguard team work to find the car. A couple of times, Kate glanced back at Bev, but all she could see was the outline of her inside the car, watching with the police officer.

The Coastguard's team wore long waders as they stepped into the thick, gloopy sand around the long metal pile. Three of the men had long metal hoses, which they used to fire high-pressure seawater down into the sand and loosen it, whilst the other two men dug. After twenty minutes, a shout went up, and a voice came over Faye's radio, confirming that they'd found a car bumper.

"We need to move fast," said Faye into her radio. "You've got thirty minutes until the tide turns."

"How do you think Bill drove Bev's car so far out in the sinking sand?" asked Tristan.

"If he left the road and crossed the beach at high speed, then the momentum could have taken him far out to the water's edge," said Kate, feeling a burst of excitement that this could be it. This could be Bev's car.

They watched as a long chain from the front of the tractor was fed out across the sand to the Coastguard team, who attached it to the car down in the sand. The tractor began to reverse, an inch at a time, until the chain was stretched taut. Its engine roared and hit a higher pitch as it pulled, and its wheels stuck and spun, throwing up wet sand. The Coastguard team dug in with their spades and used the metal hoses to irrigate the sand around the trapped vehicle.

"Oh no, the tide's already starting to come back in," said Kate, seeing the foamy water creeping closer to where the team worked.

Then there was a roar of shouting as the wheels of the tractor gained purchase on the sand, and it began to move backward. The sand in front of the metal pile began to move up and bulge, and then, rising out of the sand, came the shape of a car.

Kate looked back toward the shore and saw Bev was now standing outside the police car with her hand on the open door, staring at the ruined wreck. The tractor kept reversing and, with a jolt, pulled the wreck of the car free, up and out of the gloopy sand, dragging it back to firmer ground.

They followed the car as it was pulled up to the forensics tents pitched at the edge of the beach. The body of the car had rusted badly. The rubber of the tires had long perished, exposing the wheel rims. Kate tried to see inside, but she couldn't make out where the windows had been, and it looked as if the roof had caved in. Two forensics officers unhooked the chain, and the tractor lumbered off, back down the beach. The white forensics tent was lifted and moved closer, until it covered the rusting hulk of the car.

A tense hour passed, and Kate and Tristan went up to wait by the police van with Faye, drinking more tea. They could see Bev was becoming more anxious inside the police car until she got out and ran down to the tent. A moment later, Faye's radio crackled on her lapel.

"We have a positive ID, boss."

"Okay, on my way down."

Faye indicated that Tristan and Kate should come with her. When they reached the tent, Bev was in the arms of a middle-aged male police officer, who was half supporting her and half holding her back from entering the tent. A terrible low keening was coming from her. It was more animal than human, and it chilled Kate, making the hairs stand up on the back of her neck.

The side of the tent facing the car park was open, and bright lights inside shone down on the rusting hulk of the car. The interior was a mess of mud and sand and twisted metal.

The forensics officers had spread two large white sheets in front of the car. On the first lay the remains of a leather bag and a laptop with the plastic housing in surprisingly good condition. On a second sheet Kate could see the yellowing bones of a skeleton. The eye sockets of the skull were wide and staring. The teeth were intact, and next to the skull lay a part of the jawbone. The skeleton looked so small.

"The number plate matches. This is the car which belonged to Bev Ellis," said one of the forensics officers. "We've been able to compare the teeth from the skull with dental records. The skeleton we found inside the car is Joanna Duncan."

Bev screamed in pain and broke away, reaching out to touch the skull, but Faye and Kate moved to hold her back. Her legs sagged, and she gripped Kate's shoulder.

"My little girl . . . You found my little girl," she said. Kate put her arms around Bev and held her.

"I'm so sorry, Bev," she said. "I'm so, so sorry."

EPILOGUE

Two weeks later, Kate and Tristan and Ade were on the beach behind her house. The sun was going down, and they were sitting on a large driftwood tree, which had been washed up after a storm a couple of years ago and pulled up clear of the tide. In front of them they'd built a fire on the sand.

"You know, this nonalcoholic sparkling shite is actually not bad," said Ade. "What's the occasion for us not drinking?"

"You're a bit cheeky, considering you've crashed the barbecue," said Tristan.

"I brought meat!" said Ade.

"Thank you, and you're very welcome," said Kate, taking a sip of the sparkling fruit drink and agreeing that it wasn't bad. "We're celebrating being paid for solving the case, and the big interview that we did for the *West Country News*."

"And we're hoping it will lead to more work," said Tristan.

Jake was standing to the side of the big tree and trying to light the small barbecue that they'd dragged down from its regular place on the cliff outside the back door.

"We're also celebrating that we've finally managed to find staff to do the caravan changeovers," he said, picking up his glass of fizz. He came over to Kate, Tristan, and Ade and held it up.

"To the detective agency, the caravan site, and the end of scrubbing toilets," he said, and they all clinked glasses.

"You'll learn, Jake, that part of life is having to scrub toilets," said Ade. He took another sip of his drink. "Have you got any ice?"

"I bought some ice. I'll get you some," said Tristan.

"Bring the meat down, too, in the fridge," said Jake.

"I'll come up with you," said Kate. "There's a lot to bring."

They left Jake and Ade on the beach, chatting over the barbecue, and came back up to the house. Just when they were in the kitchen, the doorbell rang. Kate frowned. Tristan went with her, and when they opened the door, it was Bev. They hadn't seen her since Joanna's skeleton had been recovered from the sand.

"Sorry to bother you," she said.

"No, please, not at all," said Kate. Bev looked exhausted and wore a long black Lurex skirt and a black roll-neck pullover. There was an inch of gray in the roots of her dark hair. "Do you want to come in?"

"No. No. I just want to apologize to you both . . . I was in denial about Bill . . . And I never thanked you properly for finding Jo . . . I'm ashamed at how I reacted. I was in shock. I now get to bury her and put her at rest," she said.

Kate and Tristan nodded. Shortly after forensic officers confirmed the skeleton on the beach was Joanna, Bev had collapsed and had to be taken to the hospital with severe shock. They hadn't had any contact with her since, but Bev had transferred the remaining money owed for solving the case.

"This is a silly question, but how are you? You scared us back on the beach," said Tristan.

Bev shifted on her feet and hitched her handbag over her shoulder and shrugged.

"I don't know how I feel . . . He's pleading guilty. Bill, Nick, or whatever his bloody name is. Which is right and proper. There's so much evidence against him . . . for killing Jo. And those poor young men. Oh God, you must think I'm so stupid. I spent all those years with him, and I didn't know about any of it . . . I suppose you heard. The cyber-forensics team were given Joanna's laptop and a USB key the police found in her bag in the car."

"Yes," said Kate. "The laptop had been destroyed by the salt water, but they managed to recover some data from the USB drive. There was a copy of the photo that helped us crack the case—one of Bill with Max and a man called Jorge Tomassini at the commune."

"Please," said Bev, holding up her hand. "Please don't say their names. I've had to hear from the police about everything they found . . ." She put her hand up to her mouth, and her bottom lip began to tremble. "That they found DNA for that lad, Hayden . . . Bill was only ever a gentleman to me, which makes it even more difficult to hear about the things he did. The things Nick did. I've been seeing a shrink. She told me I probably saved a lot of young men's lives. I grounded that side of him. The side of him that wanted to be Bill, the heterosexual man. That's just expensive talk for what I was: I was his beard. I used to accompany him to work stuff, to show them he was a straight man. Settled down. All good and proper . . ."

"Please, Bev. Don't do this to yourself," said Kate. "Are you sure you don't want to come inside and have a drink of something?"

Bev took a tissue from her bag and wiped her eyes.

"No. Thank you. I'm not much company, as you must imagine. I had a long phone call with that Max Jesper today. It turns out, he was just as in the dark as me . . . I'm going to meet him tomorrow. That's crazy, isn't it?"

"No," said Tristan. "He lost someone too. You have that in common."

"God, I feel sick all day long. I don't want to have to deal with Bill and everything. I just want to mourn for my Jo . . ." Bev rummaged around in her handbag and pulled out a tiny square of folded-over tissue paper.

"Listen. I want you both to have this, to remind yourselves to keep doing what you do. I know it's tough out there." She handed the square of tissue to Kate, and when she opened it out, nestled inside was a tiny silver charm in the shape of a magnifying glass. "Jo had a charm bracelet. I bought it for her eighteenth, and she always wore it. They found it in the car, with her remains, when they pulled it out of the sand. I had it cleaned up."

"We couldn't take this," started Kate.

"No. I want you to have it. Please. A piece of Jo to remind you both that you did an incredible thing, solving this case and returning her to me."

"Thank you," said Tristan. Bev gave them both a hug.

"God bless you both," she said, and with a small wave, she left. A moment later, they heard her close the front door behind her.

Kate stared at the charm for a moment.

"It just breaks my heart, this case. To think how long she lay there, trapped in that car, deep under the sand," she said.

"You should be proud, Kate. You did in a month what the police couldn't do in thirteen years."

"We both should be proud. I couldn't have done it without you."

There was another moment as they stared at the small silver charm. Kate placed it on the counter and wiped her eyes. She thought of how the charm had been on Joanna's wrist for all those years, waiting to be found.

Tristan's phone beeped in his pocket, and he took it out and looked at the screen.

"That's Ade, asking where we are with the ice."

"Come on. We're lucky that's all we have to worry about—Ade's drink getting warm. Let's go and eat," said Kate with a smile.

They picked up the ice and the food, left the house, and made their way back down the cliff toward Jake and Ade, waiting for them by the warm, happy light of the fire.

AUTHOR'S LETTER

Dear Readers,

Thank you for choosing to read *Darkness Falls*. If you enjoyed the book, I would be very grateful if you could tell your friends and family. A word-of-mouth recommendation remains the most powerful way for new readers to discover one of my books. Your endorsement makes a huge difference! You could also write a product review. It needn't be long, just a few words, but this also helps new readers find one of my books for the first time.

I love to read, and I love nothing more than escaping into a story. I think that this past year, more than ever, I've relied on books to escape what's going on in the world. Thank you to everyone who has sent me a message to say you enjoyed escaping into my books. Your messages mean so much to me.

To find out more about me, you can check out my website, www.robertbryndza.com.

Kate and Tristan will return shortly for another gripping murder investigation! Until then . . .

Robert Bryndza

ACKNOWLEDGMENTS

Thank you to my brilliant publishers. In the US and Canada, the team at Thomas and Mercer: Liz Pearsons, Charlotte Herscher, Laura Barrett, Sarah Shaw, Michael Jantze, Dennelle Catlett, Haley Miller Swan, and Kellie Osborne.

At Sphere in the UK and Commonwealth: Cath Burke, Callum Kenny, Kirsteen Astor, Laura Vile, Tom Webster, and Sean Garrehy.

Thank you, as ever, to Team Bryndza: Janko, Vierka, Riky, and Lola. I love you all so much and thank you for keeping me going with your love and support!

The biggest thank-you goes out to all the book bloggers and readers. When I started, it was you who were there reading and championing my books. Word of mouth is the most powerful form of advertising, and I will never forget that my readers and the many wonderful book bloggers are the most important people. There are lots more books to come, and I hope you stay with me for the ride!

About the Author

Photo © 2020 Ján Bryndza

Robert Bryndza is the author of the Amazon Charts bestseller *Nine Elms* and *Wall Street Journal* bestseller *Shadow Sands* in the Kate Marshall series, as well as the Detective Erika Foster series, which includes the #1 international bestseller *The Girl in the Ice*, *The Night Stalker*, *Dark Water*, *Last Breath*, *Cold Blood*, and *Deadly Secrets*. Robert's books have sold four million copies and have been translated into twenty-nine languages. In addition to writing crime fiction, Robert has published a bestselling series of romantic comedies. He is British and lives in Slovakia. For more information, visit www.robertbryndza.com.